# PROLOGUE

*Once, long ago, the seven kingdoms were united under the rule of Arthur, the Golden King. But wherever peace and brilliance exist, war and darkness must by their very nature lurk beneath the surface. And so, it was the Dread Queen, that most ancient of evil, came to covet the destruction of the court of Camelot.*

*Her plans were insidious. She cursed Lancelot, chief of Arthur's most loyal knights, and forced upon him an unyielding desire for Arthur's queen, Guinevere. In the night, he took her from her chambers and brought her to the Dread Queen. There, the ancient evil used foul magics to turn Guinevere into an unholy beast.*

*And once Guinevere had been turned, she corrupted Lancelot until he too was no longer human. One by one, all of Arthur's knights fell and were corrupted beyond all saving. At last, only the Golden King and his closest councilor, Mordred Le Fay, son of Morgana and nephew of the great wizard, Merlin, favorite of Lady Fate, remained.*

*But it was only at that moment when the Dread Queen revealed the fullness of her plotting.*

*For Mordred was in league with the ancient evil, and once Arthur had no more protectors, he struck. Only the intervention of Merlin prevented his nephew's complete victory, but both men were delivered mortal blows during the battle.*

*As he lay dying, the great sword Excalibur shattered upon the ground, Arthur begged Merlin for one final favor. "Once," he gasped, "you found me and brought me to my reward. I do not believe the Lady Fate, greatest of all the gods, would craft such a destiny only to see it falter like this. She has work for me yet, and I shall return. Watch for me, old friend, though it be to the end of the world itself."*

*Merlin promised he would, and when Arthur breathed no more, the wizard gathered up the remains of his wondrous sword and bore them away to his tower in the woods. There are those who say the pieces of mighty Excalibur lie within those mystical walls still, waiting the return of the hand fit to wield them.*

*The hand fit to belong to a king.*

# SWORD OF LIONS
## BY TZ KRASNER

**TZ KRASNER**

COPYRIGHT © 2022 TZVI KRASNER ALL RIGHTS RESERVED

THE CHARACTERS AND EVENTS PORTRAYED IN THIS BOOK ARE FICTITIOUS. ANY SIMILARITY TO REAL PERSONS, LIVING OR DEAD, IS COINCIDENTAL AND NOT INTENDED BY THE AUTHOR.

NO PART OF THIS BOOK MAY BE REPRODUCED, OR STORED IN A RETRIEVAL SYSTEM, OR TRANSMITTED IN ANY FORM OR BY ANY MEANS, ELECTRONIC, MECHANICAL, PHOTOCOPYING, RECORDING, OR OTHERWISE, WITHOUT EXPRESS WRITTEN PERMISSION OF THE PUBLISHER.

ISBN-13: 9798419904170

COVER DESIGN BY: GABRIELLE RAGUSI
LIBRARY OF CONGRESS CONTROL NUMBER: 2018675309
PRINTED IN THE UNITED STATES OF AMERICA

*For my father
Brian Deane Krasner*

*August 9, 1958-July 4, 2008*

*Forever under the canopy you built for us
With your mind, your hands
And your incomparable heart.*

There are many whose aid in helping me to create this book was invaluable. Chief among them are:

Gabrielle Ragusi, for the wonderful cover.
Tim Marquitz, for the fantastic editing.
Zachariah Watson, my co-writer, who helps me craft the worlds of my stories.
And lastly, my mother, Sharon Krasner. Would that every child had a parent so willing to impart the beauty of the written word.

# CHAPTER 1

Crown Princess Janet, Duchess of Morrberry-by-the-Sea and heir to the Golden Eagle Throne of Avanna, sat in the library of the royal castle and paged through a richly appointed book of arcana. She was a slight, tiny young woman with gold-dust skin and long dark hair that fell about her slim shoulders like a waterfall. Her amethyst-hued eyes flicked back and forth from the pages of the book to the parchment beside her as she made notes on this spell or that one.

The strange color of her irises was no mere birth defect. Instead, it was a rare manifestation called the Eyes of Fate, and those who bore it wielded significant magical ability. Though, in Janet's case, she had spent much of her young life struggling to manage her power. Each day, she secluded herself in some corner of the castle to study and attempt to work on her magic. *Attempt* being the operative word.

"So," another young woman—taller and curvier, with a long blonde braid that hung over her left shoulder like a trailing scarf—dropped into the chair beside Janet, "what was wrong with Lord Sturmhalten?"

Janet sighed. Of late, besides controlling her magic, Janet sought refuge in order to not have to discuss the unending line of suitors seeking to claim her hand with her sisters.

Except for the blonde beside her—nineteen-year-old Rebecca—none of her sisters were yet of age to receive suitors of their own. As a result, the bevy of men plying for the attention and affection of their twenty-one-year-old eldest sister was a fascination to them. They did not yet realize just how frustrating it was to be only a prize, and she had a challenging time imparting that fact to them.

Preparing herself for yet another irritating discussion about how the most recent suitor had not been all that bad, she closed the book. And discovered Rebecca had not come alone.

Arrayed around the table like a jury, silently judging the accused, were three of her other four sisters. Fifteen-year-old Sonya, a slip of a girl born pale of skin, eye, and hair, was curled on a settee, nimble hands clasped around her agile legs. The studious seventeen-year-old twins, olive-skinned Jasmine and fair-complected Monica, studied her as if she were one of the many scholarly lessons they took entirely too seriously. Only the twelve-year-old knight hopeful Alexis was absent, which was hardly a surprise as she alone considered the obsessions with Janet's dilemma to be foolish.

"I see," she said, folding her hands on the table. "So, this is to be a formal interrogation. Very well. The reason I turned down Lord Sturmhalten is the man is a giant pig who paid entirely too much attention to the bosom of Lady Cornwell."

"Well," Rebecca said with a shrug, "the woman shows a truly scandalous amount of cleavage."

Janet gave her a look. "I am not interested in a husband I shall have to keep away from the servant girls."

"I hardly think—"

"He was also," Janet continued, interrupting Rebecca's protest, "inordinately interested in the way you were moving around the chamber hall. More particularly, in the way your *backside* moved."

"Oh." Suddenly appalled, Rebecca drew inward. However, when she did, the twins took up the fight.

"Sister," Jasmine began, leaning on the table to look her in the eyes, "you are nearing your twenty-second birthday."

"My how time flies," Janet replied dryly.

"Do not make light of this," Monica, always the more hot-tempered one, banged her fist on the table. "It has been nearly four years since you became of age! In that time, you have turned away no less than twenty-five suitors! How much longer do you intend to leave this kingdom without an heir?"

"*I* am the heir," Janet said with just a hint of a bite to her voice. All around them, a light breeze weaved through the room, the first signs of her unconsciously using her magic, something that always signaled she was losing her temper. "Whoever I marry will only become king through that marriage. He will *not* be of royal blood and will only be the means of continuing our family line."

She gestured to Rebecca beside her. "And should something happen to me before I produce a child, Rebecca will be next in line *not* whoever I have chosen as my husband. Therefore, rushing into marriage only serves to remove all of you from the line of succession. I will not subject Avanna to an unworthy king because you fear I am taking too long choosing."

"You can hardly blame her, Monica," Sonya said in her smoke-like voice as she smiled wickedly. "It is not as if any of the suitors wore a long-saber at their waist."

"So," the breeze blew harder, the papers, books, and tapestries rustling as Janet curled her hands into fists on the surface of the table, "That is what this is truly about. Malcolm of Bonaparte."

"It has been five years," Rebecca said, her voice soft, sympathetic.

"I am well aware of that," Janet snapped back. "He and I share a birthday, and it was on that day he left for the wars."

"You cannot—" Rebecca began, only to for a gust of wind to slap her hard in the face.

"I have told you all repeatedly," Janet snapped out as the surrounding air whipped and whirled and her sisters' eyes went wide, "Malcolm is my friend. Whether or not he returns to the castle, I have no desire to take him as a husband."

"Janet—" Monica began, eyeing a particularly large tapestry that was dangerously close to tearing loose from the wall just behind her now-furious eldest sister.

"That is enough!" Shooting to her feet, the crown princess took in her four sisters with blazing eyes as the wind whipped through the library like a maelstrom. "A thousand and one times you have brought this notion to me, and a thousand and one times I have called it silly, yet still you go on and on about Malcolm of Bonaparte and these feelings you have decided I have for him with no evidence of your idiotic beliefs! None of you have any true concept of what you speak, so until you have achieved that, open your ears, *and hold your tongues!*"

On the last word, the violent zephyrs reached their peak, exploding outward in a thunderous detonation. It threw Rebecca and the twins to the floor, tossed furniture several times heavier than any of the five young women in the room like children's toys, sent books cascading to the floors in untidy heaps, and ripped priceless tapestries from the walls.

Janet stood speechless, stunned mute as she stared around in horror at the devastated library. Then, covering her face with her hands, she rushed from the room.

* * *

Growing up, Janet's response to the embarrassing unintentional release of her magic had often been to retreat to her rooms in the Eastern Tower of the castle. There she stayed, wallowing in her misery until Malcolm would come and talk her back out. It was that which had developed their close friendship and fueled her sisters' suspicions there was more between them.

For that very reason, since Malcolm had left, she had found other methods of getting away from her embarrassment. And so, donning a light summer cloak, she slipped from the castle and out into the capital city to walk among the people.

She knew that some members of the nobility and even some of her own relations believe in keeping a distance from commoners, but she found it soothing to mix with them, perhaps because of her long friendship with Malcolm himself. And to her mind, a future queen needed to know her subjects as more than *the people*.

It was market day, one of her favorite

times to walk the capitol as the streets filled with the citizenry, come to peruse the stalls and the wares and to meet and talk with each other. The stall keepers, who at the least recognized her as nobility if not royalty, greeted her warmly when she stopped to look over an assortment of fruits or a collection of leather goods. Ever a warm and friendly woman, she greeted them back, chatting about the weather or the merchandise or even the shopkeeper's family if she knew them well.

Though she carried no money with her, the recognition she was nobility held weight for the king's own orders placed harsh penalties on any noble who would dare shortchange or steal from a merchant, and so she could order items sent to her and leave a marker that guaranteed payment upon delivery and the merchant would make no complaint.

She was deciding between a pair of bracelets—a silver one set with small diamonds and a scrolling gold one with a large amethyst that matched her eyes—when she heard a man say, "I often wonder if you spend more when you are still upset or after you calm down."

She glanced over her shoulder with a smile. "Cedric."

He was a tall man, taller than she remembered Malcolm being, and nearly as tall as her father and with shoulders broad enough to carry the world. Blue eyes laughed at her out of a roguishly handsome face topped with wavy hair, the golden blond of ripe wheat. There were many young women in the court—and a few who were not so young—who sighed behind their fans when he walked by.

To be true, she had been a little uncertain when he had become her personal guard, afraid people might make assumptions. But she had relaxed upon learning he was not only betrothed but madly in love with his fiancé and the two had become fast friends.

She made her selection—really, she had such a fondness for amethysts the dilemma had been more for the fun of it than anything else —and he fell into step beside her with a smile. "I, um, got a look at the library. Had another outburst, did we?"

She sighed, her anger and mortification having long since faded over the hour and more she had been shopping, leaving only a dim headache. "My sisters were giving me their usual going-over."

"Ah, yes. Lord Sturmhalten. Honestly, for the king's top diplomat the man can be decidedly undiplomatic when it comes to women." He chuckled. "It would, I think, be quite entertaining to see him try his more lecherous ways on my Rowena."

An answering smile spread across her lips. "Yes, from your descriptions of her, she sounds like quite the forward woman. I think I would like her."

He coughed delicately. "You, um, are aware the Loxellys are not fans of the royal family?"

"Yes." Her smile widened. "But I do so enjoy working for things rather than being handed them."

He chuckled again. "There are times you remind me so much of Malcolm."

She stopped dead in her tracks, her heart thumping in her chest. "Who told you about him?" she demanded. "Was it Rebecca? Sonya?"

"Whoa, whoa. Told me about who?"

"Malcolm. Malcolm of Bonaparte."

Now he was the one who looked surprised. "How do you know the captain?"

"His father is Martin of Avalon, the Order's blacksmith. He is my oldest friend. You called him captain. You served with him?"

"Rowena and I both. He was our commander. Well now, this is quite the surprise. We shall await them together."

"Await?" Her eyes lit with excitement. "He is returning?"

"I received a letter from Rowena not four days ago. They have been discharged and will be here within the next few days."

"That is wonderful news, Cedric." Happy for him, she laid a hand upon his arm. "Would you and she like to marry here? In the castle? Father would be more than happy to—"

"I fear Rowena would not be amenable," he said, cutting off her exuberance. "She truly does not like your family. To be honest, she may attempt to harm Malcolm when she finds out he is a friend of yours."

"This is true." But she continued to beam excitedly. "Oh, tell me of my friend, of the three of you on the battlefield. I want to hear all the stories you have."

"I will," he agreed, "but I believe I deserve some stories in trade, of my captain and his friend as children."

"That is a fine trade," she told him as they turned to head down the street leading toward the city gates.

\* \* \*

They walked and spoke for over an hour. She told him of the golden-hearted boy who had been like a brother to her and her sisters. Of him skulking through unused hallways with Sonya, delighting Monica and Jasmine with pop quizzes on their lessons. Trading barbs with sharp-tongued Rebecca or showing Alexis how to hold her sword.

And how whenever her lessons or attempts at spell craft had gone particularly wrong, and she had retreated into her rooms, it had always been he who came to find her. When she had been young, he had drawn her back out to try again or to play with her sisters. Then, as they had grown older, he had sat in her rooms with her and talked for hours on end.

Cedric's tales showed her the boy she had

known had grown into a skilled warrior and an innovative tactician. It thrilled Janet to hear of her friend slaying five mountain trolls on his own or leading an operation to flush out and annihilate a tribe of goblins tormenting a town. The creatures were an ever-present and never-ending menace that constantly popped up in the northern regions of the kingdom.

"How did you come to know him?" she asked, eyes bright and eager.

"They assigned me to a new mobile tactical unit that was being formed. He was to be the commanding officer. There were only the three of us on the team: Malcolm, Me, and Rowena."

"So, *that* is where the two of you met." She grinned. "You have been amazingly scarce on the details about your relationship with her."

His brilliant blue eyes took on a dreamy quality as his own smile spread. "She is an amazing woman, fiery and headstrong. And beautiful, so beautiful that some say she is her own ancestor, Lady Marian, reborn in the world." He laughed ruefully. "And she disliked me at first sight. I was just what she did not want to see and nothing I did was ever correct or without an ulterior motive."

"This story sounds familiar."

He laughed again and paused to inspect some high summer apples. "I suppose it does."

He gestured silently to the merchant that

he would take two and handed over a silver piece to pay for them. It was always his habit to overpay for such things and let the merchant keep the rest. He handed her the second apple and bit into his as they resumed walking.

"When a man is faced on a daily—even hourly—basis with a woman who is determined to find fault with his every action, it takes little time before he is as angered by the sight of her as she is of him."

"So, you fought often."

"Over everything from battle strategy to who would do the night's cooking."

Janet's eyes twinkled. "I suppose that last was one you could hardly leave up to Malcolm. He is a terrible cook."

"Oh, most assuredly," he agreed. "And he was always the one who would force us to decide by offering to do it. It always amused Malcolm, the way we could fight at the drop of a hat. I suppose it is always more evident to those on the outside looking in."

"Malcolm has always been rather observant."

"You would know, I suppose. In any matter, Rowena and I went on that way for months, until one night an argument went farther than we ever had before." His hands clenched and unclenched at his sides, the muscles in his jaw tightening as his eyes unfocused for a moment, as if he were reviewing the moment again. "Never, in all my life, have I ever struck a woman, save for that night."

Janet laid a comforting hand on his arm. "It must have been quite the fight to drive a man like you to such extremes."

He gave a short bark of laughter. "Aye, that it was. She struck me back. Rowena is not one to take and not return. But before she fled the campsite, I saw the tears in her eyes. The tears of a strong woman can cut a man to ribbons, regardless of how he feels about her. Or thinks he does.

"I moped about the camp for more than an hour, alternately wishing she would never return and wanting her to come back so we could finally have out what was so poisonous between us. Then, finally, Malcolm spoke, just three words. Go after her. It was all he said, for we both knew he needed nothing more.

"Her tracks were not hard to follow as she was far too upset to take any care. But when we found her, she was in the middle of an entire band of monsters. Malcolm says I laid in, riding like a demon and destroying the entire force. I do not recall it, only that they were indeed all dead when I came to my senses."

The ghost of another smile played across his lips. "She came to my tent a few hours before morning. And until they discharged me and sent me home, it was *our* tent from that night on."

Janet stopped walking, turned to look back

at the castle. "They are pushing me to take a husband, Cedric. Worse, my sisters believe Malcolm is why I have not chosen one. He is only my friend, but they will not leave it alone."

"Then you shall have to prove it to them, Princess. But remember we rarely know what we truly need until we already have it."

Janet would likely have said something nasty to that, as it appeared even he was not truly listening to her. But, at that moment, there came a commotion from the far end of the market back towards the castle. When a girl's voice cried out, "Stop, thief!" the princess rolled her eyes skyward.

"Lovely."

Cedric sighed in agreement. "Shall we intervene before the city guard gets involved?"

"After you."

\* \* \*

Under normal circumstances, a boy and girl chasing each other amid a town center would have been nothing more than a young mating ritual. This instance, however, was distinctly unusual.

The boy, a slim, almost gangly youth with chestnut hair and wild eyes, vaulted and dodged obstacles in a dash too mad to be a playful chase. The girl who pursued him did so with hate in her blue eyes and a short sword clutched in one gauntleted fist. The pair raced towards the gates of the city, the boy obviously seeking escape and the girl clearly intent on stopping him before he did.

Cedric moved quickly, angling to intercept both before harm could be done. As the boy did, the knight leaped agilely over stalls and barrels and hay bales, weaving around people without slowing down. But as fast as he ran, it became clear he would not reach the boy before the girl did.

In truth, she took her quarry with a flying tackle that slammed them both up against the side of a stall of goats. "I have you!" she spat out. "Blasted thief! You shall pay for your misdeeds!"

She rolled him over onto his back when a pair of hands grabbed her by the shoulders and hauled her off the boy. She never hesitated, spinning to slash out at her assailant with her weapon. But her blade met another, a long, thin and yet strong one that flicked like the tongue of a viper and spun like a baton. The sword flew from her grip and buried itself in a nearby hay bale.

"Really, Alexis," the stranger said, "will you ever learn patience?"

Alexis, youngest princess of Avanna, blinked at him in surprise. He was tall, nearly as tall as Cedric, though slimmer than the broad-shouldered knight. His body was lean and tough, his limbs long and somehow graceful even with their muscle. But it was his eyes, those tawny, golden eyes like a lion's hide that told her who he was.

"Malcolm!" Her enmity with the young man still lying on the ground absolutely forgotten, she eagerly leaped to hug him. "Welcome home!"

He pretended to gag, slapped playfully at the arms she had thrown around his neck until she released him. "Strong as ever," he said with a small smile as he checked to make certain the hug had not done permanent damage, which they both knew was far from likely.

"Oh, the others will be so excited to see you." Her joy fled and her eyes went cold as she rounded on the boy who had tried to get up and away. "Move from that spot," she snapped out. "And I will be forced to break your legs."

"I did nothing," he said, but settled back down.

"Oh, certainly." She leaned down and scooped up the gleaming silver bracelet that had spilled onto the ground when she had tackled him. "And I suppose you were doing nothing with *this*?"

"My lord had me take it to a silversmith," he protested. "The clasp is broken."

"Alexis." With a sigh, Malcolm neatly nipped the item from her hand and kneeled to return it to the boy. "Be off with you."

"Malcolm!" she whined as the boy scampered off like a demon was on his heels. "He was a thief!"

"Unless you saw him snatch that bracelet himself," he cautioned her, "you have no proof of your claims."

"He ran."

"You had your sword out and were yelling at him." He pulled the weapon in question from where it had landed and handed it back to her. "Most people when faced with someone in armor coming at them waving a blade are going to panic."

"As I have told her numerous times over the last year." Janet, having caught up both to Cedric and her sister, stepped forward. Her amethyst eyes flicked over Malcolm before latching onto Alexis. "What has father said about chasing thieves in the marketplace?"

Alexis sighed and rolled her eyes. "That I am a princess not a city guard."

Janet folded her arms, tapped her foot. Waited. "And?"

Another sigh, another eye roll. "To leave matters such as this to the professionals. Sister —"

Janet held up her hand, cutting off any protest. "Let us all be thankful Malcolm is as fast as he ever was and stopped you from making what could possibly have been a very dear mistake."

She shifted, looking to the muscular blond knight. "Cedric, would you be a dear and escort my sister back to the castle? I believe Master

Jeeves has a few lessons for her."

"Um," Cedric looked briefly to Malcolm, then nodded. "As you wish."

"Cedric." As his former subordinate took hold of the arm of the youngest princess, Malcolm turned and took a parcel from one of his saddlebags. "Rowena returned to Raven's Rock. She awaits you there once your duties are discharged."

With his free hand, Cedric took the parcel, and a brief flicker of disappointment passed through his eyes. "Much obliged. It is good to see you again, Captain."

Janet waited until Alexis was out of sight before turning back to him. The cold distance in her expression and demeanor was replaced with the warmth he remembered. "I appear to have dismissed my escort," she said with a small smile. "Would you walk with me?"

"Gladly."

# CHAPTER 2

"Have you gotten control over your powers?" he asked as they turned away from the market, his horse oddly following them like a trained dog without needing to be led.

She pictured the absolute carnage she had wrought in the East Library and had to fight not to wince. "No," she told him, looking away so he could not read her face and trying to keep her tone mild. "I fear my magic may never be under full control."

"I see." He waited for a moment. "What did you destroy this time?"

"Nothing!" She made the mistake of swinging back and came under the scrutiny of those patient tawny gold eyes. "The East Library."

"The East Library." He laughed, a rich, rollicking cackle that had him doubling over as he fought to catch his breath.

Her temper sparked, her eyes lit. "It is not funny!" When he sat down on the ground, continuing to laugh, she stamped her foot and hissed, "Malcolm!"

"Forgive me." Still chuckling, he wiped tears from his eyes and looked up at her furious face. "Five years, and you have not changed one ounce. What in blazes did Rebecca do, suggest we marry when I returned?"

"Not only Rebecca."

Those three words cut off his laughter as neatly as his own sword might. "Janet, I—"

She waved him off. "It is a prospect I know we both find insulting, and one I have endeavored to drive through the thick skulls of my sisters with very little success I might add."

For a moment, she feared that despite his having made a joke of it the prospect might actually be something he harbored after all, but all he said was, "If you would like, I could make my own intentions on the matter clear to them."

"No. It would do little more than fuel their beliefs. The best way to get them to leave it alone would be to simply return to as we were before you left."

"I see. Very well, if that is what you wish, then that is how we shall proceed." He got back up and brushed off his pants.

As he did so, she studied him. He had filled out during his time away. The boy she remembered had been on the verge of being skinny no matter what. But now, there was visible muscle beneath the leather armor, and he had the dangerous grace to his movements, which truly fit men carried without trying to.

His face had fined down as well and was all planes and angles.

He had gotten handsome on her, she realized, already dreading what sordid ideas her sisters would cook up upon seeing him. If there was any man in the kingdom who looked the part of a potential crown prince, she stood before him now.

"Problem?" he asked with a bemused smile that told her plainly she had looked a bit too long.

"No." Quickly she turned away, looking off into the distance for the gods knew what.

"Janet."

"It is nothing. You have just— It has been quite some time since I have seen you."

"I suppose people change after five years apart." He stepped around so he was in front of her and, to her deep consternation, angled her face up to look at her. "You have certainly become a beauty."

Annoyed, she slapped his hand away. "Would you kindly stop playing around?" she hissed, not pleased with either his action or the fact her heart was beating a little too fast.

He laughed again and fell easily into step beside her as she tried to march away from him. "It has always been far too easy to fluster you."

"Perhaps you should remember what can happen when I get *flustered* and restrain yourself!"

\* \* \*

She calmed down quickly enough and was soon back to joking and laughing with him. He was grateful for that, as even though he did delight in teasing her—always had—he was all too aware how fearsome and dangerous her temper was.

He still recalled how, when Alexis had still been leaning to crawl, a careless lord had trod on the little girl's hand. The court wizard had been forced to retrieve the man after nine-year-old Janet had sent him flying onto the roof of the castle's Northern Tower.

Still, he had told the truth. She had grown into a beautiful woman. Flawless golden skin, eyes clear as diamonds, and a smile brilliant as the sun. A generous mouth making that smile even more noticeable. And the ebony hair that had always been a mess growing up was now sleek and glossy and straight as a board.

And as attractive as the exterior was, the woman underneath was even more so. Smart, strong, and more than a match for any man. He hoped to the gods that whatever man she chose would appreciate her.

He hoped her father agreed with what he had requested. It would settle his mind to watch over her regularly.

"Malcolm?"

He stopped, realizing Janet was no longer walking beside him. Looking around, he spotted her several feet back, giving him a look of worried confusion. "Sorry." To excuse the fact she had likely been speaking to him for some time without him hearing, he rubbed at the bridge of his nose. "I rode through the night so I could come home before sundown today."

"I wondered." She continued to study him as she gestured down the alley she stood beside. "Five years does not seem long enough for you to forget how to reach the shop."

He looked at the alley, then at the buildings around. She was right. He had walked right past the route to his father's blacksmith shop. To his home.

The buildings became progressively shabbier and dirtier as they walked now. They headed towards the far end of the city, the poorer end.

For twenty years, it had been one of the most curious aspects of life in the capital that a boy who had grown up living in the poorest section of the city would be a friend and playmate to the princesses. Even more curious was those same princesses had come to this section often over the years to see him.

But here was where he had been raised by Martin of Avalon, a humble blacksmith with talent beyond his status, in a small shop next to the city wall. Unlike other sections of the quarter, here they swept the roadway clean of debris and kept the buildings neat. After all, important visitors came here, and they could hardly be expected to walk through filth.

For Martin's humble shop boasted a most peculiar item among its wares. Beneath a wooden sign carved in the shape of a prowling lion painted gold hung a magnificent weapon. A weapon that was the result of a legend known across the Seven Kingdoms.

* * *

"It was early in the reign of King Ardent and Queen Celina," so the legend went, "that the uprising came. Geoffrey de Bergiouac, Baron of Bonaparte, became outraged a commoner sat upon the throne of Avanna, proclaimed Ardent usurper, and declared he would retake the crown from the pretender. The Bonaparte Revolt lasted for the better part of a year, and much blood—common and noble—was spilled on both sides. Finally, after eight months of warfare, the two sides met at the Battle of the Idenian Plains and the commoner king struck down the Traitor Baron with his own blade.

Only a few days after the death of the last Baron of Bonaparte, the old man appeared in a village not far from the scene of the battle. He seemed at once to be both ageless and as old as time, clad in a dirty robe and tattered traveler's cloak. His beard was dingy and gray, his nose long and hooked.

He would seem no more than a vagabond to the eye of any man save for one thing. His eyes, clear and sapphire-blue, were as sharp as a finely honed knife beneath the ratty hood of his cloak.

He marched up to the village smithy and demanded, "Make me a sword."

The smith, who was a pretentious man, for this was a wealthy village, took one glance at the old man's ratty garments and sneered, "Go away. I have no time for the likes of you."

The old man, rather than take offense, simply inclined his head, turned, and left. But a few days later, he appeared in another village further west. Once more, he approached the smith and demanded, "Make me a sword."

The smith merely shook his head. "Forgive me, but I cannot. This is a poor village, and I know only how to make horseshoes and bridles. I could not make a sword were the king himself to ask me."

Once more, the old man inclined his head and departed. Yet, when the smith entered his workshop the following morning, he discovered a small pile of gold upon his anvil. The money was not enough to cause insult by turning a poor man into a wealthy one, but he and his wife and child would live comfortably on the sum long enough for him to learn the very trade he apologized for not knowing.

And so, it went throughout the summer. The strange old man would appear in a village and demand, "Make me a sword." The smith would invariably turn him down, and he would depart without another word, only to reappear in another village farther down the line.

If the refusal were rude or curt, nothing more would happen. But if the smith were polite, then a mysterious reward would be left that would enable him to do better for his loved ones.

Finally, the day came he arrived at the capitol of Avanna. While the villages had each boasted a single smithy or weapon shop, the capitol was home to ten, for nowhere in the kingdom were there housed so many knights and lords in need of weapons and armor.

As he had before, the old man appeared within the city rather than walking through the gates or sentry posts. He made his way to a shop on the edge of the merchant's district that dealt in and crafted weapons of the finest quality. The shop's owner was an impeccably dressed man whose manicured beard and quaffed hair betrayed his national origin as that of Avanion.

When the old man made his demand to, "Make me a sword," the shop owner laughed, for it also happened to be the Festival of the Joker upon which jests were common. As was tradition, he flipped a coin to the man and said, "A very fine joke, my good fellow."

But, to his surprise, the old man slapped the coin back on the counter and repeated his demand, "Make me a sword."

The shop owner raised one perfumed brow, for the silver coin had been the appropriate payment for a Joker's Sport. "I will not give more. Take the coin and be off."

The old man, for the first time, became angry, hurling the coin back to the owner as he bellowed, "Make me a sword!"

"You are mad!" the owner cried, trying, and failing to disguise his fear. "Be off with you, else I call the guards and have them arrest you!"

This answer mollified the old man, and he left much as he had with all the others. Not two days later, he reappeared, this time at a smithy near the livestock stables. He was turned away far more charitably than the previous appearance, but when he walked into a third smithy, then a fourth, word spread.

And so, by the time he entered the fifth, the man within knew who he was and dismissed him before he could utter his demand.

It went on and on for a tenday and more until the old man at last entered a smithy within the poorest section of the capitol. It was small and dingy, with a grimy door and a greasy pane of glass beside it. The owner was young, the youngest of any he had seen, and his nose was singed from the heat of his forge. But beneath the singe marks and the dirt on his face was a nobility and an honor the old man had rarely seen.

And so, rather than make his normal terse demand for a sword, he said, "I have walked the length and breadth of the kingdom to find a smith of talent and integrity to make a sword for me, the finest they can. Would you be so willing, good smith?"

The shop owner, Martin of Avalon, bowed low, an uncommonly courtly manner for one so plebeian. "Though my talents are not great, my lord, it would be an honor to do as you ask."

The old man smiled for the first time since he had begun the journey, a kindly expression that made him seem somehow younger. He outlined the type of sword, explained that whatever materials and design the man chose beyond that would be more than all right, and shook his hand before departing.

Though others would have called him foolish, for the requested sword was a difficult one to make and the likelihood the old man would be able to pay an adequate price for it was low, the young swordsmith set to making the item with the fervor of a man after religion. Day after day and long into the night, his forge rang with the sound of his hammer and the hissing of cooling metal. Hour after hour, he worked, bringing to life a creation rarely seen before in the world.

And at the end of a week, when the old man returned, the young smith proudly presented him with the sword wrapped carefully in a cloth. Desiring to see what had been crafted, the old man unwrapped it and pleased the smith with his reverent expression.

"A fine sword," the old man declared, holding it aloft.

And a fine sword it was, a rare type known as a long-saber. They were difficult to learn to use, and even harder to master. The blade, long and slim and flat, could be spun and woven so fast it seemed a veritable web of steel, yet was strong enough to turn aside the swipe of a battle ax then sever the arm that wielded it as neatly as one might chop a piece of wood.

This one seemed to gleam in the dim light of the shop, as if the very act of forging it had imparted some hidden power upon the metal. Yet, the true art of the crafted weapon was not the blade but, instead, the hilt. Most swords bore a straight, level hilt, but this one was forked, the ends of the crosspiece extended like the up strokes of the letter Y.

Wrought in gold on the ends were the regal heads of majestic lions, and another prowled from the butt of the handle, teeth bared in a snarl. Carved into the pommel was another lion head, this one with its jaws stretched wide in a thunderous roar.

And set within that wide-open maw was a glittering gemstone clear as ice.

"Hello again, old friend," the old man said quietly, as if only to himself.

The smith started to ask what he meant, when the old man suddenly turned and made for the front of the shop. Now annoyed, thinking the stranger meant to flee with the finest work he was likely to do in his life without paying for it, the younger man vaulted his counter to pursue.

But the strange elder did not go to the door. Instead, he strode confidently to the window and, turning the magnificent weapon so the blade pointed at the ground, pressed it against the grimy glass.

It seemed to the smith that for a moment the air of the shop echoed with the ring of metal on metal, as if a thousand swords clashed together all at once a great distance off. Then the old man stepped back, and the wondrous sword remained stuck against the glass, which was now every bit as clear as the crystal that had been set within it.

Speechless, his heart pounding in his chest, the young man all but tore down his own door as he scrambled to get a look from the outside. The window was now diamond-bright in the sun, and the simple if elegant crystal was now a deep, deep crimson."

\* \* \*

As they stood before that still-crystal clear window looking at the amazing weapon that stuck fast to it, Janet mused, "So many tried to lift it down over the years. They came from all over the kingdom, from all over the world. Earls and barons and counts and knights, even one of the high captains of the Five Seas."

He laughed. "As I recall, he tried to leave with five of my father's best daggers as *compensation* for failing."

She laughed, too. "That was quite the row when Sir Garret caught him. For a moment, I was afraid he would run the man through and there would be an international incident."

"All of six and you were fearing international incidents?"

"Oh, very well. My tutors were afraid. All those men who came to claim the Sword of Lions and none ever could" She turned her head to study him. "If you were not a commoner—if you were a noble or knight and could wield a Bloodstone Blade—I should wonder if it has waited for you all these years."

When he did not respond, she reached out to tap a finger on the handle of the sword he carried— a far humbler version of the same weapon. "Why did you train to use one, anyway? 'Tis an extraordinary goal to set oneself."

"He was always obsessed with the Sword of Lions," a voice said from behind them. "So, it seemed an appropriate choice."

"You say that as if it was you who taught me." Malcolm turned and, grinning, pulled his father into a warm embrace.

"Welcome home, lad." He was a short, squat man, beefy with muscle. His arms were too long for his body and marked with years worth of burn scars, a mute testament to his profession. His hair, a short, springy black liberally shot through with gray, was missing a section over what had once been his left ear, burned away by molten metal before Malcolm had been born.

Father and son, Janet thought, looked nothing alike. Until you looked in their eyes and saw the good man in their souls. Malcolm might not look like his father, but there was no doubt in her mind who had raised him.

"Come in," the older man said to them both. "Come in."

Janet hesitated, looking over her shoulder towards the castle. Her sisters were likely already whispering about her not coming back with Cedric. Best, she decided, not to give them any further fuel for their suspicions.

"Go," Malcolm told her. "I will see you tomorrow."

Still, she hesitated. "It has been a long time since I saw you last."

"I am hardly going to up and flee the city in the middle of the night." He stepped over and planted a brotherly kiss on her forehead. "I shall see you in the morning."

She nodded and said goodnight to both. Yet, before she was out of sight of the shop, she turned back to give it a last look. In the light of early afternoon, the magnificent sword hanging in the window gleamed brilliantly. And she could almost swear the lion in the center of the hilt watched her.

\* \* \*

"How long will you deny yourself?"

Malcolm, sitting in the window of the

living space above the shop, turned to look at Martin. "All my life, if I must."

"And must you?" The older man crossed the room to join him. Beyond, the city spread out in a vast tableau that rose higher and higher. And at the very end, above everything, was the castle. "Do you think she would hate you, were you to tell her?"

"Yes," Malcolm admitted without pause.

Martin sighed and shook his head. "How little you know of the minds of women."

Now Malcolm turned, giving Martin a cool look. "And I suppose you know so much more."

"Enough to know you are wrong about this."

Malcolm was about to respond when a horrid screeching rent the air. His head snapped around, eyes searching for the source. "The city gates," he said when a second hideous cry erupted.

"What are you doing?" Martin turned, but his son had already leaped off and out into the street.

Malcolm hit the ground, rolled, and was up and running across as if he had done no more than step over a fallen tree branch. Then, not five steps later, he jumped high into the air without breaking stride and landed nimbly on a rooftop.

Off in the distance, just outside the city gate, an amorphous shape formed. It was a column of blackness, too dark to be smoke, and so tall it towered over the walls. His skin crawled with an icy chill at the sight of it.

He darted across the roof and when he reached the far edge, he took a flying leap to the next roof over. Off he went, arrowing towards the gates as he leaped from roof to roof, gaining speed with every yard.

The column at the gates swirled and solidified into a gaping maw of darkness that seemed a tear in the very fabric of existence. Night seemed to fall with it, though the sun was not yet set.

Something erupted from the next roof just as he leaped to it. It was a dark, hooded figure that held a long white sword in skeletal fingers. Malcolm's own weapon was out of its scabbard and slashing across the being before it could swing. No blood sprayed as the figure fell, cleaved in two, then evaporated into grimy smoke.

He took the next two in a whirling strike that never broke his momentum and followed up by spearing a fourth through the head as he continued. He was unsure what he would do once he reached those gates, but if someone could open a portal such as the one spawning the creatures, then there was a way to close it up again.

Idly, he thought of the of Janet. Spells might be necessary to end the attack, but he dismissed the idea of going to get her. If they found it to be the case, the court wizard, Amus of Shrewsbury, would be dispatched to handle things. There was no need to bring the princess into things.

By the time he reached the market, the din of battle told him he was far from the only warrior in the city to have reacted. Through the gathering darkness he could see the glint of helms and swords and the purple cloaks that marked those of the Purple Rose. Cedric would be down there.

He found himself amused at the sight of a small form with a shock of blonde hair at the edge of the fighting closest to the palace. Running quickly, he jumped and landed beside Alexis, saving her from a sword aimed at her back. She spun, and the look on her face was comical as her eyes were the size of saucers. "Malcolm, I—"

"Always watch your back, Alexis." So saying, he stepped past her and cut down two more who tried to take advantage of her distraction. "And never take your eyes off your enemy."

At the sound of a sword being swung, he turned in time to see her destroy a figure coming at his back. She gave him a grin. "What was that?"

He started to grin, but another horrifying wail tore through the air and, as if it were a signal, the remaining hooded figures vanished. Dread coursing through his veins, Malcolm slowly turned back to look at the void.

    A giant skeletal arm slowly emerged from within, one bony finger pointing ominously at the castle. Then the arm and opening faded into smoke, too, leaving those standing at the gates bathed in the last light of the setting sun.

# CHAPTER 3

Though the city buzzed with conversation of what had happened at the gates, life went on. Two days later, the king called a court to formally endow Malcolm of Bonaparte into the Purple Rose. Though it was not normal for them to be in court, King Ardent also asked his daughters to attend, and so they did.

"Excited?" Rebecca asked Janet with a wry smile as they waited in the balcony that overlooked the hall.

Janet sighed and adjusted the cuff of her new court dress. The sleeves did not fit quite right, and it bothered her some, but not enough to go through the hassle of having another made. "For the tenth time this morning, yes, I am excited to see Malcolm join the Purple Rose. He is a valiant warrior and will make a fine addition to their ranks. No, I am not expecting to have him become my bodyguard because that is not a position given to a junior knight."

"Not traditionally," Sonya began.

"And I do not expect father to break tradition simply to indulge your idiotic fantasies. Kindly keep them to yourself, unless you wish me to do to the court what I did to the library." When the four of them gave each other sidelong glances, she hissed a further warning, "Because, this time, I shall do so deliberately."

Satisfied by the fear in their eyes at the last threat, she turned back to the balcony railing. Their father had called a full court, which in and of itself made her a little nervous. Malcolm was certainly worthy of honor, but this much was unusual for a recruit, even a war hero.

"Why must I wear this?" Alexis said plaintively, tugging at the collar of her dress. "No one can even see us up here."

"Because" Jasmine said with a roll of her eyes, "you are a princess of the realm. You will not go through your life acting like a boy."

"I can if I want to!"

"Alexis!" Janet spun back around, her voice a low hiss of warning. "Do not speak so loud in here!"

"Sister—"

With a sigh, Janet beckoned her over. "Look at everyone below. Do you see Cedric and the other Purple Rose?"

"Yes."

"Do you see how they are in their finest armor?"

"Yes."

"This is a formal occasion, one honoring someone we grew up treating as family. The armor is in tribute to him, as are the formal finery we are wearing."

"Then why can I not wear my armor instead?"

"Is Father wearing his armor?"

Alexis looked down, then sighed. "No."

"The armor is reserved for those endowed as knights of the realm. You have not been so endowed."

"Oh, very well."

Janet shook her head as her youngest sister gathered up her skirts and stomped away. "Honestly, you would think she is five rather than twelve."

"When she does not get her way, she might as well be." Rebecca rubbed Janet's shoulder in solidarity. "Let us just be grateful you are the eldest, and she the youngest."

"Hush." Monica, who had held herself from the main thread of conversation, waved to her sisters. "They are starting."

Down below, two attendants, clad in silks of the palest blue, opened the doors of the court at the direction of Lord Regis, the late queen's brother. Twin trumpets sounded with silvery blasts as Malcolm entered, flanked on either side by three full-clad Purple Rose.

Up on the balcony, Janet swallowed against a lump in her throat. Six escorts were far too many for a mere recruit. It was an honor reserved for officers and heroes. What in the blazes was going on?

The escorts walked Malcolm to the center of the court, then parted and marched away to either side to stand before the assembled officials. It was only then, with Malcolm standing alone, did Janet see the emblem affixed to the left shoulder of his armor, a rose, wrought in silver.

Malcolm, she realized with sick dread, was not being installed as a recruit. He was being installed as an *officer*.

King Ardent rose from his seat upon the Golden Eagle Throne. Even at more than fifty years of age, he was still hale and hearty. Through her mounting horror, Janet noted Malcolm and her father were far more physically similar than Malcolm and his own father. Ardent was tall and lean and moved with the ease he had possessed in his younger days.

Had she been down on the floor, she would have seen her father smile warmly as he drew his rapier, the legendary weapon that had taken Geoffrey de Bergiouac's head at the Idenian Plains. Malcolm kneeled before him and the king laid the flat of the blade on the crown of his head, not on his shoulder, as was done in a knighting ceremony. It was a gesture done only for those being named to the private guard of a member of the royal family.

The eruption that took place in the court at that moment made the devastation in the library look like a summer squall. It threw everyone to the ground- knights and lords and courtiers and royals alike. All save two.

A gust lifted Janet from the balcony and carried her to the floor, her hair fluttering madly as her eyes blazed like suns. She alighted on the floor of the court directly in front of Malcolm, who stood watching her with the patience of the ages.

He took the slap across his face without comment and watched her as she stalked angrily from the room.

\* \* \*

The castle housing the royal family was shaped like a diamond laid upon its side, with the two longest ends meeting at the point of the castle gates.

The remaining four points each held a tower, and it was within these most of the royal family had their private apartments. The tower to the northwest was known colloquially as the Crown Tower, and within its rooms lived the reigning monarchs and any children too young to live on their own. At present, the only occupant was King Ardent, as Queen Celina had perished a decade before after a life-long battle with Denorit Plague.

The westernmost tower, meanwhile, was shared by Jasmine, Monica, and Sonya, who were too young to have their own suitors. Given the interests of the three young women, the tower was often a quiet one as the twins were usually reading something, and Sonya sulked somewhere in the castle.

Two years before, Alexis had moved out of the tower and into a small suite overlooking the training field and stables. There, she indulged in her dream by putting herself through training methods of her own devising and had, in fact, developed a decent, if unorthodox, fighting style of her own.

The northernmost tower belonged to Rebecca, where she lost herself in painting and sewing for hours at a time. The irony of the idleness of her preferred pursuits when compared to her tendency towards sarcasm and bawdy teasing was not lost on her, but she had never claimed to be an uncomplicated woman.

The last easternmost tower was Janet's by right of being the eldest daughter. The library she had torn apart in her fury was her own private one, in the lower chambers of the tower, while she lived in a suite of apartments in the upper reaches. It was to those apartments Malcolm came once the briefly interrupted ceremony was complete.

Her angry outburst was frankly a little confusing to him. He would have thought she would be happy to have him become her body so her sisters could see there was nothing between them. Instead, she had created undeniable drama about the entire affair.

He stopped at the door to her apartment and knocked. He waited for a time, but she did not respond. It was the way she had acted when they had been younger and embarrassed herself with a failed spell. Back then, he would have barged in so she could not shut him out. But doing so now would only cause more controversy.

He could knock again, louder, until she finally opened it. But that would also draw a crowd.

And so, he chose another path. He had snuck about the castle with Sonya growing up. And while he was no longer small enough to use the tunnels the girl had found, there were other avenues open to him. His speed was hardly the only ability he had picked up during his years at war.

He crossed to a nearby window and climbed onto the sill. He reached out and grabbed the lip of a stone that protruded slightly and swung out into space. He climbed along the side of the castle like a spider until he at last came to another open window. Swinging down, he alighted on the sill, and then hopped down inside.

And had to duck and roll to avoid a fireball that instead shot out the window. "Janet! Stop!"

"Stop?" she snarled, curling her fingers around another fireball. "*Stop*? You collaborate with my sisters and my father to humiliate me in front of the court, and you wish *mercy*?"

"You are the one who unleashed a hurricane." He raised his hands in defense as she raised the ball to throw it. "Gods, not in here! You will burn down the entire tower!"

She kept the hand raised another moment, glaring at him, before dispelling the flames. "Leave," she snapped, jabbing a finger at the window he had entered.

"Not until you listen to me."

"Oh, fine!" Throwing up her hands, she stomped to her bed—as they were in her bedchamber—and dropped down onto it with a great deal of petulance. "Have your say, then."

He got to his feet and studied her. "I will send you flying out that window," she told him. "You will come down at the city gates."

He sighed. "No one was conspiring to ambush you."

"The gates are not far enough. I believe I shall send you beyond them."

"Oh, in the name of the gods, Janet. Pull your head from your ass long enough to unclog your damn ears."

She shot up, eyes blazing once again as she jabbed a finger at him. "I'll not marry you, Malcolm, no matter what pressure my family brings to bear!"

He was certain his jaw had landed on the floor. "What in the Five Halls of the Death God does *that* mean?"

"It means my father disregarding procedure by inducting you as an officer so he can place us in proximity is not going to make me choose you as a husband! I do not care how annoyed my family is that I have not chosen a suitor! I—"

He was across the room in a flash, clamping his hand over her mouth to cut off her tirade. "Hold. Just hold things for a moment."

He stepped back, pleased when she folded her arms rather than continue ranting. "Clearly," he said cautiously, "both of us have come into this conversation missing critical details. Janet, your father did not disregard procedure."

"Oh, bollocks to—"

"I have been a Purple Rose for nearly five years."

Her jaw nearly hit the floor. "You *what*?"

"It was my gift from your father when I turned eighteen. My intention was to go to the wars to gain experience being a leader and warrior, then to return and become your bodyguard."

"I— You— When did he gift you this?"

"He called me to a closed session of the court and offered me one request."

"I—" Her mouth worked silently for several seconds. "He made you that offer, and *that* is what you chose? You could have had anything, land, a title! *Me*, for the gods' sake!"

"Would you have wanted me to ask for

that?"

"No, but— By the gods, Malcolm! The throne could have been yours!"

"And all it would have cost," he countered. "Would have been what you hold most dear. Your freedom. Your father gave all six of you the Right of Choice, the right to choose who you marry. That is a right given to few daughters of the nobility and almost never to royals. Your own mother was betrothed to the baron of Weldentore before marrying your father."

"And she would have been married to the baron had father not unmasked him as part of the assassination plot. I know that Malcolm. But, Gods, am I so displeasing to you?"

"You and your sisters are as family to me. I love you as I would my own sister if I had one." The way she took this was not what he had expected after her actions in the court. And he had a suspicion as to what was behind it.

But before he could bring voice to that suspicion, he caught the slight shuffling sound above their heads. Recognizing it for what it was, he walked quickly over to one wall and pushed on an innocuous looking stone. It slid into the wall smoothly, and a section of the ceiling swung down into a staircase. And gray-eyed Sonya came tumbling down it.

"Ow." With a petulant pout, the spying princess sat up and rubbed at the back of her head. "That was unnecessary."

"So is spying on me." Janet flicked a glance up at the opening. "What exactly is that?"

"An escape tunnel." Malcolm pressed on a second stone, and the section swung back up without a sound. "We found it roughly eleven years ago."

"We?"

He recognized the skepticism in her voice, the annoyance, and could not begrudge her it. He imagined there were few women, if any, who would appreciate a man spying on their bedchamber. "You were at your lessons with the court wizard at the time, and I have not been up there since. Which," he added, turning to Sonya, "is apparently more than I can say for you."

The pale-eyed girl shrugged with a nonchalance belying the fear in her eyes. "I like to know what goes on."

"More," Janet said. "I think *Rebecca* likes to know what goes on between Malcolm and myself. Hoping to catch a proposal or assignation, were we?"

Sonya shrugged again, but more jerkily this time, and her gaze flicked to the windows in a manner that told Malcolm she had heard the threats Janet had aimed in his direction. And understanding Janet's own temper quite well, he chose to step in.

"Janet, am I to assume questioning why I did not choose your hand in marriage for my request has more to do with taking it as an insult than any hopes I might lean in that direction after all?" When the eldest princess nodded, he refocused on her younger sister. "Gather the others. Tell them Janet and I would like to speak with them all. Use the door," he added when Sonya jumped up a little too eagerly.

She slumped some but did indeed leave by the door.

* * *

Whether Sonya was more scared than he had thought, or whether the princesses genuinely wanted to hear Malcolm's tale, they were all assembled in Janet's sitting room inside of thirty minutes.

He pondered and studied the five younger sisters as he perched on the arm of a chair. All but Rebecca, it seemed, had changed out of their more formal gowns once the ceremony ended. What they wore now was, naturally, dependent on their own preferences. Still, it was interesting to see what they had put on.

Alexis, given as she was to her utter hatred of displaying her own femininity, had at least chosen not to wear her chainmail around her own quarters. The twins, ever studious, wore simple dresses without frill. They had never enjoyed calling attention to themselves, something he thought might change once they came of age.

Sonya, who preferred being invisible even more than Jasmine and Monica, wore leggings and a loose tunic that hung a little too loosely on her slender frame. She kept having to shift it back up over her shoulders, which suggested she had stolen it from a male page.

It cheered him to see that so much of their personalities had not changed over the time he had been at war. He was, however, worried as well, as their fascination and assumptions regarding Janet's suitors suggested they were not maturing in areas they would need to.

"Janet," he began. "Has told me you have been intimating she has been waiting for me to come home so she and I could marry."

"She has turned aside more than a dozen suitors," Rebecca accused, jabbing a finger at Janet. "She makes excuses for them, but excuses are all they are."

"No," Janet replied. "They are called *reasons*."

"Oh, please." Rebecca rose. "If you are just going to repeat this whole thing again, then I have better things to do with my time."

"Sit." Malcolm kept his voice patient and easy, but there was enough steel in it the nineteen-year-old princess sat back down.

"May I leave?" Alexis asked. She had chosen to perch on a chest of drawers at the far end of the room and now hopped down. "I could honestly not care less about all this. It is a stupid matter to gossip about and does not even affect me."

"No," was Janet's reply. "Whether you like it or not, you will be receiving your own suitors one day. You need to understand the subject."

Alexis rolled her eyes toward the ceiling and leaned back against the chest with a look of sheer petulance on her face.

"Sonya told us of your words," Rebecca accused her elder sister again. "You were outraged he did not choose you."

"No," Janet disagreed. "I was aghast and surprised that, when offered the world, he turned it down. Malcolm respects my wishes. He knows I do not love him in that manner any more than he loves me."

"You all have gotten to know Cedric." Rising, Malcolm drew the princesses' attention back to himself. "Has he told you of the story of he and his fiancé, Lady Rowena Loxley?" When they all shook their heads, he continued. "Cedric and Rowena did not fall for each other at first sight. Quite the opposite. They hated each other, could not be in each other's company for five minutes without a fight breaking out. It took Rowena nearly being killed for them both to realize they fought what they felt for each other with everything they had."

"That is far from the only course for love to blossom," Rebecca countered. "Our parents certainly did not take that path."

"That is not my reason for telling you this. They were my subordinates, my comrades.

I had to place my life in their hands, bickering all the while though they were. I did so without hesitation, only because there was no other option. Had we been in safer surroundings, I would have stayed as far from their bickering as I could, even though I could clearly see why they fought so often.

"The reason for that is this. What happens between two people is no one's business but theirs. Not so long as none are being harmed. Janet's search for a husband and her friendship with me are her concern, and hers alone. Leave your sister be because you will be in her place err long. And when you are there, you will no more welcome her intrusion than she welcomes yours now."

\* \* \*

Most of Janet's sisters appeared to take Malcolm's advice. Well, not Alexis, who, as she had so eloquently put it, considered the entire matter "stupid." But those who had cared in the beginning now backed off.

Except, as Janet really should have expected, for Rebecca. She did not come out and say she still believed Janet was secretly in love with Malcolm. Instead, she dropped little tidbits, pointing out to her elder sister how handsome and fit the swordsman was, how good a man he had become. It was all said in an offhanded manner, as if they were merely comments. But she always spoke with a slight smile and smirk in her voice, and it drove Janet crazy.

Finally, when she and Malcolm had been sitting off to one side discussing another impending suitor, Rebecca came up to them and said, "Well, you two look cozy. *Very* cozy."

Janet, who had decided to take it upon herself to alter the dress she had worn the day Malcolm had been invested as her bodyguard, threw down both dress, needle, and thread, and snapped out, "By the gods, Rebecca. Would you just come out and say it already?"

"Very well. You dislike having all these suitors come to call on you. You keep turning them aside. Why keep doing it?"

"I am crown princess. The royal line will continue through me."

"And that does not require a king. There have been rulers in our family's past who never had a co-regent. They have had a consort."

"No."

"The two of you are good together." Rebecca rounded on Malcolm. "She is not displeasing to you, is she?"

"Sit," Janet ordered, jabbing a finger at a nearby settee. When Rebecca arranged herself on the settee and looked to her with defiant eyes, Janet took a moment to focus her anger and lock it away. "There are things of which you are not aware."

She looked over at Malcolm, who watched her as well. She had kept this secret for five years. It was time. "When father called you to the court on your eighteenth birthday, you were not entirely alone in the room."

"You spied on us."

She saw the realization and shame come into his eyes and, oh, it tore at her. "I thought he would do what he did, and I wanted to hear your answer."

"Do what?" Rebecca asked. "What answer?"

"Father offered Malcolm my hand."

"*What?*" Rebecca rounded on Malcolm. "And you said *no*?"

"I am not fit to be king."

"Sister!"

Janet held up a hand to cut Rebecca off and kept her own gaze on Malcolm's. "I will admit, here and now, in this company, that back then I did entertain the notion of us being wed one day. You were good to me, and I thought I loved you. I know now I did not, and when you told father I was not what you wanted, then I let you go.

"I let him go," she repeated, turning to her sister. "And I hold no more desires in that direction. I am not what Malcolm wants, and he is not what I want. And I will not take him as my consort and bind him to me simply to save myself some aggravation, either in the form of more suitors or pressure from those who should know enough to allow me to make up my own mind."

# CHAPTER 4

Rebecca spread the tale to her other sisters, and they all promptly backed off any further insinuation. But Janet scarcely had time to breathe a sigh of relief before a new situation gripped the castle.

Ever since the night of the invasion at the castle gates, Alexis had developed a strange numbness in her hands that cropped up at odd moments. She would be training with her sword, only for it to fall from her grasp when she abruptly lost control of her fingers. The same could, and did, happen when she was eating or cleaning her chainmail shirt or saddle.

Lady Maria, the castle's healer and the consort of the late queen's half-brother, Lord Regis, could find nothing wrong with the girl. Yet, the problem persisted until the day after Janet's confession, when Cedric discovered Alexis and one of the cook's boys passed out cold in the hallway outside the girl's apartments. He carried both to Maria's hospital, where Janet, Malcolm and Rebecca arrived on the run.

"How is she?" Janet demanded the

moment she entered the hospital.

Maria rose from beside Alexis' bed. She was a tall woman, taller even than Malcolm, and a magnificent beauty with creamy pale skin and lustrous ebony hair. Her eyes—the same purple hue as Janet's, for she was also a wizard—were patient as she looked upon the trio. "She has yet to wake," the woman said. "Though she rests peacefully enough."

While Janet and Rebecca went to the side of their little sister, Malcolm walked over to another bed. There the boy slept under the watchful eye of Cedric. "Dorian," he identified at a glance. "His parents own a stall down in the market. Salted meats and fish."

"Does that make him worthless to you?" Cedric snapped, causing Malcolm to raise a brow.

"As the son of a blacksmith, no, it does not. Are you alright?"

"Fine." Cedric rubbed at his brow in a manner suggesting he experienced a vicious headache. "The boy had been after becoming a squire for some time. I suppose I took this personally."

Malcolm laid a hand on his friend's shoulder in solidarity. "Lady Maria is a wonder. If there is a way to bring him around, she will find it."

"It would help immensely if I had the slightest clue what was wrong." Maria picked up a round of crystal and laid it upon Alexis' brow.

"This would turn red if she had a fever or blue if she were cold."

"It turned green," Rebecca observed when the older woman removed her hand. "What does that mean?"

"Under normal circumstances? Pregnancy. No," she added with a laugh when both young women's heads snapped up. "That would be under normal circumstances, as I said. This is far from normal."

Just as Maria took the crystal from Alexis' forehead, the girl moaned softly. Janet all but leaped forward. "She is waking!"

"Calm yourself." But Maria's eyes narrowed in concentration as she reached out to lay two slender fingers on the pulse in Alexis' wrist.

Her eyes narrowed further, and she turned to take up another crystal, this one a translucent blue and carved in the shape of a pyramid. "A pain relief," she explained as she lay it on the girl's chest, which heaved with increasing rapidity as Alexis gasped for breath. "She is in considerable pain." Alexis arched, and she let out a bone-chilling scream of mortal agony as her entire body tensed.

"Hold her down!" Maria snapped out as the men charged across the room. Without a word between either, Malcolm moved to grab Alexis' right arm while Cedric took her left.

To give them room, Maria stepped around to the head of the bed and began weaving her fingers above Alexis' chest in arcane patterns. "*Molo tenbra, ahko ten,*" she chanted in a voice that rose and fell musically on the words. "*Zanka eti magabra kolee.*"

The crystal pulsed and glowed, the surrounding room darkening as if the stone drained the light away. Alexis screamed, groaned, and tried to pull free, but the crystal stayed put no matter how hard she writhed.

"*Mato mela kanata zata tu.*" Maria plucked at the air above the crystal as if she tried to pull something from it. "*Zota kento degata ambu moga petaro zen!*"

On this last, she seemed to take hold of something with both hands and pulled on it hard. Alexis threw back her head and screamed louder and longer than ever before, and the crystal flared with such brilliance everyone assembled turned their head away.

Both scream and light faded, and they turned back. Alexis lay still once more and, for a moment, Janet feared her sister had perished. But then the girl's eyelids twitched, fluttered, and opened to reveal blue eyes clear as a summer's day.

"Alexis?" Janet pushed past Malcolm, reaching out to brush her baby sister's hair away from her face. "How are you feeling?"

"I—" She blinked, looked blank for a moment, then shot bolt upright and reached for where her sword would be had she been wearing it. "Where is it? Where did it go?"

"Your sword is over there," Rebecca told her, pointing at the table where Maria had laid out her implements.

But Alexis only shook her head. "No, not my sword. The skeleton."

"Skeleton?"

"The skeleton in the cloak." Alexis looked past Janet to Malcolm. "You saw them."

"You mean the things we fought that night at the gates?" He shook his head. "Alexis, they all vanished with the portal."

"Then either one did not," she said, "or they have come back because one accosted me in the hallway."

\* \* \*

Despite the strange events, Lady Maria could find nothing wrong with Alexis and let her go shortly afterwards. An hour later, Dorian woke as well, though far less dramatically, and was sent home.

That, however, proved to be the last normal occurrence in the matter, for the boy never made it to his home. The last person to see him had been the guard manning the castle gates, and that had been for no more than a few seconds.

Two days later, it happened again. Cedric discovered Alexis in the stables, slumped against her horse's paddock. Though she recovered more quickly and did so without the theatrics of her first fainting spell, there were whispers, nonetheless. Whispers that got louder when one of the stable hands turned up missing.

From there, everything went downhill.

Sonya was found passed out in a corner of the kitchen. By the time she woke, a scullion had walked away from his duties, never to be seen again.

Monica fell asleep in the middle of a lesson and, a day later, her tutor was gone without a trace. Jasmine did not come down for dinner that night, and her maid was never seen again.

When Rebecca toppled off a chair mid-sentence and her bodyguard disappeared, Janet decided enough was enough. She sent a letter to Malcolm, instructing him to stay away from her. If the progression continued, then she was next and, as the person who was around her the most, he would be in grave danger.

King Ardent agreed with this as he took it a step further. He ordered his daughters locked in the Eastern Tower and allowed none inside without a contingent of guards escorting them.

"Even prisoners are given more freedom," Alexis grumbled one afternoon, perhaps two weeks after her initial collapse.

Janet smiled sadly. Out of all of them, Alexis was the most used to being active. Sitting and working on her needlepoint or weaving was all but anathema to her. "Why do you not do your lessons?"

"Because they are idiotic and all but

useless." Staying sprawled on the divan she had flung herself upon in a display of utter boredom, Alexis turned enough to pick up the lesson in question. "How on earth does it affect my life to know the name of the twelfth emperor of the Kam'We'Ta Dynasty of Mi'Kam'Wo?"

"Kohtem IV," Jasmine said, without looking up from the tome she was in the process of copying from. "Also known as Kohtem the Mad."

"Liked playing Pinochle, with the loser having to sacrifice a servant's heart on the temple altar," Monica added, pointing out a phrase for her sister while all around them their four other sisters stopped what they were doing to stare at them.

"He was finally deposed in 412 AC," Jasmine finished. "And executed by being forced to drink a bellyful of liquid gold."

The silence that fell in the wake of that statement was so oppressive both girls finally looked up. "I do not know which disturbs me more," Sonya said after another long moment, "that story, or the fact you can relay it so handily."

As everybody laughed, talking turned back to their current situation and the facts of what had led to it. "I just cannot understand the meaning of it," Rebecca said after a time. "Why do we collapse? And why does someone always vanish in the afterwards? They must be linked."

"Of course, they are linked," Monica replied. They had gone around and around on that subject endlessly since being locked up in the Eastern Tower.

"Yes," Rebecca admitted. "But what I mean to say is, what links them? What is causing this?"

"Cedric?" Sonya asked. "He has always been the one to find us."

"Unlikely." Janet put the final stitch in the needlepoint she had been doing and set the hoop aside. "This is doubtlessly magic, and he is incapable of even the simplest battle magics, let alone higher magic such as this."

"So speaks the expert," Alexis teased.

"Yes," Janet shot back, "so, she does. I may be limited in what I can control, but I know enough of the theory to know that any magic controlling behavior requires considerable knowledge of the craft. Knowledge far beyond that of any knight."

"Could it be Lady Maria?" Sonya piped up. "She is a well-learned mage."

Janet shook her head. "It would be rather foolish for anyone within the castle to be behind this, particularly someone who has been here as long as her."

"Well, it must be someone we know," Rebecca protested.

"Why?" Jasmine asked.

"Because."

"That is hardly a reason, sister. It is barely

an answer, and one far more appropriate for Alexis than you."

"Jasmine!" Alexis protested, only to be ignored.

"Why must we know the person who has done this?" Jasmine asked again. "What could possibly make that a necessity?"

"Well, why do this to us if you do not know us?"

"Why do this to us if you *do* know us?" Jasmine countered. "Never look at a problem from only one side, Rebecca. It is only when you look at it from all sides you find the answer."

Rebecca stared at her for several seconds. "There are times I wonder if you are indeed human."

They all had a laugh over that, and conversation moved on from there to other matters. There had been a young squire who had come into the city the day before their father had confined them within the tower, a handsome youth of the same age as the twins, and he had evidenced something of an interest in Monica. For Janet, it was a pleasant change of pace to tease someone else about a match, rather than to be teased.

Yet, even late into the night, she could not seem to cast aside the subject of their misfortune. She was, after all, the only one who had not yet had a fainting spell or been linked to a disappearance. Now, she dreaded what might happen to her.

* * *

Janet awoke in the middle of the night to a terrifying sight. There, leaning over the bed, was the very thing that had been at the city gates, the creature she had briefly seen upon the day of the first incident. Fear threatened to strangle the breath from her as she looked up at the hideous face beneath the black cowl. The creature blinked at her, surprised she had awakened. *Move*, she screamed in her mind and, amazingly, her body responded. Or, more accurately, her *power* responded.

Wind lashed out, driving the monstrous figure back from her bed, and with that separation the crown princess found she could move. She pushed up, summoning flame and ice to hurl at the beast, driving it towards the large window of her bedchamber. It waved its gnarled hands, movements she recognized as the arcane art of Will. It was going to overpower her!

She raised her own Will against it, fighting back with everything she had and was. Straining, she tried to force it to flee, tried to implant the suggestion to *go away*. But she tired. Her bed called to her and in some corner of her mind she understood the creature had secreted a suggestion of its own. She was losing.

So, she gave up, allowed her Will to fall away. And struck with a gout of flame.

The figure, unprepared for the tactic, went

hurtling through the window and out into the night. Janet slumped against the bed, exhausted but victorious.

* * *

Malcolm sat in his small room above the Golden Lion, looking out across the city. From there, he could see the castle rising in all its glory over everything.

It was strange, but the imposing edifice had never seemed intimidating growing up. It had been the home of his friends and their family. His second home in a genuine sense.

Yet now, in the fading light of a beautiful cloudless day, it seemed almost sinister. There were no clouds in the sky, yet a dark shadow appeared to hang over the castle. He feared the darkest days were still ahead.

"I wonder, do you see her when you watch from here?"

Malcolm smiled to himself. "Sometimes."

Martin crossed the small room to lay a rough-skinned hand upon his son's arm. "You should be with her."

"They lock her up for the safety of all, Father."

"Yes, so they did." With no further words, the old smith left him to his thoughts, and Malcolm went back to watching the castle. He could see Janet's window from where he sat, and seeing it now made him feel as if he were still watching over her.

When the black form leaped from Janet's window, with a gout of flame chasing it, it was so sudden it took him a full thirty seconds before he realized something had *exited* the tower.

He did not bother with the stairs to the ground level, instead leaping from the window as he had the night of the attack at the gates. Landing light as a feather, he took off running for the castle.

He had no way of knowing where the specter headed but reasoned it would make for a quick escape. And so, he aimed to head it off halfway to the city walls.

He did not get far before he saw the first shadow. It stepped into his path with its sword striking out for his head, and only his well-honed instincts enabled him to roll beneath the strike and past his attacker. Coming up on one knee, he drew his sword in one swift motion, spinning it around to stab backwards into his opponent's torso.

He felt his blade bite deep, but when he glanced over his shoulder to look, there was nothing there. The shadow had vanished rather than dying.

Another blade flashed out of nowhere, forcing him to drop to the earth and flick his weapon up to take the hand holding it off at the wrist. Both sword and hand vanished into wisps of black smoke that quickly faded from sight. He annihilated close to a dozen shadowy swordsmen in short order, using his speed and his sword's inherent versatility to outmaneuver and surprise each he encountered.

But he had to alter his trajectory with each, for though the fights were quick, they still took time. The specter had to be throwing them in his path to slow him down, and it was drawing closer and closer to the gates with each encounter. There would soon be no chance of catching it.

And so, he pushed that speed to its limits, rocketing forward and ignoring the shadows that continued to pop into his path. They followed him, he knew, and would catch up while he battled the specter. He just hoped they would not enable it to escape.

\* \* \*

Rebecca stared at Janet in disbelief as her elder sister finished recounting the tale. "Do you have the slightest clue how completely mad that sounds?" she asked.

"I know how it sounds," Janet said, "but if you were to come with me right now, I could show you the scorch marks on my windowsill."

As it was not the length Janet would normally go to make a tale believable—in fact, Janet was rarely one for telling fibs of this magnitude—Rebecca swallowed and nodded. "Very well."

Together, they woke their remaining sisters, including Alexis, and all repaired to the tower's library as the twins insisted there must be an answer.

"There has to be something," Sonya said as they searched the books and volumes and papers of six centuries of Avanna rulers.

"Here," Jasmine said, beckoning over her twin to where she had found a gargantuan leather-bound treatise. The two girls struggled to lift the cover as their sisters joined them, and Janet ended up helping.

The moment she saw the first illustration, she cried out, "That is it! That is what I fought!"

Stepping forward, Alexis peered at the title below the drawing. "La Reine de L'effroi?" she asked, hopelessly mangling the pronunciation. "What on earth does that mean?"

"It is an Avannionian treatise," Monica explained. "From the time of the fall of the royal family of that land. It means—"

She stopped and looked slowly to Janet. "It means the Queen of Dread."

"The Dread Queen," the eldest Princess whispered. "The ancient evil that used the Black Counselor to destroy Camelot."

Monica spun back to the treatise and scanned her eyes over it. "According to this, unlike what they say today, the royal family of Avannion did not die in an accident. The Dread Queen cursed the women of the family into Dread *Mothers*, a kind of demon. They..."

"They what?" Janet asked quietly.

"They began having fainting spells, as did men around them. And those men vanished, never to return."

"Just as is happening now." Jasmine sank into a chair and lowered her face into her hands. "We are doomed."

"Cursed," Rebecca murmured, stepping away.

"Is there any way to remove it?" Janet asked.

Monica shook her head. "The book does not say. An alliance of heroes drove the Dread Queen off, including Arsene Lupin, but they had to destroy the royal family during the fight. They were too far gone."

Of a sudden, Rebecca turned and stalked across the library to a portrait at one end. She looked up at the painted figure of their mother for a moment. "Forgive me," she whispered, then reached up to tear it open.

"Rebecca!" Janet cried, running across to her. "What are—?"

Rebecca turned with a chain grasped in one hand and thrust it out to her elder sister. "Take it."

"What—"

"Take it!" Rebecca reached out and grasped Janet's hand to shove what she held into the woman's grasp. "Our mother's amulet."

Janet stared down at the circular pendant, set with six round-cut diamonds. "The Seven

SWORD OF LIONS

Moons Amulet? Rebecca—"

"Mother used that to survive the Denorit Plague as a girl," Rebecca said. "It can ward off any disease or curse for seven days."

"Yes, but—"

"The Forest Tower is six days' ride from the capitol."

Janet's eyes went wide. "The home of the wizard, Merlin? Rebecca, tell me you are not serious."

"If she cursed us," the girl stated. "Then you are the only one who can go. The Dread Queen must have been laying the curse upon you when you woke. You may have avoided it."

"And what if I have not?"

"Then the amulet will give you time to reach the Forest Tower."

"Sister—"

"Seek the aid of Merlin," Rebecca pressed. "The Dread Queen is an ancient force. It will take the magic of the Favorite of Lady Fate to undo her curse."

"And how am I to leave the castle? Father barred us in."

"Find a way,"

Janet looked at her sister, then at the younger ones, each in turn. They looked back with confidence and hope, and a note of barely restrained despair. She was their only chance, she realized. "Alright." She held up the amulet. "But I'll not wear this until I am sure there is no other choice."

"Find Malcolm."

"Oh, Rebecca, honestly."

"Do you have a better idea for a traveling companion?"

Janet sighed. "Very well. But do not get any ideas."

She left the library, planning out her escape as she went. There was no way from the tower, save for one: the very way the specter had fled.

The windows were still open, and Janet changed quickly into her favorite riding dress. The purple garment had a skirt that was only two long sections, which kept her modesty and allowed her black-trouser-clad legs freedom of movement. She paired it with soft half-boots of the same black and a bracelet interwoven with a few handy little dweomer that her mage craft instructor had made her when she had come of age. Two rings containing small amounts of ointments and unguents joined that, and she deemed herself ready.

She took a last look around the room—so dear now she was leaving it—and went to the window. She climbed up onto the sill. Drawing in a breath, she focused on her powers. She had rarely attempted this kind of magic, and never on herself. But there was no other way down to the city.

Closing her eyes, she leaped feet first into

thin air. As she plummeted, she clasped her hands together, the right with her index and pinky fingers extended, the left with the thumb outstretched. She muttered a spell in the ancient language, her voice rising with each word. "*Dota melek, zanta fee. Moreg tantu elif!*"

The wind caught her halfway down, a soft zephyr that somehow possessed enough strength to slow her descent. It carried her out into the city, out along the avenue to the market, where it deposited her upon the roof of a market stall.

Though she was a princess, Janet was no weakling. The castle guard had trained her and her sisters in various athletic talents at the king's direction. She allowed her knees to buckle as she landed, turning it into a roll that took her across the roof to the edge where she hopped down as nimbly as a mountain goat.

Purpose and anxiety sped her steps as she arrowed straight for the old shop and Malcolm.

\* \* \*

Malcolm's sword spun and slashed, cut and sliced. He cleaved limbs, shattered weapons and severed heads and torsos. Yet, no matter how many he slew, more took their place. He fleetingly wished for Rowena or Cedric, just to have some help, though he knew the first was leagues away, and the latter would be no more successful at fending them off.

No. He would have to finish this fight on

his own. And he had a feeling he knew how.

He fell into a more defensive style of combat, using his sword to knock weapons away rather than destroy them. He struck out with the flat of the blade rather than the edge. And he turned endlessly, holding off the mass of attackers with little effort.

He saw a pattern he realized after a time. The shadows moved with a form of synchronized unity. There was a method, and in battle method could become an exploitable weakness if one knew how.

He spun faster and faster, his circles tighter and tighter until he turned in place and his sword almost seemed a steel cocoon around him. But the speed with which he moved was even greater than that, for the sword flicked out and cut and sliced in the space of a breath, carving each up in a hundred ways without the strike even being noticed.

Until they all flew apart, shattered into swiftly dispersing shadows, and he dropped to one knee in exhaustion. It was rare for him to use that much of his ability, and the exertion forced him to prop himself up with his weapon. He leaned his forehead against the cool metal of the hilt and fought to slow his breathing.

The specter had gotten away. Of that, there was no doubt. But it clearly watched the city, for it had laid a most powerful trap to hold him in check.

It had best come for him next time, he vowed. For if it did not, he would make certain to come for it instead. He would end it for putting all of them through this. For putting Janet and her sisters through this misery and using them for its unwholesome ends.

When he was certain he could walk home, he climbed down off the roof and made his way back through the city. Night had fallen during his battle, and only his memories of the streets guided his steps.

He arrived back at the Golden Lion and nearly took down the slim figure, which stepped out of the shadows before him. Only those lovely amethyst eyes stayed his blade from a death blow. "Blast it all, Janet," he hissed, shoving his sword back into its scabbard. "I nearly took your head!"

"That would likely have done me a favor."

He studied her for a moment in the dim light spilling down from his window. He knew her face, knew to read her emotions in it. Fear was almost naked upon her, a bone-deep terror that wrenched at his own soul. "Tell me what is wrong."

She shook her head. "No, Malcolm, we must go. Now."

"Go where?"

"To the Forest Tower. I-I need to seek the aid of Merlin."

"We can hardly set out on a month's

journey without provisions or supplies." He beckoned her towards the door. "Come."

He saw her eyes accept, then go wide with shock. "Malcolm!"

He rolled, drawing his weapon once again. And found himself at the point of Cedric's sword. "She is coming with us," the blond knight said in a voice cold and hard as steel.

"She is my responsibility," Malcolm countered.

"You have been relieved of your duties."

*Like hell*, Malcolm thought and slapped aside the weapon with his own. He came up, elbow slamming into the soft spot beneath Cedric's chin. The knight stumbled back a half-step but got his broadsword up in time to block Malcolm's long-saber before it bit into his throat.

Malcolm spun the other way, then back the first way again, his sword flicking out like the tongue of a snake. Cedric parried with ease. Malcolm tried going low, but that, too, was avoided. He tried coming up with a rising fist, but Cedric stepped aside and hit him with a backfist that buckled his knees.

Now, Cedric came on the offensive. The hilt of his sword smashed into Malcolm's shoulder. His knee drove itself into Malcolm's solar plexus. His open hand shot out and grabbed the swordsman by his throat and lifted him off his feet as if his weight were only that of a small child.

Then he pivoted and hurled Malcolm through the gleaming window of the front of the shop. The enchanted window that had withstood grime and dust and damage for over twenty years shattered into small diamonds that fell like rain around Malcolm as he hit the ground.

He dimly heard Janet screaming his name as everything went black.

# CHAPTER 5

"Malcolm!" Janet screamed as she fought against the iron grip of the two Purple Rose Knights who carried her between them. They held her so firmly she could not even touch her feet against the ground as she struggled and kicked. "Blast you, unhand me! Malcolm! Help me! Malcolm!"

"Be silent." With a cold finality, Cedric backhanded her across the face.

She took the blow but glared at the man who had once been her friend through eyes teary from pain. "Why, Cedric? Why are you doing this? Why did you attack him?"

"Be silent," he said again and stepped around the two men who carried her between them to take the lead in the little group.

They were out of sight of the Golden Lion now, and Malcolm still was not coming after them. She feared he would not wake until the morning and despaired he might attempt to raid the castle to get her back. Even with his ability, the fight would be bloody, possibly suicidal and take far too long.

They needed to go now. Which meant she

had to free herself.

She delved inward, gathering her energies to break herself free. But her energies would not coalesce. She had spent too much of her power escaping the castle by flying herself from her window to the market. She he did not have enough left to do more.

She turned her head, hoping to find someone watching through the windows who might come to her aid. But there was no movement within any of the houses. She would have been certain the fight between Malcolm and Cedric would have alerted nearby residents. Yet, no one seemed to have heard anything.

She could hear nothing either, she realized. Nothing but the blowing of the wind. A wind getting louder and closer.

A sudden howl rent the air, a roar that seemed loud as a thunderclap. Her mind registered it as the roar of a *lion* just before something rushed up on the rear guard.

The first Purple Rose went flying into the side of a building with an impressive crash. He bounced off the wall and landed on the ground in a heap. A second flew headfirst into a garbage pile while a flurry of blows lifted the third three feet into the air before he came crashing back down.

Janet stared in amazement. The person who stood where the three knights had been just a moment before had his head down, but it was unmistakably Malcolm of Bonaparte.

"Take her!" Cedric shouted to the two who held Janet, drawing his sword as he stepped past them. Malcolm blurred, and Cedric's sword spun away to bury itself in a nearby wall as Malcolm appeared before him with his own sword swept out.

No sooner had Malcolm appeared then he vanished again, leaving Cedric to drop to his knees. Malcom reappeared beside one of the knights holding Janet and grabbed the man by the back of his head. Malcolm spun, tearing the man's hand off Janet's arm as he hurled him face-first into the wall next to Cedric's sword. He slid down the wall into a boneless heap.

The last knight released Janet and went to draw his sword. Malcolm brought his own sword up. The slim blade flicked out like a steel whip against the man's hand, forcing him to drop his weapon.

Cedric hit Malcolm from behind, looping his arms under Malcolm's, holding him fast. "Take her!" he commanded the last knight again as he tried to haul the swordsman away.

But Janet had recovered enough to act, and she spun towards the knight. Her foot came up hard between his legs—a woman's ultimate defense—and the man crumpled.

Malcolm slammed his foot down on Cedric's instep, jerked his arms up, and then down to break the hold, and pulled free. He spun back around, smashing the hilt of his weapon against the knight's skull, dropping him to his hands and knees. He finished the attack by driving his knee into Cedric's face, breaking his nose, and knocking him cold.

Janet stepped up beside him, looking around at all he had done. It was more than she had ever thought him capable of, and she turned to say so. But as she did, she caught a glimpse of gold and red and looked down. He held a longsaber, but not the one he had brought home from the wars.

Clutched in his hand was the Sword of Lions.

"It was mine, after all."

She raised her eyes to his, swallowed against a sudden lump in her throat. "It would seem it was," was the best she could manage.

He slid the weapon into the hilt at his waist, then held out his hand for hers. "We should go," he said. "There will be others after a time."

She hesitated for a moment, then took the offered hand, and the two of them ran for the smithy.

* * *

Martin waited for them when they got back to the shop. He had already saddled Malcolm's horse and prepared two traveling bundles for them. Janet nearly asked where he would have gotten women's clothing for her, then stopped herself. Malcolm's mother, she remembered, had passed away shortly after his birth, and by all descriptions had been roughly her own size.

That the man would have held on to his late wife's clothing for over twenty years only to pass them to her touched her deeply. As did Malcolm's attempt to get his father to come with them, though all involved knew the man was no warrior and would slow them down more than he would help.

But she raised a brow when Martin told Malcolm he recognized what had happened as being the same as *that* incident. She wanted to ask how the blacksmith knew of the deaths of the Avannion royals when it had happened two hundred years before his birth, but there was no time.

They took the city gates at a full gallop, afraid the guards might attempt to stop them. In truth, one guard did try to bar their path, but he quickly dove aside when he realized they were not about to slow or stop.

Malcolm rode his horse—a strange breed she could not recognize, with a shiny black hide and white mane—hard for hours, and Janet chose not to distract him by asking any of the many questions in her mind. Actually, if she was being entirely truthful, she was still sorting out some of them.

The chief question was how he could be the destined wielder of the Sword of Lions. There had never been a case, to her knowledge, of a commoner being linked with a bloodstone. There had been some raised as commoners who were in fact the children of nobles or royalty, but Malcolm was undoubtedly Martin's son.

So then, how did he come to possess it?

"What flew from your window?"

Malcolm's question was so sudden it took her several moments to realize he had seen the specter fleeing her bedchamber. "It was trying to curse me. I woke in the middle and managed to fight it off, but—"

"Did you grab your mother's amulet before fleeing the castle?"

The sudden change of topic threw her, and she yet again was forced to reorient her mind to answer. "Yes, but—"

"Put it on. Now."

"It is only a precaution."

"I said put it on." He snapped something to the horse, and the magnificent black beast slowed to a stop. Once it had, he turned around to look at her. "We will not be going another step until you do."

Her temper flared. "You do not give me orders."

"I do when your safety is at risk." Swinging his leg over the saddle, he hopped down and moved to sit at the base of a nearby tree.

Appalled and angered by his actions and tone, she snatched up the horse's reins. "Ya!" she said, giving the reins a snap.

The horse did not move. She snapped them again, harder. "Ya!"

"Shadow is trained to take orders only from me," Malcolm called out. "And as I have just given him an order to remain where he is, you will not be traveling onward until I am satisfied you have done what I asked. Come down, Janet. I believe it is time we talked about a few things."

More than a little annoyed, she slid down and gave him a haughty look as she crossed to sit before him. "Very well, have your say."

He slid the sword, scabbard and all, from his belt and laid it across his lap. The golden handle and bloodred stone glittered in the dawning light, for they had ridden out the rest of the night. "I know you have wondered how I might be the one meant for this. Commoners are not supposed to be able to wield bloodstones, as they rarely have the means to trace their bloodlines."

"You are not going to tell me Martin is really a noble."

"Not Martin, no. But I am."

He could not have stunned her more. "Your mother?"

"I do not know who my true parents are. Martin and Shana, his late wife, were barren."

"Then how—"

"There is an element of the legend of the Sword of Lions that you…that no one has ever heard. When Merlin left the sword attached to the shop window, he told Martin its owner was, at that time, too young to wield it. He would need watching, a home, and instruction in humility. And then he produced an infant from beneath his cloak."

"You." Her anger fading away in the face of astonishment, she looked at the weapon in his lap. "Then you—"

"Have known all my life I was the sword's true owner? I have."

"You lied to us. To me."

He shook his head. "Think back, Janet. Think back to every time you or one of your sisters has made a comment about the sword waiting for me. Not once have I ever responded. I never said a word on the subject."

She did think back, and she realized he was right. His response each time throughout the years had been to change the topic of conversation. "Whose son are you, then?"

"As I said, I do not know. Only that I was never a commoner." He reached out and gently pried apart her fingers, revealing the amulet she still carried. "Put it on."

"No."

"Janet, are you familiar with the fate of the Avannion royals?"

She sighed. "So, your father *does* know the truth."

"Avalon, where Arthur lies in his tomb and where Martin is from, is in Avannion.

Martin's family has been castle blacksmiths for generations. One of his ancestors was a victim of the incident. I know what happened, and I have no intent of letting that happen to you."

* * *

She gave in and put on the amulet, though the chain locking behind her neck sounded entirely too much like the door of a dungeon slamming shut for her liking. Putting it on bound her soul to it for the rest of her life, just like her mother.

They rode on for the rest of the day without incident, covering a considerable distance as the day waxed and waned. Malcolm's horse was a most unusual creature, able to run for hours without pause. She thought to ask him what the breed was shortly past midday.

"They call them Shadda-dar," he replied. "The warriors of Kahn the Conqueror first used them, during his conquest of Qin Han. They are bred specifically for war and are never ridden until the age of three. The warrior who breaks them is their master for life."

He patted the horse's gleaming black neck. "Shadow here took me three months to break. He has been rather gentle since then, rather like a pup."

The horse gave a whinny at that moment, which sounded like a laugh to Janet, and promptly bucked. "Alright," Malcolm laughed, patting the horse's neck again. "Alright. He dislikes when I call him that," he explained to her with a broad grin.

Janet's laugh was a trifle strained. The horse's little protest had nearly thrown her from the saddle, and she had been forced to cling to Malcolm's waist to keep her seat. The feeling of being pressed close against his broad back had been one that was not unpleasant, and she was not entirely happy about the emotions it brought up.

Gods, she had buried those emotions long ago. Why were they coming back now?

\* \* \*

They reached an inn just as the sun headed towards the horizon. Though there were a few hours of light remaining, they elected to stop and find lodgings for the night.

"I suppose I will be doing the cooking after this," Janet said as they sat down at a small table. "Unless you have gotten loads better in the last five years."

He chuckled, but before he could reply, a passing figure—small and cloaked—went suddenly flying across the room. Even as Malcolm got to his feet and went to check on the figure, Janet knew they had attempted to steal the Sword of Lions. Now that its owner had claimed it, it seemed the sword violently rejected all others who tried to take hold of it.

She followed him, then stopped as she got a look at the thief's face. For whatever bizarre reason, they had crossed paths with the very boy her youngest sister had chased the day Malcolm had returned.

Pieces shifted into a new pattern for her, and she regarded him with folded arms and a raised brow. "Where exactly *did* the bracelet come from?"

The boy gave her a cheeky grin. "The castle is not nearly as impenetrable as one might believe, m'lady."

Janet had to laugh. "Alexis. I might have known. She wears her jewelry so rarely she would never recognize it if it sat on her bedside table."

"'Twas really somewhat disappointing." He hopped nimbly off the table. "Come. My cousin wishes to speak with you both."

He led them to a table at the far end of the room where a solitary figure sat in a forest-green cloak. The form beneath was obviously that of a woman, but there was an obvious rough strength more common to an adventurer than a lady.

*Or*, she realized as Malcolm's steps faltered beside her, *a soldier*.

As if suddenly given prescience, Janet knew who the woman was before she pushed back her cowl. She was as lovely as the tales of her intimated, with hawk-like eyes of emerald green and short copper hair. "Lady Loxley, I presume?"

Rowena Loxley, fiancé of Sir Cedric

Ivanhoe and fourteenth-generation descendant of the venerated Archer, Robin Hood, cocked her head and a brow as she studied Janet. "Captain," she drawled out, drumming her fingers on the mug of ale before her. "The next time you lie to me, you will need a healer."

"To be completely correct," he replied, pulling over another chair. "This is only a lie of omission. How are you, Lieutenant?"

"Singularly annoyed with you." She sighed and gestured to a serving girl scarcely older than the boy. "Though, I suppose that is nothing new. Have a seat."

The girl came over, and Janet noted she favored the youth with a big smile before promising to come back with food and drink. As she walked away, Rowena turned to Malcolm. "I can guess easily enough you and the royal are close, but I do not believe you are foolish enough to have run off with her given the stories going about. So, pray tell, what are you doing this far from the capital?"

Janet and Malcolm traded glances, and then she began, "If you have heard of the trouble—"

"I did not ask you," Rowena snapped, never looking at the princess. "And this is not the castle, so you will wait until I have asked you before replying."

"Rowena, that is enough." Malcolm's tone carried a note of iron. "I know well your family's problems with the royal line, but rein in your tongue. Janet has done nothing to you."

"Oh, perhaps she has not," Rowena agreed. "But then, her family continues to blame mine for something that happened two-and-a-half centuries ago."

"As your family continues to blame mine for the actions of a man dead for nearly twice that," Janet countered. "John the Greedy was a bastard, Lady Loxley. I will freely admit that. Can you admit that Jacob Loxley betrayed his own nation?"

"Oh, aye. But there is a key difference between the two of us. Been to your lands lately, Princess?"

"My ancestor did not provide a staging ground for an invasion from Avannion."

"Still, you blame us. Two hundred and fifty years!"

"It is not a matter of blame, Lady Loxley." Janet spread her hands as if gesturing to her whole kingdom. "Whose lands should we give you? Which noble house should we slight so Loxley can have its own lands again, when they have been no friend of the crown for nearly three centuries?"

"There were dozens of lords who sided with de Bergiouac!"

"And their lands were gifted to knights who stood with my father at the Idenian Plains! A battle, mind you, that your own father was conspicuously *absent* from!"

"Enough." Malcolm's calm voice cut through the argument as neatly as the sword at his side. "Rowena, you and Cedric went round on this very subject when we were at the front, and you know well Janet speaks the truth. Your family has done nothing to earn back the trust of the crown, and so can hardly expect the crown to favor you."

When the light of triumph lit Janet's eyes, he rounded on her. "And as the crown princess, Janet, you know full well the argument you just made is in no way any sort of attempt at diplomacy or a way to bridge this divide."

"We do not need to bridge the divide."

"Oh, aye," he said. "We do. The two of us are not enough if we face what we face."

He turned back to Rowena. "The troubles you have heard of are true, and worse than you know. Janet's sisters are cursed by the Dread Queen herself, and we ride for the Forest Tower to seek Merlin's aid. I ask you to join us."

"Malcolm!"

He waved off Janet's protest with a single raised hand. "My skills are not enough if she turns her full power upon us, and your magic is still often uncontrollable. We need help."

Rowena looked back and forth between the pair. "I shall think upon it overnight and give you an answer in the morning."

\* \* \*

"Why must I share a room with her?" Janet demanded.

"Because a place such as this does not run to private rooms," Malcolm replied wearily. "And I do not think it is proper for us to share a bed."

Janet paled slightly. She had not considered that before, and now an image of him so near in the dark flitted into her mind and nearly made her stumble physically back. "Very well," she said, trying to maintain some of her dignity, though she wanted to run in the opposite direction as fast as her feet could carry her. "But be it on your head if I end up blowing this place apart because she could not hold her tongue."

She turned and went to the room Rowena had been sharing with Andre, the one the two women would now share instead. Inside, the woman had removed her cloak and was reclining in bed wearing only her forest-green undertunic and leggings. The cloak, Janet saw now, had hidden a tough, disciplined body so unlike her own. Somehow, that made her feel inadequate.

"I snore," Rowena warned her, toeing off her boots and letting them fall on the floor with twin *thunks*.

"According to my sisters, so do I." Janet slid off her own boots and laid them neatly beside her side of the bed. And sighed. She did not want the woman joining them. But she knew Malcolm, and she knew what his true motivation was for inviting her along. "Lady Rowena—"

"If you think to make an apology or some let us be friends speech, save your breath. My hatred for your family runs deep."

Janet closed her eyes, forcing down her rising temper and the bile over what she was about to do. "What I was going to say is Malcolm has been my closest friend since childhood, and I trust his judgment. If he wants you to come along with us, then I bow to his wishes."

Rowena clapped three times in a slow, thoroughly insulting fashion. "Am I to be impressed?"

"No, but if you served with him for as long as Cedric says, then you should be able to trust his judgment as well. Would the man you served with be so blind as to risk his life for me if I were as truly horrible as you believe?"

For a long moment, there was silence from the other side of the bed. "I know Malcolm," Rowena said finally. "And my Cedric. He wrote to me of being your guard, and he had little but praise for you and yours."

"I consider him a friend." An idea occurring to her, Janet shifted to face the woman. "And a good, honorable man who deserves more than an empty title with no land attached. If you come with us, and we save the kingdom, then I promise you I will carve off half of my own lands to be the new Loxley Hall. As a wedding present for you both. Will that satisfy your honor and outrage?"

Rowena studied her for another long, silent moment. "'Twould not be the first time one of your line has lied to a Loxley."

"True. But, as I said, I trust Malcolm's judgment. He wants you with us, and so he shall have what he wants if it be within my power. I ask not for your loyalty or friendship, Lady Rowena, not freely, for those are things that must be earned. I ask only for your bow and your arm, to aid me in saving this kingdom as your ancestor once did."

She held out her hand. "Do we have an accord?"

Rowena hesitated a moment, then shook the offered hand. "We do."

# CHAPTER 6

When the two women came downstairs the next morning, Malcolm was cheered to see neither sported bruises or wounds. Even better, they seemed to have come to something of a truce as they walked together to himself and the boy, who had introduced himself as Andre before they went up to bed.

"Before we get this underway," Rowena told him, "I want to know why Cedric is not with you if you are indeed in such danger."

When Janet, standing somewhat behind his old lieutenant, jerked in surprise, Malcolm deduced she had not given Rowena that particular piece of information. It made him wonder just what she *had* told Rowena, and how she had convinced the archeress to join them.

With a sigh, he told her of what had happened in the capital city since his return home. And when he reached the fight with Cedric and the other Purple Rose, her eyes went to cold chips of green ice. "So, you fought with him, injured him. Defeated him. And all without losing so much as a drop of blood yourself? At what point in the last three months did you decide I was an idiot?"

Whatever temporary truce had been forged between Janet and Rowena shattered like glass as the princess grabbed the archeress' arm and spun her around to jab a finger in her face. "Your fiancé tried to abduct me and nearly killed Malcolm. The only reason he won the fight is the Sword of Lions. Its powers—"

"I do not care what kind of powers the blasted thing has!" Rowena snarled. "He and Cedric are so equally matched any true battle between them would be long and bloody and leave both in need of a battalion of healers."

The brewing fight was cut short when a roar of, "You thieving whore!" came from the dining hall. Malcolm and Rowena, spurred by the instincts of veteran warriors, ran for the door with Janet hot on their heels.

But it was Andre who got there first. The boy shot into the hall, leaped onto a table, and bounded off in a twisting, arcing leap towards the fat man in the green silks who held the serving girl by the front of her simple cotton dress. His elbow shot out, breaking the man's grip by breaking his wrist. His other flashed up, driving the V of his index and thumb into the man's throat.

The fat man stumbled back, grabbing for his throat as he fought for air from the blow. His face went even more red than it had been, and he reached for the boy. Only for Malcolm to grab his arm, spin him about, and pin that arm behind his flabby body at a painful angle.

"If you all will excuse me, I believe the gentleman will be leaving now." So saying, he frog-marched the man out of the room and the inn itself.

When he came back, Andre was getting the girl a glass of water. "Did you kill him?" he asked, his eyes hot and angry.

"No," Malcolm told him calmly, sliding his perfectly clean sword back into its scabbard. "But he desperately needs to change his leggings and will ride for several hours before he can. Let that be enough."

\* \* \*

They went out to the stables, and while Malcolm and Rowena saddled their horses—the redheaded archeress had a mount of the same breed, though its hide was dappled with white here and there—Janet turned to the boy, who had calmed down once the man was out of his sight. "The serving girl is the daughter of the owners, yes?"

"Yes," Andre said cautiously.

"I think they would be a better recipient of the merchant's money than you, do you not agree?"

As both Malcolm and Rowena stopped and turned, Andre's eyes slid away from them all. "I do not know what you mean."

"Oh, I very much doubt that." Janet smiled sweetly. "Your instincts are very proper regarding rescuing a lady, Andre, but only someone who knew what money the merchant had lost, and the girl had not taken it would have acted so fast."

"You would have him admit the theft?" Rowena demanded. "And admit he placed their daughter in danger?"

"Oh, hardly. I am quite certain an intelligent young man could produce a believable lie about how he found the money out here on the ground." With a smile, Janet leaned in towards the boy and said quietly, "I am also quite certain a young maiden might be rather... *thankful* towards someone so gallant."

Andre, who had paled degree by degree as she had exposed his perfidy, perked back up, and Janet grinned as he scampered back to the inn. Her grin faded, however, when she saw the look on Rowena's face. "What do you find wrong now, Lady Rowena?"

"Why not tell the merchant he had it if you are so determined for Andre to do the right thing?"

"Because" Janet replied evenly, "I recognized that merchant. My father had him banned from the capital market after the guards arrested him for trying to buy a thirteen-year-old girl from her parents, then attempting to abduct her when they refused. The man is a gigantic pig who has avoided the gallows solely because his brother is a member of court in good standing."

Rowena put up her hands in surrender, then caught the glint of light off the golden hilt of Malcolm's sword. "So, was that how you crossed the room so quickly in there?"

"It seems to boost my speed," was his reply, "beyond even what I have trained myself to have. It is why I could defeat Cedric without a mark."

"Hmm." She crouched and started to reach out for it, but he quickly snagged her hand.

"No. I alone seem able to touch it safely."

"You mean it is a bloodstone?" As she straightened, Janet watched understanding come into the woman's eyes. "Of course. You said your father was a blacksmith. Martin of Avalon."

"His adopted father, apparently."

Rowena turned to look at Janet, and for the first time there was no hatred in her gaze, as curiosity had overcome it. "Adopted. Yes, I suppose that would make sense. A commoner could never use it. Do you know who your true father was, Malcolm?"

"No." He shifted, looking out towards the road. "Merlin did not tell Martin my true identity. Only that I am of noble blood."

"Hmm." Rowena pondered him. "I have heard the legend of the weapon, naturally. I doubt there is anyone in the kingdom who does not know it, though clearly none know the entire story. Did not Merlin first appear in the wake of the Battle of the Idenian Plains?"

That piece of information had not occurred to Janet before, but the idea now sparked her mind. "You think him the son of one who feel in the battle? It could be. There were many lords and knights slain that day, and more than one likely had a child out of wedlock."

Rowena's dislike roared back in a heartbeat. "Why are you assuming he is a bastard?"

"Because were he the rightful son of one of the fallen, there would have been little need to spirit him away in the dead of night."

"Even if his father had sided against you?"

Janet gave her a wry look. "My family is not in the habit of executing children for their fathers' crimes. You live, do you not?"

Rowena conceded the point with the slightest inclination of her head, then turned to look at Malcolm again. He was still staring at the road, fingers tapping lightly on the hilt of the magnificent weapon at his side. "I suppose it hardly matters who your father was. It was not he who raised you, and so he is nothing to your life."

He turned at her words, one brow arched high. "Quartermaster Toblermane's words? From you?"

This time, Rowena shrugged, but said no more, for at that moment Andre came back with a strut to his walk and a big smile on his face. His alternate reward appeared to be one he was quite pleased with. "Shall we go?"

* * *

Janet had been quite tired the day before, and more than a little upset. As such, she had not taken her usual notice of the scenery while she and Malcolm had ridden along on their quest. But now that they rode off from the inn, she studied the brilliant day around them.

The sun was warm and bright, the sky such a clear blue it nearly made her forget what they rode from. The trees were a gorgeous green, almost like emeralds, and here and there she saw fruit hanging from boughs. She could hear the twittering of bird song and caught flashes of brown and black scampering along branches that were squirrels and other tree-dwelling woodland creatures.

She had not been on the road like this in years, not since she had been sixteen and last visited her lands. It felt wonderful, even if Rowena still seemed cold towards her. Attempting to bridge the divide, Janet passed the time by relaying a disastrous escapade of Malcolm's in the castle kitchen.

They had put him to work on a state dinner, and the cook had set him to seasoning a grand pheasant. It had turned out horrible because he had substituted the cook's usual spice blend with another concoction. It had made the central guest of the dinner—a diplomat from the northern plains of the kingdom of Zula—so ill he had had to delay his meeting with the king until he could safely get beyond the easy access of a chamber pot.

"I was ten," Malcolm protested. "What does a ten-year-old know of cooking?"

"Had you bothered to listen to directions," she said loftily. "You would have known he had dietary concerns and could not stomach even the smallest amount of oregano."

"The man ate like a horse," Malcolm shot back. "You have no proof his condition was not the product of eating five helpings of goose along with three full potatoes and two treacle tarts. It was a miracle he could stand up from that table at all."

"Cedric and I could not allow you near the cooking pot," Rowena said, suddenly joining the conversation. "It was the first thing we ever agreed upon. You tend to experiment, and it rarely goes well."

Sensing an opportunity, Janet turned her focus to Rowena. "Cedric told me some stories of the two of you, but I would love to hear it from your side."

"No," Rowena replied brusquely.

It was not the most heartening response Janet had heard, but Rowena had responded at all gave her hope. And so, she told a story of her own. "My parents did not entirely get along when they first met. Of course, that may have partially been because father was an assassin hired by my mother's cousin. It often seems to me the best matches hate each other at the start."

"Malcolm," Rowena said, interrupting her in a tone far more warning than complaint.

"I know," he said. "Just keep riding."

Janet opened her mouth to continue her story, then gaped in astonishment as an arrow flew past her head. "What on earth?"

She turned to look back and saw a full two score of riders thundering towards them. "Where did they come from?"

Malcolm's magnificent sword flashed out, neatly cutting a second arrow in two with the ease of swatting a fly. "Our friend from last night seems to have regained his courage."

Janet, too, had spotted the merchant riding at the back of the force of men. Judging by his clothing and expression, he had been less concerned with his revenge than finding new trousers, which explained why they had waited so long.

"Take these," Malcolm said, and when she looked at him, she found he held out the reins to her.

"Your horse will not respond to me," she reminded him.

"No, which is why you will be safe." He thrust the reins into her hands and swung one leg over the side. "He will not turn around until I return."

"What in blazes do you think you are doing?" she demanded.

But it was too late. He had already flung himself from the saddle.

\* \* \*

Malcolm heard Janet screaming his name. He heard her screaming for him to stop, for him to come back, but he ignored her. His duty had never been to obey her orders, but to keep her safe. And damned if he was going to allow whatever rabble that fat, useless piece of trash had bought to place her in jeopardy now.

One rider in the group's lead fired off another arrow, heading straight for his face. Malcolm never broke stride as he reached down to draw the Sword of Lions.

The weapon was out of its scabbard so fast that, rather than cut the arrow down, the blade caught the arrowhead and deflected it into the trees. He rotated his wrist, spun the sword, and sliced the tips off the next two in midair.

In the back of the group, a man whirled sling over his head in fast circles, then loosed the bullet. Malcolm simply ducked, rolled, and came back up as the projectile hit the ground in a harmless puff of dust.

Another arrow flew past his head, but from behind him. It flashed across the distance, straight and true, and took the slinger off his horse with a dead center hit. Malcolm grinned, knowing Rowena had his back, but that grin faded quickly as he spotted Andre leaping from branch to branch in the trees.

The boy set, bunched his legs and launched himself at the men on horseback, knocking three to the road with the weight of his body. When he came up, there were gleaming butterfly blades grasped in his hands. He kicked the first to rise in the chest, slashed the second across the face and took the third down with a backhanded swipe to the throat.

It was an impressive display, and one that caught the attention of the other riders. Six quickly dismounted, surrounding the youth with drawn swords while their remaining fellows rode for Malcolm and the two women behind him.

They met within seconds, and Malcolm put all his speed and agility to work in dealing with them. It was the same as when he battled the shadows the night they had fled, with him turning and sweeping in tight circles, blade flicking out here and there.

He slashed a leg, cut a bridle strap. One rider fell to the ground as his saddle was neatly cleaved just above the buckle. Before the man could regain his feet, he took a kick behind the ear that put him down for good.

Rowena jumped over his battle in a flying arc, loosing three arrows from her bow. A man who had been raising his sword for a blow at Malcolm's back collapsed, an arrow in each shoulder, and the third pinning his leg to the saddle.

She landed and her hand blurred to the quiver slung over her shoulder, drawing another arrow that flew into the back of one of Andre's opponents. When another of the riders Malcolm was dealing with attempted to strike her down from behind, she dodged the blow without looking. Spinning around, she put an arrow through his windpipe in one fast, accurate shot.

From there, the fight was quick, bloody, and brutal. All twenty assailants lay dead, bleeding, or unconscious. But as Malcolm looked around, he noted their equipment was far better than ordinary brigands or sell-swords. "These are merchant caravan guards. The bastard had his own men stationed nearby."

Rowena smirked. "We have cost him more money, then. Good."

"Malcolm!"

They whirled. The fat merchant had somehow gotten past them and now had his arm around Janet's throat as he attempted to drag her into the trees. He had had his hand over her mouth, but she had briefly gotten free to call out.

His fingers tightened on the hilt of his weapon, and he heard a sound like a lion's roar in his head. The next thing he knew, he had his hand around the man's flabby throat and pinned him against a tree several feet beyond Janet.

"Please," the man whispered, all he could muster with Malcolm cutting off his air, "have mercy."

"I warned you," Malcolm hissed in a voice not his own, "that if I ever saw you again, I would send you to the Death God."

"Malcolm. Malcolm!"

Whatever had taken him over ignored Janet, even as the rest of him fought to call out against what he was doing. For he stepped back and raised his sword to end the man's life.

And then Rowena was there, grabbing his shoulders and yanking him away, placing herself between him and his victim. "Stop!" she demanded of him but spoke no further as he instead swung at *her* neck, forcing her to duck and roll clear of him.

This time, when he came around, it was a blast of wind that took him off his feet. He slammed into the tree, his brain rattling in his skull.

And the last thing he saw was the bottoms of a pair of feet coming right at his face.

\* \* \*

"Was it necessary to hit him so hard?" Janet demanded of Andre.

"Yes, it was necessary." Rowena answered for her cousin as she stoked the fire. "Something was wrong with him. He tried to kill us."

"I understand trying to subdue him," Janet snapped back, "but he has been unconscious for three hours."

"And you have cared for him all this time." Rowena scooped up a small spoonful of the stew she was making and tasted it. Shaking her head, she took out a small pot and sprinkled a finger of powder into the pot. "You shall make him an excellent wife one day."

Janet scowled at her but said nothing else. She knew the woman was only needling her. Rowena considered Janet not worthy of Malcolm, which was truly fine with her as it was one less person to press that particular fiction.

Still, the fact was Malcolm's inability to wake worried her. She needed his aid if they were to reach the Forest Tower and, if he remained unconscious, they were going to be in considerable trouble.

"Princess," Rowena finished stirring the pot and tasted again. Evidently, it now met with her approval as she nodded once. "If you are going to walk off your worry, perhaps you could go to the stream and get some more water. We will need to refill the waterskins before leaving in the morning."

Janet had not even realized she had stood up, let alone taken to pacing back and forth, worrying at the bracelet. Because she had, and because it mortified her, she took the small bucket from Rowena's saddle and went to draw water without complaint.

She had always enjoyed riding through

the countryside and camping beneath the stars. But now there was a wary unease beneath the enjoyment. She had little doubt the Dread Queen would try to stop them, and the odds were the fight that day had been the easiest they were going to have.

Gods, she needed Malcolm to wake up. Talented though Rowena and Andre were in the ways of battle, even her unpracticed eye could tell Malcolm was a level above them. If something especially dangerous came after them, they would need him.

She paused beside a tree as the memory of the fight came back to her mind. In particular, the weapons Andre had summoned from out of nowhere. The boy had considerable athletic ability, and Janet did not think it resulted from combat magic.

So, where had the boy gotten those swords from? They hardly matched anything that would have come down from any of the Archer's compatriots.

Could they have come from the other side of his family? The boy's athletic and acrobatic talents were well-developed for one so young and seemed to speak of a Qin Han heritage. And when you added in his nimble fingers and penchant for thievery, she thought he might very well have a blood tie to Aladdin or Alibaba.

Shaking her head as she remembered she had a task to perform, Janet started walking again. She got only a few steps before realizing she could no longer tell what direction she headed in.

Night had fallen while she ruminated, yet unless she had been completely off, she had left the campsite with nearly an hour of daylight remaining. And there was a cold mist creeping along the ground that was inconsistent with the time of year. As the chill seeped into her bones, she decided she would be far safer returning to the campsite.

But no sooner had she turned around than she came face-to-face with an inky black shade holding an equally black sword.

# CHAPTER 7

Her throat closed shut as if squeezed by a gauntleted fist. She did not know what it was, but she knew it was evil, and she had to get away, had to get help.

When it reached for her, she dodged right, spun, and jammed an elbow into the midsection. Though she put her full weight behind the blow, it barely fazed the creature, and she had to dodge away again.

She shoved out her hands, trying to use just a whisper of her power. Whether it was the immediacy of the situation, or her luck was improving, she did just that. The spell took the creature off its feet and sent it rolling along the ground for a few feet.

She, meanwhile, turned and ran like an army of demons was on her heels. She had no clue where she headed, and she did not care. If she ran all the way back to the capital, then as long as she got away from the thing, so be it.

She raced headlong through the underbrush. Branches that just minutes before had seemed normal, even friendly, now reached out like evil hands to stop her. Nails scratched at skin and fingers tore at her clothes until she feared they would leave her naked and bloody, yet still she ran on.

It was after her now, racing in her wake and howling at her in an inhuman screech. Even without looking back, she knew it was gaining ground, knew it would catch her before long.

And then, up ahead through the gloom, she caught sight of the flickering of the campfire. Her heart sang at the knowledge salvation and safety were near.

"Malcolm!" she cried, all but diving for the glow of the flames. "Rowena! Andre! H—!"

She shot through the trees and stopped dead. Rather than her allies, two more shadows stood beside the campfire. One held two wicked short swords, the other waved a vicious-looking club back and forth as if fending off a bear.

Oddly, she seemed to have surprised them somehow, for they hesitated. Her mind, fueled by adrenaline as it was, reacted in that single heartbeat of time. She shot a hand toward the fire behind the two, then closed it swiftly into a fist as she spat out, *"Zane metlo!"*

The fire erupted in a burst of heat and light, a detonation that threw the sword-wielding shadow to the ground while its companion rolled clear. It came up on one knee and hurled the club at her, but she slashed out with her hand, spat *"Motra!"* and a gust of wind slapped it aside.

But to her horror, the club tumbled end over end back to its wielder as the shadow creature ran, jumped, and kicked off a tree to throw at her again.

This time, she dodged the thrown weapon, hissed another incantation, and sent a lance of wind at the shadow creature instead. She caught it in the side, and it spun down, down, down until it hit the ground with a thud and moved no more.

She darted for the tree she had left Malcolm lying against, but he was gone. The horses still stood where they had left them, but there was no sign of anyone else.

The shadows had captured them, then. Or they had fled into the trees. *Gods, please let them have gotten away.*

The first shadow emerged from the trees just as she regained her feet. In desperation she reached out to the fire again, determined to have a weapon that could counter this one, for it did not hesitate as the others had. It rushed at her with unnatural speed, its horrifying hands reaching out to grab her and wring the life from her body.

She tried to sidestep, to get clear so she could summon the flames to immolate the monster. But, instead, it collided with her, spilling them both to the forest floor. They rolled, and she ended up under it. Its breath was ferocious, the sounds it made as it clawed at her hideous and sickening. She fought at it with all her might, shoving it off her with a vicious gust of wind.

It scrabbled up again, and she shoved more wind at it, fighting it off in sheer desperation. Then, through her terror, she thought she heard Malcolm's voice, and she called out, screaming for him to help her. But he did not come, and the thing redoubled its efforts to get to her. Her will and magic crumbled bit by bit until it broke through and pinned her down once more. She drew in air to scream for Malcolm's aid one last time.

And the shadow shouted at her, "Come back!"

A hand smacked her across the face, stinging her cheeks and jolting her with pain. "Damn you," he snapped down at her. "Come back now!"

Through tears brought on by terror and pain, she recognized the face above her. "Malcolm?"

His face, so full of fear and worry, relaxed at that. "Thank the gods," he whispered, shifting to take his weight off her. And as he did so, she scrambled back, looking around frantically for the shadows, for whatever evil had attacked her that he had obviously driven off.

But the fog and the unnatural darkness had vanished, and, in place of the shadows, she had felled two familiar forms lay unmoving upon the ground. "Andre!" she sobbed. "Rowena!"

Oh, gods. What on earth had she done?

\* \* \*

"I suppose I should be grateful you did not incinerate me," Rowena growled as Janet brought her some stew. She and Andre had turned out to have nothing worse than a few bumps and bruises, but the archeress was still spitting mad, and Janet could not entirely blame her.

"You should be grateful for your own reflexes." As soon as she handed the woman the bowl, Janet checked Rowena's eyes one more time. When Rowena scowled and jerked away, Janet ruefully shook her head. "To fall that way and incur neither broken bone nor concussion is truly a marvel. You are a formidable woman."

The need to insult warred with simple courtesy on Rowena's lovely face for a time before she finally sighed. "I had heard your talents with magic were well below par. It would seem whoever thought that was mistaken. Nothing has struck me that hard since a hobgoblin got lucky and rammed its club into my midsection."

Janet smiled. "And I am sure I got off much easier than it as well."

"The trip is not over yet." But Rowena smiled, too, as Janet returned to the fire and the cooking pot.

The fight seemed to have created

something of common ground between them, which Janet was thankful for. She had not looked forward to a week of travel, sniping and bickering all the way with the woman.

As she stirred the pot some more, ladling out another bowl for herself, her gaze landed on Andre. The boy was plowing through the stew with an appetite only the young had. "What line do those swords come from?"

He froze, the spoon halfway to his mouth as his shoulders jerked once in shock. Then he shoved the spoonful into his mouth and spoke around it. "My father's lineage."

"Ah," Janet said. "So, that is why Rowena is heir rather than you. Your mother is the Loxley."

"Not...exactly." With a sigh, he put the spoon and bowl down and scrubbed at his face with his hands. "I am not truly a Loxley. My stepfather is a cousin of Rowena's father. My mother and I are from Avannion. Her grandfather was Arsene Lupin."

"Lupin?" Janet sat back, considering. "I suppose the Gentleman Thief makes sense. Was your father kin to Aladdin or Lord Alibaba, then?"

"Um, no." Andre shifted nervously. "My last name is actually Le Fay."

"You are in no position to judge someone else's heritage," Rowena snapped quickly. "Not with what lies in your family tree."

Janet cast a weary look at the woman. "Do

you suppose at some point you might allow me to speak before taking offense at my words? The Le Fay family might have included the Black Counselor, but there are no less than twelve royal functionaries across the world with blood ties to him. All are men whose reputations are above reproach, and one of them is my father's personal chamberlain. Malcolm and I have both known him all our lives."

She turned back to Andre, her eyes kind and smile warm. "And as for your mother's grandfather," she continued, "Arsene Lupin may have been a thief, but he was an honorable man who once counted Holmes as a close friend, and their teacher, Dupin, had nothing but praise for his mind. He did what was needed in a kingdom where evil hides behind a friendly smile and a hand extended in friendship might disguise a knife in the other. I will not disparage a man hailed as a hero by many beyond his kingdom's borders."

Andre gave her a grateful smile, though Janet saw Rowena's scowl out of the corner of her eye. There was still a considerable distance for them to cross, despite the initial bridging of the gap.

They talked about nothing in particular for the next little while until Janet accidentally let slip her continuing problems controlling her magic. Rowena pounced immediately. "So," she smirked, "the rumors are true after all. Your powers are weak."

Janet rolled her eyes. "My, but you are a determined one, Lady Rowena. Do I need to check you for a concussion again?"

As it was a rather good comeback, Rowena's snarl lacked most of its punch as she hissed, "Had I not held back, you would be dead now."

"Enough." Malcolm raised a hand to stall the mounting argument, although Janet caught the quick tremor of his lips that betrayed his suppressed amusement. "We shall travel together for some time to come. I would appreciate if you would not spend that time bickering constantly."

While Rowena took to muttering under her breath, Janet changed the subject. "I suppose we shall have to keep watch for those shadow spells from here on. They seem to be the Dread Queen's signature."

"Is that what we looked like to you, then?" Malcolm asked. "Skeletal shadows in robes?"

Janet paused. "No, you seemed made of oily blackness. When did you see skeletons?"

"The invasion at the city gates." Malcolm looked confused. "Why would the spell look different out here?"

Janet thought for a moment, and then her eyes widened. "They are different spells. The creature who tried to curse me matches the skeletons you fought at the gate and what my sisters saw, but not what I saw tonight. It was a different spell."

"It sounds like one of the defensive spells employed by my family," Andre piped up.

"Your family?" Janet asked, surprised. "The Dread Queen may have set Morgan Le Fay upon the Eternal King in order to destroy Camelot, but why would she have access to magic created by the Le Fay family?"

The boy stared at her as if she had lost her mind. "Princess, you have been speaking of the Dread Queen all this time. Do you mean to tell me you have been speaking without knowing her actual identity?"

Janet glanced at Malcolm, but he looked equally as surprised as she. "Her identity? You mean you know who she truly is?"

Andre nodded. "She is the mother of the Black Counselor, and sister to Merlin himself—Morgana Le Fay."

\* \* \*

It was not the best revelation to go to bed on. One of the most powerful wizards ever born had cursed Janet's sisters, and perhaps her as well. Things had quite suddenly gotten much, much worse.

So, when Malcolm did not get up with the rest of them the next morning, they initially thought little of it. Until Janet brought him breakfast and could not wake him.

They tried every method they could

devise, yelling and shaking and throwing water in his face. Janet even tried kissing him, though it made her unbelievably uncomfortable to do so. But nothing worked. At most he would shift slightly and murmur something incomprehensible, then settle once more.

"This is your fault," Rowena accused Janet.

As she had just attempted the kiss, Janet was not in a forgiving mood at that moment, and she responded harshly. "I did nothing to him. What did *you* put in that stew last night?"

"We *all* ate the stew."

"And Malcolm is the only one I did not take down with my magic during the fight last night, so do not blame me for this."

"Why did you not take him down?" Rowena demanded, her green eyes bright. "You got away from him, took Andre and I down. Why?"

Janet stared in amazement. "Are you truly that dim? I did not recognize *any* of you!"

"So you say."

"Enough!" Taking the risk all men rightly dread, Andre stepped between the two women who were heading towards fury. "By the gods, can all the two of you think to do is fight?"

"She starts every fight!" Janet snapped.

"And you respond."

All three whirled around. Malcolm sat up and rubbing at his eyes. "By the Gods, I feel as if I have slept for a week."

"Malcolm." Anger fading quickly into relief, Janet kneeled to lay a hand upon his brow and check his eyes. "Are you alright?"

"Groggy." He shifted, then laid a hand on his stomach. "And starving. Is there any food left over?"

Fortunately, they had saved the remains of the leftover stew, and he wolfed it down as if he had not eaten for three days. In between bites, he relayed a dream he had had while he slept.

"I was running through an endless field. There was a lion following me. Not chasing me or stalking me. It kept pace, step by step, mile after mile. Every footstep. There was nothing around in any direction. It all looked the same.

"Yet it felt as if I had to keep going the way I was. That to deviate even by one step would destroy everything. Would cost me more than I could imagine."

It was an interesting dream, and one that made Janet feel oddly uncomfortable, though she could not exactly say why. But one element of it gave her an idea. "You said a lion followed you. Do you suppose that could have meant your sword?"

He stopped to think for a moment, chewing over both question and food. "Yes," he said at length after he had swallowed the latest mouthful, "that could have been it."

"What does it matter?" Rowena scoffed. "'Twas only a dream."

"Perhaps," was Janet's reply. "But perhaps not. Bloodstones are magical artifacts and semi-sentient by nature. They must discern one's bloodline, after all. The lion Malcolm saw might be a manifestation of the sword's will."

"Its will," Rowena said skeptically.

"Yes. Do you recall how he acted yesterday when the merchant grabbed me?"

"That was berserk. He has done it before."

"How many times at war did you witness men going berserk?"

Rowena shrugged. "Dozens, I suppose."

"And did a loud roar ever precede it? Did any of them speak in a voice not their own?"

Rowena blinked in surprise. "No."

"I did that?" Malcolm asked. "That happened?"

Janet nodded. "It was one of the most terrifying things I have ever seen. I would scarcely have recognized you for the utter rage on your face."

"And you believe that was somehow his sword exerting influence over him?" Though Rowena had doubtlessly meant to sound incredulous, her voice carried heavy notes of amazement and interest.

"More than that," Janet continued. "I believe it may explain why he slept so long and why he was so hungry when he woke. Such a possession can use up one's energy reserves."

"You know a lot about this," Andre

observed.

"I have done a lot of research into the effects of diverse types of magic. There are entire tomes on mind magic and their effects." She turned to look at Malcolm again and found him watching her and smiling as he chewed the last mouthful of his breakfast. "What?"

"It occurs to me," he said as he set his bowl aside, "that as studious and scholarly as Jasmine and Monica are, you have always outshone them in the ability to comprehend and remember certain subjects."

"If this is all true," Rowena said, cutting into the moment. "Is it something we shall need to watch for?"

"Unlikely," Janet replied after another moment's thought. "This was the first time it happened, and it did not until the merchant tried to abduct me."

"Oh, so as long as we keep you out of danger, we should be fine."

Janet smiled at the sarcasm in Rowena's remark. Despite herself, she was coming to enjoy the woman's acid tongue. "It will likely not be easy, I grant you. I am the one the Dread Queen cursed, and she will likely have her servants attempt to capture me and bring me back to her. Something tells me her plot will not be complete without the full set."

"She'll be quite disappointed, then." Malcolm pushed himself up and gained his feet, then immediately had to put his hand on the tree he had sat against in order to avoid falling.

"And you will take more time to rest." Janet moved so he could lean on her, and Rowena did the same on his other side, so they supported him between them. "I will guide the horse for today."

* * *

It was not the easiest thing for them to manage, as Shadow flatly refused to follow her commands even with Malcolm's instruction. Eventually, they discovered that so long as Malcolm's hands were on the reins, Shadow seemed to believe he was the one controlling things. And so, with both his hands and Janet's holding on, they were able to go.

But for Janet, it was only half a victory. The arrangement forced her to sit snug in Malcolm's arms as if he surrounded her on all sides. It was not something she was comfortable doing with any man, but she was most uncomfortable because it was with him. In particular, because the feel of his lips from that insane moment of trying to wake him by kissing him had lodged itself firmly in her mind.

What in blazes had she been thinking, agreeing to try that? She should have been more insistent Rowena do it, especially given it had been her idea to begin with.

The worst part was it reminded her of being fourteen, that day at her estate in Morrberry-by-the-Sea. The day she had impulsively kissed him, intending it to fluster him as he so rarely was. And instead feeling a flutter in her own stomach at the taste of him, the smell of him, that look in his eyes...

*No.* By the gods, she would *not* think in *that* vein. Not now. Not after all this time.

Desperate for a distraction, for any form of subject to alter the course her mind took, her gaze landed on the bow and quiver strapped to Rowena's saddle. The quiver looked quite full, though she recalled the woman had not retrieved so much as a single arrow from the fight with the merchant's guards.

"It is an enchantment," Rowena said when Janet voiced question. "It refills any arrow used against a foe, though that makes it rather useless for hunting."

"How would it even know that?"

"The quiver and bow are a set," Malcolm told her, his voice somewhat sleepy, which set her stomach to flutter again. Gods, she had entirely too much of a reaction to him just lately. "The bow normally cannot miss, and so knows what the wielder aims it at."

"Is it the Archer's?" Janet asked, eyes going wide.

"No," was Rowena's somewhat amused reply. "My ancestor's legendary talents resulted from his own skill. My bow and quiver belonged to Robin and Marian's son, Robert. The enchantment was necessary as Robert lost his thumb as a boy, and we have passed them down through the line since."

Janet hesitated at that. The next question was rather obvious, but she was uncertain whether it would anger Rowena to ask.

Rowena, clearly seeing what was coming, headed her off. "I have talent with bow and arrow myself. Any member of the family can string a bow by the time they walk. But the legendary accuracy is part of the lore about us now, so we make use of the artifacts."

Janet wanted to point out that this essentially made the entire thing a fiction, but decided not to. She was once again building a bridge with Rowena, and she did not wish to destroy it. So, instead, she turned to Andre. "You mentioned your father's heritage when I asked about your blades, but you never told us anything about the blades themselves."

Andre grinned. It seemed the boy always had an impish smile on his face, as if he found the entire world amusing. "Watch."

He shook back his sleeves, and Janet saw the glint of gold on the skin of his wrists before the blades were in his hands. With a wink, he pivoted in the saddle and threw both into the trees.

"What—" Janet began, then blinked as, with another glint of gold, the swords were once more in the boy's hands. "How on earth did you do that?"

"They are blood-bound," he explained, making them vanish once more with a flick of his wrists. "So long as I have the strength, I can summon them again and again. It is a ritual passed down through the family, like Rowena's bow and quiver, though the weapon takes a different shape for each. Legend has it, this is the spell that struck down Arthur."

"Quite impressive. You are an absolute font of surprises, Andre." And Janet could not help but wonder what might happen if the boy ever came to odds with her baby sister again. Alexis' short sword had its own enchantments, laid by the court wizard himself.

And then something occurred to her. "Malcolm," she asked, "when Alexis fainted while training with her swordsmanship instructor, was she using her sword or another?"

He thought for a moment. "I believe she was using a training sword, but I cannot say for certain. Cedric was the one who found her, remember?"

The moment Malcolm mentioned Cedric, Janet saw Rowena bristle. Inwardly, she cursed, certain the woman was about to make some angry remark that would once more ruin whatever progress they had made towards peace.

But before Rowena could speak, there was a hideous wailing, like a scream of mortal agony issuing from a thousand throats at once.

Following it was a series of slow, rhythmic *booms* that sounded like trees being crushed under a mountain.

"What on earth is that?" Janet demanded, looking this way and that for the source of the sound as the scream came again. "Is that the Dread Queen?"

"No." Malcolm sat up straighter and took full control of the reins from her. His eyes glinted hard as coins. "That is something much worse."

She was about to ask what he meant by that, when she saw the massive horned helm cresting above the tree line.

# CHAPTER 8

"Ride!" Malcolm ordered, kicking Shadow into a gallop.

"What is that?" Janet cried as the scream ripped through the air again.

"Dread Knight!" was Rowena's shouted reply.

"A *what*?"

But there was no need for either the swordsman or the archeress to reply to that, for just at that moment the creature came into full view behind them. It was over eleven feet tall and covered in what looked to be plates of blood-colored iron fused to its blackened skin. The head was a horrific visage that was half hideous mask and half demonic helm, complete with wicked-looking horns spiraling up from the temples.

"They appeared on the battlefield about a year ago!" Malcolm nearly had to put his mouth next to Janet's ear as the creature's cries were growing louder.

"It must have been an early move on the Dread Queen's part!" she shouted back. "They are obviously her creatures!"

"If they are," he responded, "she has a most formidable weapon! They are extremely difficult to slay! I have seen them mow through the better part of an entire battalion of infantry! Those plates on their bodies are harder than steel!"

"And they are relentless!" Rowena called out. "They seek battle endlessly until someone brings them down! We will never outrun it!"

"Aye." Grimly, he pulled Shadow to a stop. As if the beast had waited for that response, its cries died away, and it stopped running after them. "Stay here," he told Janet as he swung down from the saddle and drew the Sword of Lions. "Rowena, Andre, with me."

"Wait!" Janet barely caught the collar of his armor before he went for the monster. "What if this is a diversion? What if they come for me while you fight that thing?"

"Here." Rowena pulled her dagger from her boot and held it out to Janet. Their eyes met, and the redhead nodded. "You will stand, Princess. Do not be afraid."

Janet swallowed. Her actual fear was not that the Dread Queen would come for her, but that Malcolm would overdo. In Rowena's eyes, she saw the recognition of that fear, and the understanding of it. The woman, she realized, placed herself amidst the battle in order to take the weight off him.

"Very well." Janet's hand shook slightly as she took the dagger, but her eyes were level and spoke volumes.

Rowena nodded again, and the trio turned to make for the creature. Janet watched them, though she made certain to keep enough of her focus back in case something else waited in the wings to come at her.

Malcolm took the lead. It seemed to her he was always the one to step into danger's path first. His amazing speed carried him the last distance in the blink of an eye, the glittering metal of his sword's blade flashing in the sun as he carved a line of blood into the beast's left ankle. He rolled through, came up, and stabbed backwards with the weapon, only for it to bounce off one of the metal plates of its skin.

The monster howled again, reached down for him, and it was only his speed and agility that got him clear of that reach. The Dread Knight was faster than its size suggested.

Andre came in next, hurling his summoned swords at the creature's face with all the might his young arms could muster. It got its hand up in time to block them, but the move temporarily blinded it to the boy's position, and he quickly took advantage. Where Malcolm had gone for the left ankle, Andre dove for the right, and his newly re-summoned swords dug deep lines.

It seemed a strange strategy to Janet. Though the cuts drew blood, they would be only scratches to a being of that size. Their blades were too short to do true damage to it. They would have better luck if Malcolm used his unfathomable speed and jumping ability to go for the eyes.

While the two men hacked uselessly at the monster's ankles, Rowena scaled a tree by nimbly hopping back and forth between its trunk and that of another. Once in the branches, she climbed up and up, higher and higher until she was level with the creature's shoulder. Only then did she unsling her bow from her shoulder and take aim.

As she did, Janet finally understood the strategy. Malcolm and Andre were not hacking futilely at the beast's ankles. They knew their weapons could not do actual damage. They were the diversion.

The arrow flew, streaking across the distance to the eye-slits of the mask-like face. It was only at the last possible second the face turned just enough for the arrow to bounce off the metallic skin. The creature, now warned of the true focus of the attack, reached for the tree in which Rowena perched.

"Rowena!" With a mighty leap, Malcolm flew high into the air and used his magnificent weapon to slap the arm up and away. But the move, noble as it was, opened him up to counterattack. The monster's hand came back, smacking Malcolm with such force he flew back down and crashed into the ground hard enough to bury him several inches into the earth.

Janet had had enough. Her fingers flicked through arcane signs as she intoned, "*Meto mana itali zenta!*" and sent a gust of wind hurtling at the creature. But she had misjudged the strength of the spell once more, and it hit with a furious detonation that not only knocked the beast down but shattered several trees.

Only Rowena's quick thinking and reflexes allowed her to jump just prior to the explosion, so she rode the bubble of air. She arced up above the falling monster, took aim, and fired. The arrow hurtled from her bow, down, down into the eye-slit she had first targeted.

The dull ringing of stone on metal accompanied the massive boom of the monster hitting the ground. But Janet did not care. She was too busy jumping down from the horse and running across the distance to get to Malcolm's side, fear pushing her steps to speeds she rarely took. He had to be alright. He *had* to be.

Amazingly, *incredibly*, he was. By the time she reached him, he was already climbing out of the hole, completely unharmed. Even so, she all but fell on him, patting him down as she asked, "Are you alright? Are you alright?" in a voice on the edge of panic.

"I am fine. Janet." Malcolm grabbed her shoulder and lifted her chin to look at him. "I am fine," he repeated, his tone calm and level. "The sword appears to have other abilities besides increasing my speed."

The sword. Janet looked down at the splendid weapon, still clutched in his grip. The inner light of the red stone in the lion's maw flickered, and that flickering seemed almost amused for some reason she could not entirely fathom.

"As long as you are alright," she said, stepping back and deliberately placing her hands behind her back as they wanted to reach for him again.

"Hey, everyone?" They all turned to look at Andre. He pointed. "You should see this."

What he was pointing at was the fallen body of the Dread Knight, which was now shrinking bit by bit, its ponderous body seeming to melt away. It got smaller and smaller until at last it was the form of a young boy of twelve in a dirty blue tunic and brown hose. His hair was a wavy dishwater blond, and Janet knew if his eyes were to open, they would be a dull green.

For she recognized the boy all too well and, by the set of his shoulders, she knew Malcolm did as well. "Dorian," he said glumly as Janet's knees buckled, and she sank to the ground with a sob. "Well, now we know."

\* \* \*

"It does no good to dwell on it," Rowena told Janet as they made camp that night. They had ridden the rest of the day without incident, which was fortunate as Janet had brooded and worried over the implications of what they had seen the entire way.

"Oh, no," Janet snarled, pacing back and forth, and worrying at her lip. "What could come from dwelling on the fact that my sisters have become monsters, and I am close to following? That we are turning the men of the kingdom into beasts? That Avanna is on the way to falling as Avannion did one hundred and fifty years ago?"

"Princess—"

"This is what you have wished for!" Janet rounded on Rowena, eyes alive with temper and fear. "You and yours have long wanted to see the royal family fall for what you believe we have done to you!"

"And you think I rejoice over this now?" Rowena replied coldly. "You think that a fate I would wish on anyone? If that were true, why would I have risked my life to slay that thing in the first place rather than simply run and save myself?"

"The only reason you are even here is I bought your service!"

"And if you are so doomed, what point is there to my staying?"

"Janet." From where he had been building the fire, Malcolm rose and walked over to lay a hand upon her shoulder. "None of us are fleeing you. We will see this through, and we will save the kingdom."

"Oh, fine!" She shoved his hand away,

paced off five steps' distance before whirling back. "You will be the one I turn first, Malcolm. I feel it in my bones. I will destroy you."

"No, you will not. Gods, Janet, do you think me so dim-witted? We know now what to expect, and I can watch for you to behave oddly."

"Can you? If I try, do you have what it takes to end me?"

His expression went hard as stone. "That will not be necessary."

"You see? You place my safety and security above your own. You always have. You cannot stop me because of that, and so it will doom you."

"Does not the amulet hold you in check?" Andre asked. He had stayed by the horses, brushing them down after the long day's ride and had watched the exchange with not an inconsiderable amount of trepidation. "That is its function, its power, no? To hold off a curse or disease for seven days. We have time."

"Oh, do we?" Janet nearly tore her dress open, yanking the object in question out for all to see. "Look. Three of the diamonds are black! Three! Almost half the time gone! And even if we make it to the Tower, then what? In the treatise, there was no way to return the Dread Mothers to normal! I have lost my sisters, and their victims are to be monsters for the rest of their days!"

She spoke her last sentence through tears as all her fear and worry finally broke her. As she wept, Malcolm crossed to her again. When he reached out to take her into his arms, she pushed him away, but he only reached out again.

Her next attempt to keep him back was only half-hearted, and when he pulled her in a third time, her will was too depleted to stop him. And so, held in his embrace, she lay her head on his chest and let the tears come.

He gave no words of comfort, made no soothing sound as she wept. He never did. Throughout her life, whenever her emotions had become too much for her, he had allowed them to run their course before speaking. How he had ever realized that words of any kind would only upset her further when she was like this, she did not know, but she was grateful for it.

When at last her tears were done with, he released her, allowing her to regain the distance she so needed for her own stability. "I am pledged to protect you," he told her. "But I will not leave you alone to face your fate, not ever. We will find a way to stop the Dread Queen, and if a way exists to save your sisters, then we will find that as well. You have my word on it."

She said nothing, did not even look at him. Instead, she only held the amulet for a time, looking down at it. Malcolm had insisted she put it on at the start, she remembered. She was bound to it now, but her fate...

With a sigh, she slid the amulet back beneath her dress. Whatever would happen, she decided, would happen. Worrying about it just now would not help.

* * *

It did not entirely surprise Janet when she found herself unable to sleep that night. There were far too many thoughts running through her mind, and entirely too many of them centered on Malcolm.

Blast it all, *why* had it felt so good, so comforting for him to hold her? It was not supposed to be like that! Those feelings, that *idiotic* idea of them being together, she had buried all that years ago!

Yet the fluttering in her heart at hearing his declaration he would never leave her side had been very real. Gods, was she so dependent upon him after all? Did she need him to prop her up even now? Had all the time she had spent building her confidence and backbone been nothing but wasted effort?

"Blast it, no."

"Princess?"

Realizing she had spoken the last aloud, Janet winced, then turned over to look at Rowena. The redhead had elected to take first watch and even now sat beside the fire, giving her a curious look. "Did you have a nightmare?" Rowena asked.

"No." With a sigh, Janet sat up and pushed back her bedroll. "I cannot seem to sleep."

"Ah." For a moment, both women looked at each other, saying nothing. Then Rowena shifted and patted the ground beside her. "Join me."

Reticent, but seeing little else to do, Janet did as bidden. "Are we to have a heart-to-heart?"

She had meant it as a joke, but Rowena did not laugh. She looked out at the darkness for a time before speaking. "You have surprised me."

Given the woman's stated opinions about Janet, the royals in general, and the events that had transpired that day, the princess waited for her to elaborate. When she did not, Janet finally asked, "How, exactly?"

"I always thought you royals would sacrifice anyone, even your own, to get what you wanted."

Janet sighed. "There have been some in my line who were like that. Men and women for whom blood ties meant nothing in the face of their petty desires."

"But not you."

"Not I. Nor my sisters. Our father is a man of noble bearing, even if he is not of noble blood. He taught us honor and compassion from birth. Oh, my sisters and I may bicker and fight amongst ourselves over unimportant matters. It is the nature of family. But we would rip the heart from an outsider who tried to hurt any of us."

"As would he, I expect," Rowena said, looking at where Malcolm slept by the horses. "Tell me of them."

Surprised, Janet could only ask, "What, my

sisters?"

"Yes," was Rowena's response. "My family line is small. We rarely have more than one child a generation. Andre is my only cousin, and I have only known him a handful of years. What is it like having a large family?"

Janet thought for a bit, trying to decide how to describe what had always seemed so natural to her. "You never lack for companionship," she said after a time. "And you can say things to them you would tell no one else. Malcolm has been my confidant all my life, but there are things you cannot say to a boy no matter how close he is to you."

"Even one you love?"

Janet nearly snapped out an angry reply on pure instinct before she remembered Rowena was not aware of the long-running argument she had had with her sisters. "My sisters have made the same assumption, but we are not in love. I love him, yes, but as the brother I never had not as a potential husband."

She explained, as she had to Rebecca, what had transpired on Malcolm's eighteenth birthday, then added on how her sisters had taken things the wrong way since. "Well," Rowena said when the tale was through. "So, that is what happened. I wondered why you seemed to always stiffen when he got close."

"After three years of intimation, it feels a little strange for him to be that near." Janet shook her head. "My sisters are still young. When they have grown a bit more..."

She trailed off, remembering it was entirely likely that her sisters would get no older than they had been when last she saw them. "I suppose when this is over, I shall have to be a bit more focused on finding a husband for myself. The kingdom will need the stability."

"You may be surprised about that. People rarely know what they need until it is already theirs."

"Cedric said something similar." Janet caught the sudden flicker in Rowena's eyes and winced. She felt as if she had just slammed shut the gate on their bridge again. "Rowena, forgive me. I know you miss him."

"It is nothing." The redhead pushed up and strode to her own bedroll, where she had left her bow and quiver. "As you are awake, I believe I shall patrol for a time. If I am not back in a quarter hour, wake Malcolm, would you?"

Without waiting for an answer, she strode into the trees and disappeared, leaving Janet cursing herself beside the fire.

\* \* \*

If Rowena had known Janet was cursing herself for bringing up Cedric, she would have thought it was because the princess rued not being able to draw her in deeper. Despite how she had spoken and acted, the archeress was certain the dark-haired woman had lied to her all along. She was certain Malcolm was lying, too, though whether his lies were his own or whether Janet had bewitched him, she could not be sure.

The woman's magic was the starting point of the distrust. For someone who claimed to have such poor control over her powers, Janet had a considerable talent. It seemed to Rowena that Janet was deliberately having small slipups in her casting now, and then to maintain the fiction.

And then there was the fight Malcolm claimed to have had with Cedric in the capital before the two fled. Even with the undeniable powers of the Sword of Lions, he could not have beaten her Cedric so handily.

And why would Cedric attack Malcolm at all? Because of the Dread Queen? That was nothing but a myth. The proof was the creature they had fought that day. If the other princesses were creating the Dread Knights, how had the beasts shown up on the front lines more than a year before? It was impossible.

The true villain was likely Janet herself, and she and Malcolm had probably fled the capital because they had made some power play and been thwarted. The royals were notorious for such backstabbing political moves.

There was just one minor problem with the theory, though. The amulet. Rowena knew of the Seven Moons Amulet, both its power and its curse. If everything she suspected were true, why would Janet have subjected herself to that fate? And why would it be progressing as if she truly were cursed?

It was like a melody with a single discordant note. The one sound that disrupted everything, turning a beautiful creation into a hideous mess worthy of nothing but scorn.

Unless you changed the melody to match that note. But doing that would mean believing Janet and Malcolm's entire fantastic tale.

The curse being real would mean the Dread Queen—or some equally powerful wizard that necessitated such extreme measures—had laid it. Which meant they really had fled the capital, and Malcolm really had fought Cedric, which was something she refused to accept.

It could not be real. It simply could not. And so, there had to be another side to it. There had to be some fact, some piece of information she had not considered.

"Rowena."

The voice was so unexpected, so out of nowhere, she had half-drawn an arrow before she realized who it was. "Cedric!"

Her bow fell from her fingers as she threw herself at him. She wrapped her arms around his neck and buried her face against his neck to breathe in the scent of him. "You live!"

"Why would I not?" he chuckled as he held her close.

"Malcolm swore he struck you down."

"Malcolm." He drew back, his warm smile falling away and his eyes going cold and flat. "Malcolm is hunting me. Janet tried to take the throne and when the court wizard thwarted her, she laid the blame upon *my* head. I had threatened to kill the younger princesses, she claimed, unless she took the throne and married me."

"You— She—"

"I have been on the run ever since. Malcolm's task is to find me, and Janet has hied herself along in order to ensure my silence."

Rowena's mind burned with rage. Cedric's words infuriated her, and his explanation answered many questions to her satisfaction. But not all.

"The amulet," she said. "Janet wears the Seven Moons Amulet. Cedric, it counts down."

"A counterfeit," he explained. "It does not measure the progress of a curse, but the time she has to catch me before her father renders judgment upon her head rather than mine."

"Does Malcolm know the truth?" she demanded. "Is he complicit in this?"

"No," Cedric snarled. "He is infatuated with the princess, and the entire city plans their wedding. When she voiced her lie to cover her scheming, he flew into a rage and tried to take my head in the street, and I barely got away with my life."

"I will stain the earth with her blood!"

Rowena snatched up her bow. "Come, let us end this here and now!"

"No." He grabbed her arm before she could hurry back to the campsite and take her vengeance. "If she dies, the truth dies with her. The lie will be set in stone, and I shall be a fugitive all my days."

"Then what are we to do, Cedric? How can we possibly prove you innocent?"

"I am not her only goal. Janet seeks to fool the Ariagne, the men-spiders who live under the crown's protection and ordain the rulers of Avanna by right of ancient treaty. She seeks to have them name her and Malcolm rulers, but that shall be the flaw of their plan.

"Their cave is half a day's ride in the direction you have been heading. Lead them close, then find a way to lose them. They will go to the cave and when they emerge with the honor guard we shall confront and denounce them."

"And Janet will incinerate us on the spot, then ride off to claim her crown with your head tied to the saddle."

"No. Doing so would void her pronouncement. Once such an accusation is made, the queen of the Ariagne is duty-bound to find the truth of it. Her crystalline caverns are the greatest truth-telling magic in the world and will reveal the perfidy."

"And trap her," Rowena nodded. "You

always were a genius at creating tactical plans on the ground."

On impulse, she grabbed him and kissed him, hard. "I love you. Never let me forget to tell you that again."

The last she saw of her beloved before she went back to trap those who had tried to trap her, he grinned that same grin that had stolen her heart long before she had realized it was gone.

# CHAPTER 9

Janet could see when Rowena returned the woman was in no mood to talk. In truth, she did not even look at Janet as she walked to her bedroll, set aside her bow and quiver, and laid down to sleep. And so, it was left to Janet to sit the rest of the shift, then wake Malcolm to take his turn on watch.

She was groggy when he woke her in the morning, as she was unused to staying up so long. Even so, she insisted they set out at the first opportunity as they had lost considerable time the day before.

Rowena's silence for much of the morning was oppressive. She did not even look at any of them and spoke only when spoken to. And even then, she said little.

But as the morning wore on, Janet noticed the woman's head would cock one way or another now and then. And there were brief movements, birdlike tilts, and subtle sweeps from right to left or the reverse.

Watching those telltale shifts, Janet suddenly remembered the Loxellys were known for more than their skills at archery. They were expert woodsmen and trackers. Unless she missed her guess, the redheaded archeress was not being silent because she was sulking, but because she was expecting another attack.

Then without warning she gave a shout and spurred her horse into a gallop. The action was so unexpected that Andre fell off the back of the saddle to land in a heap on the ground. The boy's reflexes took over, and he quickly rolled, shouting "Go!" at Malcolm as he gained his feet and made for the nearest tree

Malcolm had already spurred Shadow forward, shooting off after Rowena like a bolt of lightning. They hurtled through the trees, trying desperately to keep Rob and her horse in sight. Whatever the woman chased, whatever she had seen, led her on a mad chase, making her weave this way and that.

"What is she doing?" Malcolm growled as he weaved Shadow in her wake.

"She spotted something." Janet had to duck to avoid having her cheek lacerated by a low-hanging branch. "She was distracted as we rode, tracking. She must have seen something."

"I do not know what. There was nothing I saw."

That surprised Janet so completely she nearly caught the next branch full in the face. If Malcolm had sensed nothing, then what was Rowena chasing?

\* \* \*

When Rowena finally shook off Malcolm's pursuit of her, she continued to ride in that same weaving fashion for another fifteen minutes. She knew her former captain had skill as a tracker himself, and she wanted to make certain she had truly lost him.

She mourned the loss of her cousin. There had been no way to warn Andre, and she had little doubt the boy was doomed. He was not wrapped up in Malcolm and Janet's power play, and they would have to slay him before entering the cave, so he did not give them away. She just hoped she would be able to find his body so he could be given a decent burial.

When she was at last sure Malcolm would not be able to find her, she slowed her horse to a walk. Idly, she wondered if Psyche would miss Shadow, who was her broodmate. For Rowena's part, having to kill Malcolm's horse would be the saddest part of the whole affair, but there would be no leaving him alive once his rider was slain.

"Problem?" Cedric asked her as he rode out from behind a tree to join her.

She sighed. "A number of them. Malcolm was our friend once. We found each other because of him. Now I shall lose him and Andre both."

Cedric reached over to lay a comforting hand on her arm. "This is not your doing."

"No." Her jaw tightened, and her eyes fired.

"It is the princess'. And I vow she shall pay for it all."

* * *

It was several minutes after they lost Rowena when Andre at last returned. The boy dropped nimbly from the trees to land atop Shadow's saddle. The horse, annoyed, immediately bucked and threw him off. Unlike when he had fallen off Rowena's horse, however, Andre flipped in midair to land on his feet like a cat.

"Did you find her?" Malcolm asked.

"Not a sign." Andre looked to Janet. "Are you alright?"

She nodded. They had given up the pursuit when she had finally been knocked off by a branch that had caught her shoulder. It had torn her dress some, and she was now treating a scratch along her collarbone with some of the unguents from one of her rings. "Rowena disappeared quite fast," she observed, closing the ring back up. "Is she usually so?"

"If she does not want to be found, she cannot be found." Malcolm shook his head. "You are wrong, Janet."

"Am I?" Janet began studying the tear in her dress. It was not bad and could be mended easily enough. "She pretends to spot something, takes off at such a speed she ditches Andre. And vanishes so completely he cannot find her. What am I supposed to think, Malcolm?"

"She is not the kind to abandon comrades."

"And since when does she consider me a comrade? I am a royal, and she has made her feelings on my family abundantly clear."

"That is not the woman I know."

"The woman you know," she said evenly. "Did not know you know me."

"Malcolm," Andre said as Malcolm opened his mouth to respond, "we are not alone."

It was true. While they had been talking, a familiar fog had rolled in along the grounds. And shadowy figures were flitting back and forth among the trees.

* * *

What came from the trees were not the black figures Malcolm remembered from the capital. Neither did they match Janet's description of the shadows she had seen when she had fallen under the fog spell's influence.

Instead, they were gray-skinned monsters with human-like torsos and arms that had one joint too many. Their heads were hairless and mouthless, with bulbous multi-faceted eyes of iridescent blue. And from the waist down they had the bristly, many-legged bodies of giant spiders.

There were perhaps twenty of them in all, carrying jagged-edged weapons running the gamut from clubs and maces to spears and swords of various lengths and makes. And it was exceedingly clear they were ready to use them from the way their fingers were flexing on the hilts.

And so, Malcolm elected to strike first. His hand flashed to the hilt of the Sword of Lions, and he flew at one of the sword-wielders. His magnificent weapon flashed up in an arc of silvery steel, slapping up and away the curved blade held by his target. In that same fast motion, Malcolm spun around and drove the length of his weapon through the center of the chest.

From there, however, it went wrong in a hurry. While on a human that blow would have been instantly mortal, the monster he had struck simply plowed a clenched fist into Malcolm's chest. The blow was so hard he lost his grip on his weapon and went flying into a tree trunk.

Still, when the monster attempted to remove the sword from its own chest, the bloodstone rejected it. As the unmistakable roar of a lion filled the air, red lightning coursed up the monster's arm, and it dropped to the ground, twitching and jerking.

Andre, meanwhile, engaged a full five of the beings all at once. He danced here and there in a masterful performance, his magically summoned butterfly blades weaving in circles and batting away every weapon. No matter how hard the creatures tried, they could not land a blow or stab him, for his swords flicked them away as neatly as one might pluck off a bit of straw.

A spear-wielder tried to skewer Malcolm, only for the man to catch the spear just below the head and rip it away. The butt of the newly stolen weapon clubbed the creature across its hairless head before Malcolm thrust the spear into the lower body of a mace-wielder that had tried to come upon him from behind. The attacker fell with a wailing cry that appeared to come from its entire body.

While the two males had been battling, Janet had been flitting around the trees. Worried she might lose control at a critical juncture, she avoided using her magic directly. But the dweomer in her bracelet came into play at last. She had blinded three of the creatures and confused two more with a mirage of armed knights.

She tried to get to Malcolm, hoping to free him up to retrieve his sword, but she could not find an open path to him. Each time she stepped from the cover of a tree trunk, another of the monsters spotted her, and she had to duck back into hiding before they grabbed her. After all, the magic contained within the bracelet had its limits, and she could ill afford to use it up so fast.

Now, she was as far from him as it was possible to get, clear on the other side of the battle. The original creature he had attacked lay between them. She had a thought that if she could just move the Sword of Lions from the corpse somehow, she might be able to surf it along a current of wind to him. Then he could fight off the men-spiders that—

She stopped. Men-spiders. By the gods, these were *men-spiders*! They were Ariagne, the monsters that had an ancient covenant with her family! They were battling allies!

Certain now of the course she needed to take, she fell into the magic she had thought too dangerous. She built the wind, weaving it into a delicate pattern as her teacher had taught her. Perhaps it was because of the situation—the need to stop the bloodshed and the immediacy of the moment—but she found it far easier to maintain the mental construct than she ever had before.

Finally, when she was certain it would do what she needed it to, she unleashed the spell. Typically, however, she had misjudged the strength of the wind and instead of just separating the fighters she sent everyone spilling to the ground in a tangle of limbs. But she stopped the fight, and as that was the primary goal, she continued with her plan.

"Stop!" she shouted out, walking from the trees with her hands raised high to demand attention. "I am Janet, Crown Princess of Avanna, and Duchess of Morrberry-by-the-Sea! We are not your enemies!"

"What are you doing?" Malcolm called out, pushing up from where he had fallen. "Have you lost your mind?"

"They are the men-spiders," she told him. "The Ariagne. By royal agreement, we permit them to live here unmolested, and they bless each monarch in return."

"Your mate attacked us." A spear-wielder pushed himself up to his feet.

"Malcolm is my bodyguard," she replied, still making certain to keep her hands in sight as she crossed slowly to him. "He has spent five years on the front lines of the monster wars and reacted to what he thought was a threat."

She stopped before him and bowed, low and respectful. "We have been on the run for our lives. Please, forgive us our overreaction, noble warrior."

The Ariagne studied her for a time, its head cocking this way and that. "Why do you come to our lands?"

"'Twas only by accident, though it would be a happy one." Slowly, she straightened and met his gaze. "The Dark One has cursed my sisters, and we ride for the Ancient One's Tower to seek his help."

He studied her for another moment, then turned and headed for the trees they had first emerged from. "Come. The queen will discover the truth."

\* \* \*

"How *exactly* do you know these...things?" Malcolm asked as they followed the Ariagne through the trees.

Janet sighed. It was an unhelpful time for him to suddenly become suspicious, but she could hardly blame him. Few people had any trust in the non-human races, even the ones that were friendly or ambivalent towards humans.

"As I said before," she explained patiently, "my family has an ancient treaty with the Ariagne. We permit them the right to live unmolested by the army and adventurers who make their living fighting monsters are to leave them be. In return, they bless each generation of Avanna rulers."

"Bless."

"Yes, bless. They are connected to Lady Fate via the crystalline caverns they inhabit, and it affords them powers of sanctification and truth telling. They were the ones who crafted Excalibur for Merlin, along with the stone and anvil so he could find the missing Pendragon heir."

"They have been here that long?" Andre asked in wonder.

"Indeed. And they become vexed if they believe someone has violated their dominion, so keep control of your sticky fingers."

Andre winced, then sidled over to the Ariagne walking next to him. To Janet's amusement, the boy tapped him on the arm and held out a trinket he had obviously stolen, murmuring what sounded to her like a sincere apology. She hid her smile before he came back and thought once again, he and Alexis would be an interesting pairing if her baby sister ever took an interest in boys.

When she turned back to Malcolm, she noticed the way he watched the Ariagne around them. Recognizing he was worried, she reached out to loop her arm through his. "They are not dangerous to us."

"I killed three of their own," was his reply. "People tend to hold that against someone."

"People. Not them. The Ariagne prize honorable battle and to die facing a worthy foe is the most honorable fate imaginable. It is rare for a human to best an Ariagne warrior in single combat, let alone three. Regardless of what else happens, they see you as someone worthy of great respect."

"What else happens?"

He would have picked up on that one detail, she thought. "The crystalline caverns read the truth of the world rather than the truth of the word. If we have been wrong about any assumptions we have made, the queen will reveal it to us, though she may choose not to reveal the entirety of it."

The warriors led them to the hidden mouth of a cave and through into a stunning marvel. The walls were lined with glittering crystals that glowed like the faint light of a setting sun. And as they walked on and on, the air pulsed and hummed with an unseen energy.

When Andre wandered over to the walls and reached out to touch, Janet had to let go of Malcolm's arm to grab the boy. "That is not a good idea. Humans who touch the crystals are never the same afterwards."

Andre blanched, and not only yanked his hand away from the wall but shoved both hands behind his back. Janet turned to look over her shoulder at Malcolm and saw he had a faraway look in his eye, as if he were seeing something that was not there. A flicker of red caught her attention, and she looked down to see the bloodstone on his weapon glowed, pulsing in time with the energy in the air.

The pulsing stopped suddenly, and he blinked and turned towards her. And just for a moment, there was a look of such pain and sorrow in his eyes that her throat tightened. A look that made her turn away, and when she did, she found the leader of the Ariagne watched Malcolm as well. And his featureless face seemed somehow pensive.

All around them, she realized each of the Ariagne warriors stared at him with that same contemplative air. Yet, when she turned back to him again, he still watched her. His hand resting on the sword's hilt. And the pulsing hum grew louder and louder until she wanted to clap her hands over her ears to drown it out.

"Janet. Janet!"

She jerked, blinked. She was on her back

on the floor of the cave, with Malcolm kneeling over her. "I said back off!" he snapped to someone outside her field of vision. "Blast it all, give her room!"

"She must sit up," an unfamiliar voice said, fluid, soft and female. "Remaining on the ground will only disorient her further."

Malcolm turned back to her. "Can you sit up?"

"I...think so."

It turned out the answer was actually *no* because the moment she tried, her head swam, and Malcolm's face doubled. She collapsed with a groan.

"You must get her up," the female voice insisted. "The dizziness will grow worse the longer she lays there."

"Very well." Malcolm gently took her hand. "Take it slowly," he instructed her. "Slowly and easily."

Slowly and easily was exactly how they went, easing her into a seated position bit by bit. Each time her vision went blurry they would stop, Malcolm supporting her with a hand on her back. Finally, she sat, and he released her hand, leaving her to get her bearings.

A moment before, they had been standing in the tunnel leading from the cave entrance. Now they were in a grand cavern the size of the royal court. A rainbow of soft colors washed soothingly across the glittering crystals that filled the walls, ceiling and jutted up here and there from the floor in foot-high spikes. The energy running through the air was like a soft, warm summer breeze, and the hum was the continual echoing note of a silver bell.

It was, she realized with a start, the queen's cavern. She turned to Malcolm. "How on earth did we get here?"

Rather than answer, he asked, "What is the last thing you remember?"

"What do you mean, what is the last thing I remember? We stood in the tunnel leading from the cave mouth not twenty seconds ago! You had your hand on your sword and listened to the hum of the cave energy!"

"Janet, that was nearly an hour ago."

"What? *What*? An *hour*? Have you lost your senses?"

"No, Princess, you have lost your memories of the last hour."

She rounded on the speaker. It was another of the Ariagne, but with the body of a female rather than a male. Lustrous black hair spilled down from its scalp in an ebony waterfall. "Queen Zat'Rat?"

"I am pleased you still recall me," the Ariagne said. "You were quite young when last we met, and it has been a long time in the lifespan of a human."

"Nearly fifteen years," Janet agreed. "But I did not lose my memory back then."

"No. But I did not verify the veracity of what you told me back then. I did today."

"But that has never caused memory loss before."

"There has never been a royal with the Eyes of Destiny before."

Janet blinked. "I-I do not understand. What do my powers have to do with this?"

"My powers to determine truth come from Lady Fate herself. The crystals of this cavern are a link to her domain. The Eyes of Destiny are a mark of her blessing. When two elements of her power interact, there are often results that are unpredictable."

"I see." Realizing her backside had gone numb sitting on the ground, Janet pushed up to her feet, which was much easier than sitting up had been and did not involve the entire room spinning like a cartwheel.

She looked down at her riding dress and discovered the tear in the shoulder had been seamlessly mended, but the whole thing was rather dusty. As she brushed herself off, she asked, "So, we are truly being pursued by the Dread Queen, then?"

When no answer was forthcoming, she stopped brushing herself off. "She is not behind this?"

"Janet." Malcolm laid a hand on her arm. "That was not what she wanted to verify. They attacked us because a man had warned them that bandits came to raid the caverns for the crystals in the walls."

She felt a chill go down her spine, and she had to swallow because her mouth had gone suddenly dry. "A man?"

\* \* \*

Rowena paced back and forth, up and down, chewing at her thumbnail continuously. It was wrong. It was all wrong. It just did not fit.

She had watched, hidden among the trees, as the trio had battled the men-spiders. Cedric had said the creatures respected strength, and so Malcolm slaying three was not strange. But why had they not taken the opportunity to murder Andre? Her cousin would never go along with their plan, so why let him live? Why bring him into the cavern with them?

"Perhaps they seek to kill him there," Cedric said when she voiced her concerns again. "The crystals in the caverns have strange properties. They might try to use them to do the work for them."

It was too much. If Andre still lived, then it was not too late to save his life. "Take me to the cave," she demanded, moving to mount Psyche.

"It is far too early to confront them," he replied dismissively. "The endowment will likely take another hour at the least."

"I do not intend to confront them outside the cave. Andre is my only family still living. I will not abandon him to death when I might save him instead."

He considered her, then with a sigh moved to mount the black charger he had ridden out to meet her on. "This course of action is most likely to result in a fight," he pointed out.

"Good. I would prefer an outright battle to all this skullduggery."

Because he knew where the cave was, and she did not, she allowed him to lead the way. She followed, half-lost in her mind once more while the other half guided her steed.

She wanted to save Andre. Besides Cedric, her young cousin was all she had left. But her mind kept worrying over why Janet and Malcolm had allowed him to live. It would have been far easier to allow him to die during the fight, even with the boy's skills with his blades. A simple *failed* spell by the princess could have ended it without raising a single eyebrow from even the gravest skeptic.

And come to think of that, why even bring them along when both she and Andre would end up nothing but a liability? Certainly, it would afford an opportunity to silence Cedric's only defenders. But the night Janet had attacked her and Andre, she could have easily slain them both.

And Malcolm had stopped her from continuing, had pulled her from the trance she had claimed to be in. That suggested she had truly been under a spell, for it would have been the easiest thing at that moment for him to finish her and Andre. However infatuated her former captain might be with Janet, he was not a fool.

Her attention fastened upon the horse Cedric rode. Like her and Malcolm, Cedric had a Shadda-Dar of his own. But he rode an unfamiliar horse. He had brought his armor and sword, but not his horse. That made no sense.

"Cedric. Where is Sprig?"

He sighed. "I was hoping you would not realize that."

He whirled around and on pure instinct she attempted to get to her bow. She never made it.

# CHAPTER 10

"We need to find Rowena," Malcolm said as the Ariagne escorted them back through the caverns. "If Cedric's pursuing us, he may try to harm her."

Janet worried her bracelet around and around her wrist, saying nothing. She was busy piecing together the information they had, and it was painting a worrying picture.

Cedric's manipulation of the Ariagne had been perfectly timed. The queen had confirmed he had warned them only the night before, which meant he had known exactly where they were. Yet, he had used a catspaw rather than attack them directly, and his tool had been one who would easily recognize her as a royal.

And then there were Rowena's actions. Her long walk the same night Cedric had involved the Ariagne. Her refusal to engage with any of them throughout the morning. And then her sudden disappearance right before the attack.

It was all a touch too convenient. And it confirmed her worst fear. Rowena and Cedric were working together.

But that caused something of a problem. Malcolm, she knew, trusted Rowena completely. He would not be receptive to the idea she had betrayed that trust.

They emerged out into the open, and it surprised her to see Shadow nosing around in the grass scarcely a foot from the mouth of the cave. "You have trained him well," she remarked to Malcolm. "For him to remain here for so long without needing to be tied up is remarkable."

"Not entirely." Malcolm reached out to stroke the horse's nose, and it flicked its tail in greeting. "They foal Shadda-Dar in isolation, and the first human the colts meet is their rider. Shadow imprinted on me, as Psyche did on Rowena and Sprig on Cedric."

"Sprig?" she asked. "Cedric has one of these horses?"

"Oh, aye." Malcolm grinned. "He was quite the playful little colt, and he grew into a fearless steed. We used to worry he would try to run down a mountain troll."

She watched it come over him, just for a moment. The fear and grief over having to face in battle a man he had called comrade and friend. Then his back straightened, and his shoulders squared off. It was, she thought, a warrior preparing himself, and it made her wonder once again how much he had changed.

But the way he got himself under control gave her the courage to bring up her concerns. In hindsight, she should have stuck with her initial decision.

"I'll hear none of this," he snapped.

"Malcolm, you have to at least consider it."

"That is not the woman I know."

"Would the woman you know abandon the field this way?"

"I'll not hear it!" he shouted. It was the first time he had ever truly yelled at her, and he added to it by jabbing a finger in her face and snarling, "You did not like her from the start!"

"And she did not like me." While he was losing his temper, she fought to keep her own under control. This was not the time to scream at each other. "Malcolm, think this over logically."

"I am! Rowena is out there, and she likely encountered Cedric and trusted him only for him to betray her!"

"Or she has collaborated with him all along and betrayed you."

"I said I would not hear this!"

"Malcolm—" Andre flinched as the irate swordsman rounded on him with a snarl worthy of any big cat.

"She is your cousin!" Malcolm's voice was so loud at this point even the Ariagne warriors were flinching back. "You are her only family!"

"And that automatically requires him to defend her?" Janet stepped around, placing herself between man and boy.

"He knows her!"

"And if you did not, what would your reaction be? If you did not have such a long history with Rowena, would you be so quick to dismiss suspicion of her?"

"She and I have held each other's lives in our hands."

"Members of my grandfather's court were at Geoffrey's side at the Idenian Plains!" She had held her temper in check, but his boneheaded refusal had frayed her control. "Of the five knights who slayed the Morresy Woods banshee, two died wearing the crest of the de Bergiouacs and another died in prison five years ago! Those bonds do not hold when men have their pride injured!"

"And what could I have possibly done to so injure Rowena's pride? You? If she were so ticked off you and I know each other, then why would she come along in the first place?"

"Cedric is out there! The man she loves! Do you truly mean to tell me the idea she might have worked with him all along is so out of the question?"

Malcolm waved that off without hesitation. "She is not so stealthy as that."

"And if she is another catspaw?" Janet countered. "If he used her the way he used the Ariagne?"

"To what end?" He spread his arms, turning to gesture at the entire area. "To get us here? Why? If he has known our location the entire time, what need is there to bring us to this specific point?"

Unfortunately, he had hit upon the one hole in her theory. If Cedric had had them in his sights all along, why had he not already struck?

During the latter portion of the discussion, once Janet had drawn Malcolm's attention back to herself, Andre had wandered away towards the trees. His head had cocked now and again as he roamed, as if he were listening for some faint sound. But now, he threw his arms out to the sides, summoning his blood-bound blades into his hands. "Malcolm."

Just as both swordsman and princess turned to him, the first thunderous footstep reached the ears of all. And just behind it was a hideous screech that was all too familiar.

* * *

Rowena awoke with a mighty headache pounding at her temples like tiny hammers. The sunlight only made things worse, and she quickly closed them again with a groan. But they soon popped wide once more as a familiar screech answered her groan, accompanied by thundering footfalls.

She tried to sit up, to get to her weapon and Psyche before the Dread Knight was upon them. But she could not seem to rise from the ground and could only move her head and fingers.

Remembering what had happened, she was fearful Cedric had tied her to the ground. She started to scream for him to let her up, and then she realized she was not tied to the ground.

In fact, she was not on the ground at all. She floated several inches above the treetops. Floated...and *moved*.

She turned her head this way and that, fought to move and get free. The way she moved, how high up she was, and the scream of the Dread Knight told her the story. Cedric had somehow fastened her to the back of the creature.

And the implications of that had her blood running to ice.

"Cedric!" she hollered at the top of her lungs, uncertain if he was even in earshot. "Cedric! Damn you, what in the seven hells of the Death God are you about?"

"Ah, awake, are you?"

She jerked her head about, trying to see him, but could not turn far enough even to see the bloody iron of the monster's flesh. "Where are you?" she demanded, temper holding off panic by a slim margin. "Dammit, where are you?"

The pace of the cacophonous footsteps changed, seeming to echo strangely. The reason became apparent quickly as a second Dread Knight came into sight. It fell back from where it had trod beside the one she was on, and on its shoulder rode the man she had loved. "Really, my love," he said with a sigh. "You always wake up in such a foul temper."

"What in blazes have you done, Cedric?"

He gave her an innocent look. "I, my love?"

"Stop that!" she snapped. "That is a term you have never used in public! What has happened to you?"

"I told you already. Princess Janet has framed me for her failed coup."

"And that is a load of manure!"

Now he looked injured. "Really, Rowena. Doubting me in favor of a royal? Have you given up on your beliefs?"

"I am not the one consorting with the Dread Queen!"

"Consorting? You wound me, Rowena." The slap across her face came out of nowhere and was most unexpected because he never left the shoulder of the Dread Knight he rode. "You will be quiet!" he snarled at her, his expression having suddenly gone hard as stone. "And do as a woman should!"

Her eyes bulged. "You are not Cedric! He would never say such a thing!"

"Oh, I am afraid I am indeed he, my love. But I am not the weak little man you knew. My lady has freed me from the bonds of sniveling niceties which he used to keep me locked away. And now we shall together do what you have long dreamed of! By day's end, the royals will lie destroyed at our feet, shown for the monsters they are!"

And with those words, he leaped from the Dread Knight's shoulder and vanished into the trees, leaving her alone. For some time after, she screamed his name, demanding he return, that he free her and stop this madness. Even though she knew he was no longer able to hear her.

* * *

"Well?" Janet asked as Andre returned.

"That way," the boy replied, pointing to the south. "Cedric leads two Dread Knights."

"Two?" Janet turned to Malcolm. "We barely took down *one*, and that was with Rowena on *our* side."

"She is still on our side," he shot back.

"Malcolm—"

"Fighting amongst yourselves? After only a few days out here? You disappoint me."

They all turned. There was Cedric, the midday sun gleaming off his armor and greatsword as he sneered self-righteously.

"Where is Rowena?" Malcolm growled, drawing the Sword of Lions.

Cedric lifted his weapon off his shoulder and studied the blade as if fascinated by it. "Is one woman not enough for you, old friend? So much for the noble Malcolm of Bonaparte."

"Enough games, Cedric. Where is she? What have you done with her?"

"What does it matter? You cannot help her. You cannot even help yourself. You doomed yourself when you withstood my lady."

"Very well." Malcolm twirled the Sword of Lions as he started for the man who had once been his comrade. "I shall beat it out of you."

There was the now-familiar roar that signaled he had tapped into the powers of the bloodstone, and he was abruptly before Cedric. But when he swung his weapon, the knight easily blocked with his own sword. Malcolm swung around the other way, his blade slicing through the air fast as lightning, but again his strike was intercepted.

"Did you think my lady would send me after you unprepared?" Cedric taunted, shoving him back. "I am her champion, and you are but ants before her power."

"Malcolm!" Janet cried out, but he did not need to turn. He had heard the footfalls getting closer and closer and knew the Dread Knights were on them.

"You can handle this!" he shouted to her. "Center yourself and concentrate!"

From the other side of the clearing, she gaped at him. Center herself? Concentrate? That was the best advice he could give her? But there was no calling to him again, for he had closed with Cedric, and the two traded blows of such speed and ferocity they were scarcely more than blurs.

"Janet! Look out!"

She shifted her focus to see a massive hand reaching for her. Without even thinking, she hurled wind at it, shoving the hand away. Surprised at the power and speed of her casting, she looked down at the hand she had used to direct the spell. *Center myself and concentrate? Alright, then.*

When the creature that had tried to crush her recovered itself and went for her again, she drove her fist out at it. The wind lanced out, magnifying from the point of release to strike the beast dead in the center of its chest. With her other hand, she made a motion as if grabbing hold of something and snapped her wrist. An arc of flame shot out like a whip, scorching its legs.

The Ariagne had fled back inside their caverns, not willing to fight such powerful creatures. And so, while Janet dealt with the one, Andre took on its companion. But where before he had gone for a death by inches and used his blood-bound swords as throwing weapons, he now took a different tactic. For the binding magic held another power, binding the user to the swords.

He threw one blade, which the monster predictably batted aside. But as it went for him, he summoned himself to the thrown weapon, appearing high in the air to curl his fingers around it again. And as he did, he spun and threw the other sword, which buried itself into the monster's shoulder.

He summoned himself to it again, intending to use the position to strike a potentially lethal blow. And spotted the woman on its back. "Rowena!"

"Andre?" She shifted, obviously unable to turn her head far enough to see him. "Andre, for the gods' sake, get me down from here!"

He was about to reply when the creature's hand came up to slap him, and he had to jump clear. He deliberately jumped to the rear of the monster, arcing through the air to land in the branches of a tree behind it. From there, he scrutinized his cousin's situation.

She was all but crucified on the monster's back, with her arms spread out and her legs together. Nothing he could see held her there, which suggested magic, though what he could not say. But he could never free her himself.

Down on the ground, Cedric had gone on the offensive, and only the unique properties of Malcolm's weapon held him off. The tawny-haired swordsman spun his weapon, deflecting the blond knight's attack away with the angle of the blade. But the force of the blows continually threw him off balance, and only the fact Cedric had to regain his own balance allowed Malcolm to recover in time to meet the next attack.

It was a stalemate, a neutral standoff. The deciding factor would be whoever had the stronger endurance, and under normal circumstances, that would have been Malcolm. He had always been the faster and more enduring of the pair. But the Dread Queen's magic had obviously augmented Cedric's powers, possibly beyond Malcolm's own talents. He could be in real trouble.

Janet found the battle no easier. Though her wind magic and flame whip were holding the monster at bay, she could not do any actual damage to it. Her powers were next to useless in targeted attacks, as she had never learned to focus them to a killing edge.

She could try immolation, but with her lack of control she could easily start a forest fire. And there was absolutely no chance of her sending the thing flying. They were outmatched.

And then the worst happened. Her worrying over the problems of the battle cost her control of her magic. The flame whip fractured and faded away, and at the same moment the wind she had been creating got away from her. It flew apart in a mighty gust that knocked everyone to the ground, including the Dread Knights.

Janet, for her part, went flying into the cliff face. Something hit the rock beside her head and fell to the ground with the unmistakable clatter of metal. When she turned her head to look, she saw with horror it was the Sword of Lions. Her errant spell had unarmed Malcolm!

A grunt of pain and the sound of metal striking flesh had her head snapping up. Cedric had recovered quickly and delivered a punishing punch putting Malcolm down, and now he rose with a look of grim triumph on his face. His sword came up, up, up, ready for the killing blow.

\* \* \*

The pendant had come off. Rowena had no clue how, but Janet's failed casting had finally been good for something.

She had felt the chain and its small adornment bumping against her chest as she had fought to get free. It had not taken a wizard to tell her it was what had kept her bound to the monster's back. But now she was free.

She rolled over, gaining her feet. And saw Cedric plow his fist into Malcolm's face. She never hesitated, scarcely even thought. One of the long daggers she kept in her boots was in her hand and flying through the air in the time it took to blink.

The hook-pointed weapon caught Cedric in the elbow, tearing a deep line and rendering the arm numb. Rather than plunge into Malcolm's side the knight's sword clattered to the ground as he stumbled back, holding his wounded arm.

His eyes burned across to her, and she felt her heart tear at the naked hatred in them. Then, before she could blink, he was there in front of her. His backhanded blow was so hard she was thrown a full foot before she crashed to the ground.

Andre leaped to her defense, planting both feet into Cedric's chest in a leaping kick. The boy came on hard, his blood-bound blades whistling through the air as he drove the knight back. But try as he might he could not land a blow, for Cedric was much too fast and only toyed with the youth.

When Cedric finally struck back it was quick, effective, and brutally efficient. An open-handed shot to the throat stunned Andre. A knee to the belly doubled him over. And a forearm to the back of the head put him down for the count.

A lance of wind staggered the knight, another nearly took him off his feet. It was Janet, using the only weapon she had, her magic. She threw air at him, solid, invisible shafts that flew one after the other to crash against his powerful frame.

She pushed him back bit by bit, driving him towards the trees and away from them all. But the strain of the battle took its toll, and her spells gradually lost their punch as she weakened. Finally, she sagged, fell to her knees, and toppled over.

Cedric laughed. It started as a wry chuckle, then grew and grew until his head was thrown back, and he was crowing his success to the sky. He had won!

When the hilt of the Sword of Lions caught him in the stomach, it was a complete surprise. Malcolm's fist followed a second later, striking his cheek with such force the bone shattered with a loud *crunch*.

The lion's roar was louder than ever as Malcolm delivered a storm of punches and kicks and slammed the hilt of his weapon repeatedly into Cedric. It was not the graceful dance of a duelist, the skilled assault of a warrior. This was the frenzied, furious assault of a man driven beyond all reason to erase his foe. And beneath such a mauling neither man nor beast nor monster stood the slightest chance.

Cedric would die if it kept up. Rowena held no illusions about that. The only reason he stood at all was the rapid assault of blows. And though her warrior's instincts said to let their enemy die, her heart shouted at her that Cedric dying this way would destroy both her and Malcolm. So, she closed her fingers over the only weapon with even the slightest ability to stop her friend's assault, whispered a quick prayer to Lady Fate and let fly.

Though her intent was stopping Malcolm it was not he she had aimed for. Not even her fabled ancestor could have hit such a target. The silver chain of the pendant seemed to glow as it shot through the air, turning it into a shining missile that flew straight for Cedric.

The chain clasped itself around his neck as she had hoped it would, and he was hauled off his feet. He flew like a doll thrown by a petulant child, slamming into the trunk of a tree where he stuck fast.

Malcolm whirled around, staring at her

with angry eyes glowing gold. She struggled to rise, to attempt to defend herself or at least try to talk him down.

And then from behind her came that awful screech. The Dread Knights were not dead yet.

Malcolm shot forward with another disembodied roar, angling for the creature. The gargantuan hand that had been coming down to squash her like a bug instead flew through the air to crash against a tree.

And Malcolm did not stop there. He raced up the length of the monster's arm, slashing and slicing as if he planned to butcher it. The thing howled in agony, but he kept going until at last he took its head off in one mighty spinning blow.

The other monster was up by that point, gathering itself to lunge. He beat it to the punch, coiling his legs and launching himself like a ballista bolt. His magnificent sword led the way as he pierced the creature's torso and burst out the other side.

The beast dropped to its knees, shrinking back to its original form as it fell to the ground. Malcolm stood for a moment, shoulders heaving as if he was trying to catch his breath. Then he too collapsed.

In the silence following the carnage, Rowena finally gained her feet and stumbled two steps towards Cedric. She got no farther before there was the sound of a bell followed by rushing wind.

And he was gone.

# CHAPTER 11

It was fortunate Malcolm had a death grip upon his sword, or they would have gone no further that day. As it was, getting Shadow to move took some doing, for the loyal steed was not stupid and knew that his master was unconscious. In the end, it was the appearance of faithful Psyche, who had trailed her mistress at a discrete distance throughout the woods, which enabled them to go on as they were able to coax Shadow into following his broodmate.

Between the battle, the struggle with Shadow, and their own exhaustion, they rode only for a few hours before making camp. Malcolm never woke, and it took some doing between the rest of them to get him out of the saddle again as none had recovered much. He dropped the Sword of Lions in the midst of it, and they let it lie where it fell, knowing only Malcolm could wield it.

While Rowena and Andre busied themselves with gathering wood, water, and cooking supper, Janet tended to Malcolm and thought upon the events of the fight. She had done something unbelievable when Cedric had turned his attentions to Rowena and battled Andre. Malcolm had needed his weapon, their best hope for survival. And he had gotten it, but not on his own.

She was not entirely certain of the exact circumstances. One second, she was on the ground against the cliff face and the Sword of Lions was within reach. The next second, she crouched next to Malcolm and pressed the hilt into his hand. There was the sound of a lion's roar, and he was up and going after Cedric.

"I picked it up."

"Picked what up?"

She blinked, then looked over her shoulder at Rowena, who watched her with a raised brow. "Sorry?"

"You said you picked *it* up," the other woman said. "What did you mean?"

Janet swallowed, and her gaze shifted back to the magnificent weapon lying where it had fallen from Malcolm's fingers. Though she was painfully aware of what could happen if she were wrong, she rose slowly to her feet and walked over to the sword.

"No!" Andre started forward when she crouched down, but Rowena grabbed his arm and stopped him.

Janet flicked another glance at them, then reached out a shaking hand to touch the ornate hilt. It was only the lightest brushing of fingertips over the metal, but she felt the power surge into her arm and heard that roar in her own head. She pulled her hand away, and the roaring stopped.

Her lips had gone dry, and she wet them again before reaching out once more. This time she curled her fingers around the handle and picked up the sword. The roaring sounded once in her mind, then subsided, and she turned to find the other two staring at her with mixed amounts of surprise, shock, and confusion. But they said nothing as she returned to Malcolm and slid the weapon into the scabbard on his waist.

"How?" Andre finally asked. "How is it possible?"

"I do not know." Janet looked down at her hand, then at the unconscious owner of that wondrous sword.

"Perhaps it is a clue to who he truly is," the boy suggested. "Perhaps you are actually kin."

"He is not my brother. There would be no reason to hide away an heir like him."

"No, not a brother," Andre agreed. "But your mother had a half-brother, and nothing is known of your father's family."

"A cousin?" Oh, she would have loved if that were the case. If he were blood it would put to rest all the whispers and those sneaky feelings that kept coming back at the wrong time. But... "No. Lord Regis was one of those who tried their hand at claiming the Sword of Lions. If he were Malcolm's father, even illegitimately, it would have responded to him. Blood is blood."

"There is more than one kind of blood," Rowena said quietly, her gaze level. "And it takes more than one person to create a bloodline."

The cooking fire popped, loud as a smith's hammer striking iron. The soup Rowena was cooking hissed, and the woman was forced to scramble back from the pot to avoid being scalded by splashing water.

"You do not know what you speak of," Janet growled, her eyes purple flames. "There is nothing of that sort between Malcolm and I, so hold your tongue!"

Though she had been startled by the eruption of fire and soup, Rowena stayed calm, even defiant as she stared down the angry princess. "I will perhaps be the only person in your entire life who is not cowed by your wrath, so listen closely. You fool yourself, Princess. *That sort of thing is what has been between the two of you all along.*"

"Malcolm and I are not you and Cedric," Janet snapped back. "Do not measure our friendship by your own experience with your fiancé."

"You are correct," Rowena replied, still calm, still even keeled. "You are not Cedric and I. My resistance to Cedric was because I did not think he was truly what I wanted. Your resistance to Malcolm is because he has always been what you wanted, but you do not want him to be."

"I— You— How dare you!"

Rowena simply shook her head. "It is always so difficult for women like us. We want to stand alone, want to chart our own destinies. And we are fools for thinking so. As strong as we are, we are all the stronger when we stop running and recognize love is not a weakness. It *requires* strength."

She rose and brushed off her hose and armor. "Do not make the mistake I did, Princess. Do not wait until near the point of death to accept what is in front of you. It is something you will regret."

And so saying, Rowena walked away from the campsite to the river, leaving behind a princess struck dumb by such personal advice given so freely by someone who had thought the worst of her until that night.

\* \* \*

Memories flitted through Janet's troubled sleep. Ghosts of the past, of a childhood once so dear and warm to her. A childhood now viewed through a different lens.

She and Malcolm running and laughing in the halls of the castle, little Rebecca toddling in their wake. Malcolm shaking a rattle to entertain the twins in their crib while she and Rebecca played with their dolls. The two of them helping precocious Sonya learn to walk. The whole group of them passing a ball around Alexis while she shrieked with laughter and clapped her hands.

Memories of growing up joined those of early childhood. The uproar when her eyes changed color, the mark of a wizard manifesting in the royal line for the first time ever. The loss of her mother, so frightening to a child of only ten. The way her powers suddenly flared beyond her control in the aftermath as if that loss had been a key in a lock.

Her sisters and family shrinking away from her, pulling back, and sending her deep into self-loathing. The secret moment she had never told anyone of, that terrible moment when she had looked out the window of her chamber and thought of jumping. She never had because, almost as if he had read her mind, Malcolm arrived. The laughter he had finally gotten from her after trying so hard had been the most glorious thing she had ever experienced.

She recalled how he was always around after that. Whenever she turned around, he was there in her sight, always supportive and friendly. Always there for her and her sisters when they needed him.

And in the way of young girls, she admitted here in her mind, she became smitten with a boy who seemed genuinely concerned with her welfare. She fantasized and dreamed of a royal wedding with him as groom, of being his wife and having his children.

Now, finally, came the one memory that lived closer to her core than any other. She was hiding in the upper balcony of the court and listening to Malcolm refuse her hand in marriage. Listen to him refuse her.

She felt the pain of her fantasy shattering, of her heart being ripped in two. The most central hope of her life destroyed in the space of seconds. She had slipped from the balcony and run back to her chambers with tears stinging her eyes.

And there, she wept. Lamented. And, ultimately, let him go. For in the end, she knew he was right. If they had truly been a match he would have leaped at her father's offer.

And so, when he had left to go to the monster wars, she had bidden him goodbye with an easy conscience and a grateful heart. For he had given her one last gift, one last lesson of life. Her right to choose was precious and a great responsibility. She could not make the selection lightly.

A noise woke her then and, for a moment, she lay there trying to discover what it was. It sounded at first like nothing most than the whistle of the wind through the trees. But as she continued to listen and her mind cleared, she made out words.

Someone was singing. A woman. *Rowena*.

She rolled over. The redheaded woman sat

by the fire with her back to Janet, entertaining herself with a quiet little tune. She had a fine voice, and it made Janet smile to see another side of this woman she had been arguing with for days.

Until she recalled the topic of discussion before dinner. The conversation that had, she was certain, been the genesis of the dream from which she had just woken.

"Cannot sleep?" Rowena asked, turning to look at her.

Janet shook her head as she rose from her bedroll and walked to join Rowena beside the fire. She wanted to ask what the woman had meant at the end of the conversation, wanted to ask why she was so sure there truly was something between her and Malcolm.

But she could not bring herself to say the words. It was too humiliating. So, instead, she asked, "Tell me of life on the front lines of the army."

Rowena blinked at her for a long second, obviously surprised. "I would not think that is something that would interest you."

Janet's eyes drifted over to where Malcolm slept. "There are parts of his character that have changed over the last five years. I would know what changed my friend so." She deliberately placed an emphasis on the word 'friend'. So help her, they were *not* having that conversation a second time in one night.

"I cannot say how he has changed," Rowena said, shifting so they sat side-by-side, two companions talking by a fire. "To me, he is the same man I first met when they assigned Cedric and I as his subordinates. Brave to the point of suicidal, and undeniably talented with a sword. He and Cedric are alike in that way."

"Cedric told me his version of how you two were back then."

Rowena chuckled. "I suppose he said that I was always at his throat. I was, come to that, but it was hardly one-sided. By the gods, we bickered from the minute we laid eyes on each other. And poor Malcolm, caught in the middle. Was he always willing to take lumps when he had no stake in things?"

"Oh, always."

"Hmm. In any case, Cedric and I just could not get past it. You know how there might be someone you just cannot stand? No reason for it, they simply rub you the wrong way." Rowena sighed. "I suppose there was a reason for it after all, though. Gods, I never thought I would feel anything like I did the moment I caught sight of him. It was not what I wanted to feel, but I could not help it.

"After a time, fighting seemed our way to get through the loneliness of life in the army. Everyone has a different way of coping with being so far from home and normality, with watching those around you die or get maimed.

You have to cope, or you cannot get up in the morning, and it becomes extremely difficult to want to defend yourself.

"Cedric and I had nothing at home to keep us going the way Malcolm did, so we latched onto each other. That can create a special bond, I suppose. He became...necessary for me, even before we realized what we felt for each other."

"What about your parents," Janet asked. "The way Malcolm's father got him through."

Rowena turned, her green eyes seeming to gleam in the flickering light of the fire. "Princess, when I suggested earlier there was something between you and Malcolm, I meant no offense, but I also made no assumption. It was not Malcolm's father that got him through, for no man would re-read a letter from his father every night before going to sleep."

"A letter." Janet was suddenly sick in her heart as Rowena's implication was all too clear. She had only ever written Malcolm one letter, early on in his tour of duty. If he had read it each night...

Rowena's head whipped around. Her eyes searched the surrounding trees. "Wake Andre," she instructed, reaching for the bow and quiver she had set nearby. "We are not alone out here."

* * *

What came on them was an utter onslaught of monsters. Goblins and orcs and bugbears and trolls in numbers so vast it seemed entire warrens of the creatures had been loosed upon them. There was no time to call out to each other, to organize the defense. The battle was joined.

Rowena's first arrow slew two of the goblins at once, taking one through the left eye and the other through the right. Before it had come out the other side and zipped into the side of a tree, she had drawn another arrow and put that into the throat of a bugbear.

Andre spun, slicing the end of a spear as neatly as one might snip a twig, then continued the spin to take off the hands which held it. A jumping kick took the orc in the chest before it could cry out in pain, and it stumbled back only to have its head chopped off by one of its fellows when it got in the path of their bone sword.

The sword wielder had time to blink stupidly at the orc it had just killed before Andre's blades crossed over its neck and its head went flying without the rest of it.

Janet had reasoned the problem with her magic was creating rather than using what was available. And so, she drew from the cooking fire, recreating the flame whip she had used earlier that day. It was turning out to work well as she scorched creature after creature to death with deadly precision.

Rowena weaved in and out and around, working with the two horses as if the trio could read each other's minds. Psyche kicked her steel-clad hooves in the face of a troll, distracting it long enough for Rowena to put an arrow through its brain, negating the creature's inherent healing powers.

Shadow bucked, slamming his broad shoulder into the torso of an orc hard enough to send the monster stumbling away. Before it could recover, the redheaded archeress jumped onto his back, into the air, and pinned the orc to the ground with two arrows through the throat.

Andre did not make use of his fast-travel sword throwing technique, as it was far too risky in the crowded circumstances. But the agile boy nevertheless moved around the fight like a jumping flea. One second, he was here, taking off a bugbear's hand with a quick sweep. The next, he was there, driving his blood-bound blades up through the belly of an orc.

Janet had turned her flames on the contingent of trolls that were amongst the assaulting monsters. The fires were the beasts' natural enemy and overwhelmed their inherent tolerance for damage. She roasted them, immolating them into dust.

It was at that point, when they seemed to be holding their own, that things started going wrong. Almost inevitably.

Andre rolled a touch too far without realizing it. When he came up, he caught a hard kick in the chest that sent him sprawling. He managed to lose hold of one sword, letting it tumble away seemingly without intent. Yet, when the bugbear that had kicked him tried to skewer him, he summoned himself to it and hamstrung the beast.

Rowena, meanwhile, got into trouble when she tried to spin around Psyche's hindquarters to snipe at a trio of goblins. At the same moment she made the attempt, the horse reared up to kick at an orc. She had just nocked the arrows onto the string when she ran smack into the mare's flank, and they fell like a bundle of firewood as the collision flung her to the ground.

All save one projectile, which flew from the bow and scored the back of Janet's knee as it pinned her riding dress to the earth. She cried out as her leg collapsed beneath her and with her concentration broken, the flames got away from her.

She watched in stunned horror as the controlled funeral pyres, freed from the yoke of her power, erupted. At the same time, the power she had been pouring into that control instead flowed into the source she had drawn from. The cooking fire turned into a bonfire in seconds and threatened to get bigger by the second.

She was not sure why she did it. Perhaps it was merely instinct, that lifelong assurance he had always been there for her. But she reached out for him or tried to. She could not get the words out, for her throat filled with smoke.

And so, she closed her eyes and reached

out with her mind, a style of magic she had only ever read about. *Help us,* she begged, focusing on a mental image of him. *Please, help us.*

Her eyes opened again as she heard a loud catlike growl. And she saw his hand close over the hilt of his weapon, the growl becoming the familiar roar. His own eyes popped wide, and in them she saw the ferocity of the king of beasts.

He vanished, and she heard a cry of mortal agony above her. She rolled over and saw an orc, sans head, falling back as its weapon slipped from nerveless fingers. Malcolm, though, was already off to the next, and then the next.

He ran through their enemies like a river through a field. Wherever he struck, blood and soul were a gruesome harvest. It took him mere seconds to annihilate the surviving goblinkin, though a few bugbears managed to raise their weapons. His magnificent sword made short work of limb, weapon, and body in unison.

The orcs were more difficult, though not by much. They were, after all, more intelligent. Half a dozen actually had time to swing at him before their innards spilled to the earth or their heads went flying. Before ninety seconds had passed, it was over, and the last few bodies hit the ground in a great crash.

Janet watched him for a second, heart in her throat as she feared he might collapse once more. But he flicked the blade of his weapon to clean the blood from it, then slid it back into its scabbard without the slightest trace of exhaustion in his movements. And when he turned to her, his eyes were clear, alert.

And hard as iron.

* * *

Malcolm was livid. Other than that one fulminating glare, he deliberately avoided looking at her as he directed them to pack up. They had lost enough time, he said, and their enemy grew desperate. They would need to move on.

His body was stiff as they rode, his back ramrod straight. She knew his body language well enough to recognize he was furious with her. Why, she could not entirely say. But then, she had other worries on her mind.

She had never experimented overmuch with mind magic, though she was familiar with the theory of it. It was difficult enough to make unfamiliar minds connect to one another under normal circumstances. The frantic chaos of battle was not a normal circumstance.

Even so, she had reached Malcolm's mind with ease. It was not something which sat well with her. Only minds well-used to each other could link so easily, and the friendship she shared with him was not enough to create that bridge.

As they continued to ride, she closed her eyes and slowed her breathing. She wanted answers, and the only way to get them was to delve within.

In the darkness behind her closed lids, she blocked out everything bit by bit. First was sound. Picturing her ears as portcullises, she slowly lowered the gates. The clip of the horses' hooves, the creak of the saddles and the jangling of Malcolm's sword and Rowena's bow faded away.

Second came smell. The scent of the horses, of the earth and the trees. Of leather and metal. Of him. She stripped them away one by one until all were gone.

Last was touch, the only remaining sense that could distract her. The feel of Malcolm's waist beneath her fingers. The movement of horse and saddle beneath her. She shut them off as if slowly snuffing out a candelabra flame by flame.

And when it was done, when she was alone in the emptiness and the utter quiet, she formed the door. The shimmering white gate she opened was not a portal into Malcolm's mind, though. The answer she sought was not within him. It was within her.

She had traveled to the dreamscape once before, not long after Malcolm had left. Back then, she had found it necessary to use it as a method to lock away certain improper emotions. She had no intention of releasing them now, but there were things she needed to examine.

The landscape of her soul took the form of

a garden. It was lush and beautiful, though far too haphazard to be called peaceful. She was a woman with quite a few problems in her path, after all.

Still, she was certain it had not been *this* lush when she had last visited. The trees were so thick with leaves their branches drooped and bore fruit so ripe the juices nearly dripped through the skins. The flowers were an abundance of color and scent that bloomed beyond the wildest of imaginings.

There was too much color, too much scent. Too much *life*. This was wrong. This was *very* wrong.

She hurried to the far end where a great oak stood. Its leaves were not green, but rather a shimmering, liquid silver, and its trunk gleamed like gold. At its base lay a great ornate chest, spangled with flawless gemstones. It was the greatest vault of her heart, the innermost secrets of her very soul.

And it lay open and empty.

Her fingers curled into useless fists at her sides as she stared down at it. She had sealed her feelings for Malcolm within that chest, had sought to lock them away forever. But the overflowing garden which surrounded her provided mute testimony to what had happened to those emotions.

They had taken root within her soul. And they had grown into something she could scarcely control. She had not let him go.

"Janet!"

The dreamscape abruptly shattered, thrusting her back into reality. She sat up with a groan and immediately grabbed for her arm as it began throbbing painfully. "Ow."

"Are you alright?" Malcolm asked. He kneeled before her on the earth and seemed to be forcing himself not to reach for her.

"I believe so." Gingerly, she tested the arm. Nothing was broken, though the shoulder was a bit tender. "Forgive me. I must have fallen asleep."

She would not look at him. Could not. He was always too perceptive when her emotions were stirred up. She could not allow him to see what she felt.

Deliberately, she got to her feet and directed her attention at dusting off her riding dress. "We should continue on," she said, making a considerable effort to keep her voice light. "There is not much time remaining on my amulet."

When nobody said anything, she stopped dusting herself off and looked up again. "What?"

"We are going to have to waste some time," Rowena informed her, removing her bow from its hook, and slinging it over her shoulder where it was easier to reach. "Andre was scouting ahead and, well..."

Janet's heart sank. "How many?"

"An even hundred."

"A *hundred*?"

"And a Dread Knight," Andre supplied helpfully. "The Dread Queen appears determined to stop us this time. I suppose the beating Malcolm gave Cedric has upset her."

"Andre," Rowena admonished. "Really."

"Sorry, cousin," he answered with his customary cheeky grin. "Shall we go, then? Should not keep them waiting."

Janet turned to remount Shadow, then stopped and looked sternly at Malcolm. "This time," she told him. "You shall be the one to stay back."

# CHAPTER 12

Malcolm rested one hand on the hilt of his sword and gave her an icy look. "I beg your pardon?"

"I am running out of time," she pointed out again, pulling herself into the saddle. "We cannot afford to lose another day because you have collapsed again from overusing the bloodstone."

He plucked her back down again as easily as if she were a young child. "And can we afford the time it will take for the three of you to try and fail as you did last night?"

"We did not fail." She shoved at him in an effort to free herself from his grip, but his fingers were like iron bands on her arms. "Blast you, unhand me!"

"You had to reach out to me because you were on the point of death!" He shook her hard enough to make her teeth rattle. "You were pinned to the damn ground and mere seconds from being skewered!"

The familiar hideous screech of a Dread Knight interrupted the brewing argument. It did what her futile shoving could not. He released her, stepping away and drawing his weapon.

She had to lunge to catch him and found her own strength surprising. She actually hauled him back, held him back. "You *will* stay back!" she shouted at him, shoving him so hard he actually stumbled back two steps. "You will let *us* handle this! I will not let you harm yourself for me!"

"Malcolm!" Rowena called, and both turned to see the first line of goblins coming through the trees.

Janet's temper sparked higher than it had ever gone. For the first time in her life, she reached not for flame or wind, but for earth. Her hand shot out, fisted, and yanked upward as she spat out a single vicious oath. "*Molek zano ta!*" Spikes of rock shot upward, shredding the creatures in a shower of blood, bone, and gore.

With her no longer blocking his way, Malcolm shot forward. The magnificent blade of his weapon sliced through the spears so neatly and so quickly they fell in tidy piles with the sound of a hailstorm. He continued his momentum, arrowing straight for a lumbering hill giant. The poor beast never stood a chance, and the last thing that went through its mind was that its body looked strange missing its head and right arm.

Janet folded her thumbs into her palm, then stabbed the remaining fingers of both hands at the piles of rock. "*Zatra menos!*" They lifted on eddies of wind and went hurting through the air like bullets thrown from slings the size of mountains. Her targets were the ten massive hellhounds in the back of the assembled army, and she found her mark unerringly.

Howls of mortal pain died into whining yips, then the weakening scrabbles of mighty claws struggling to find purchase as the body died. The earth ran orange with lava-like blood from where the spears had pierced and pinned the bodies.

Malcolm worked his way through the giants with the grim efficiency of a headsman. Every sweep of his weapon sent fingers and hands and arms and heads and sections of club falling like a gruesome rain. He was a whirlwind of destruction and devastation.

From where they stood, Rowena simply gaped. There was nothing for her and her cousin to do in this battle. Malcolm's powers were already incredible, but Janet's destructive magic went beyond that and into the realm of spectacle. The way they fought, staying clear of each other's work, and yet making use of it all at the same time took it still farther.

It reminded her of the way she and Cedric had fought on the frontlines. And that made her smile. That smile widened when she glanced at Andre and saw the boy was staring in wide-eyed, slack-jawed amazement at the carnival of carnage before them.

They mowed their way through the entire

force before the Dread Knight even arrived and faced it together.

"*Mola zen!*" Janet sent a massive spear of stone lancing up from the ground, so the monster walked right into the pointed end. It dug deep into the chest, securing the Dread Knight in place.

Before it had stopped moving, before the spear had even stopped growing, Malcolm ran up the length of it. He picked up speed as he ran, his sword held low and ready at his side. Then, as he neared his target, he shoved it forward, and the wind arced away from the razor-sharp point.

He did not so much burst through the Dread Knight's head as obliterate it. He rebounded off a tree trunk, redirected, and landed in front of Janet before the body had shrunk down to its original size.

"Well," she said. "That was entirely unnecessary."

"I quite agree." He cleaned off his weapon and returned it to its scabbard. "But you did it anyway."

"*I* did it anyway?"

"I am glad you admit it."

She struck him, a closed fist shot that had his head snapping back. "You bastard!" she screeched. "I try to spare you from over taxing yourself because I care for you, and you have the gall—"

"Gall?" His golden eyes lit with fury. "You

wish to speak of gall? Your little tantrum had the potential to bury all of us under several feet of earth and rock!"

"Not if you had stayed out of the way! You did not need to risk yourself—"

He grabbed her once again, and she gathered her strength to shove him away. Before she could manage to do anything, though, his mouth came down on hers and her mind went utterly blank.

How long he kissed her, she could never be sure. Time seemed to have no meaning. The world faded away as easily as the dreamscape. And when he pulled back, he looked as confused and conflicted as she.

* * *

They would not talk about it. They absolutely would *not* talk about it. On that point, Janet was quite firm with herself. The kiss had undoubtedly happened, there was no denying it. But she was determined to act as if it had not.

Malcolm seemed perfectly happy to comply, as he had yet to so much as look at her since they had mounted up. By silent, mutual agreement, she rode with Rowena rather than him, while Andre leaped between the branches overhead. This was very much not the time for her and Malcolm to be near each other.

To distract herself before she yet again started dwelling on a subject she was absolutely *not* going to dwell on, Janet instead turned her mind to her ever-developing powers.

She had never tried to use earth magic before that fight. Her studies had always focused on wind and flame magic because they were supposed to be easier to manage. Yet, she seemed to be better with the more difficult earth magic, just as she appeared to have little trouble using mental magic.

It was almost as if there was something about her powers that made the easy hard and the hard extremely easy. No, that was incorrect. She had managed extraordinary feats with wind and fire magic, so long as she had not gotten distracted. In fact, the secret to her powers almost appeared to be *not* thinking.

A wry smile played at her lips. Her mother's one criticism of her had been her tendency to dwell upon matters to the extreme. She should really have listened.

When Rowena suddenly pulled Psyche to a stop, Janet looked up. The moment she saw what was in their path, all the blood drained from her face.

Before them was the reason earth magic was so difficult to use. With fire or wind magic, you could create what you needed from the energy within and the surrounding air. But with earth, you were not creating anything. Instead, earth magic made use of what was already there. Creating upthrusts like she had done pulled the ground from somewhere else.

And the result now faced them like a waiting band of assassins. The hole was enormous, and so deep a man would spend half a day climbing to the bottom only to spend the rest of the day climbing back up.

"We will lose a full day going around this," Malcolm observed with a shake of his head.

Janet immediately panicked. "We do not have a day!" she cried, grabbing at her head in despair. "Already, we have lost so much time we shall arrive at the Forest Tower with less than six hours to spare!"

"Well, unless you can somehow put it back, I am afraid we are stuck with the time loss." Rowena rubbed at the bridge of her nose. "And please, do not start arguing again. We have enough headaches at the moment."

Janet slid down off the saddle. "Leave me," she told them. "I will go on alone."

Malcolm maneuvered Shadow into her path. "Have you lost your mind?"

"I'll not place you in mortal danger, Malcolm!"

"I have been in mortal danger since we left the capital."

"Not from me!"

"Enough!" Rowena raised both voice and hands to stop the brewing fight. "We all took on the risk of your curse when we agreed to come along, Princess. Even me," she added when Janet turned on her. "No amount of land is payment enough if I end up a Dread Knight."

"That is why you should all leave me to my fate!"

"Really, Princess. You should know I do not abandon my comrades."

Janet jabbed a finger at Malcolm. "Then convince your comrade to leave me so you are not in danger."

"Abandon one comrade to save another?" Rowena smiled. "After all these days, now you suddenly wish to act like what I thought you were? I do wish you would decide who you want to be, Princess."

That Rowena was now calling her a comrade along Malcolm only made things worse. Did they not see they would all surely perish if the curse took her over?

"More than our lives are on the line." Malcolm reminded her. "If we fail the kingdom falls."

"Oh, hang the kingdom!" she snapped. "Avanna still stands! She will live if my family dies!"

"I will not."

She shut her eyes so as not to see what was on his face. Gods, of all the times, now was the worst moment for *that* look. "You will die if I turn. There will be no stopping it. Please, Malcolm. Do not let it come to that. I beg you."

"There is another way." Andre had landed on Psyche's rump with none of them even noticing.

"What way?" Janet asked. "You know of a shortcut? A way around?"

Andre did not immediately answer. He looked off into the trees and rubbed at his mouth with a thumb as if he needed time to plan an answer. "There is a path nearby, well-hidden, and uninterrupted. It will save us as much as a day's travel."

"Then take us to it!" She moved immediately to climb onto the saddle behind Malcolm, her discomfort with being near him forgotten in the face of hope. "Lead the way!"

When Malcolm stopped her, she shot him an angry glare. But he was looking at Andre, who still stared off into the trees. "A path with such convenient access to the Forest Tower is something I would expect more to know of. What else are you not telling us?"

Andre sighed. "The path is only accessible by my family. It is convenient, but far from easy. Guardians protect the way, and only Merlin himself can pass through without being challenged by them."

"Are they dangerous?" Malcolm asked.

"Quite dangerous." Andre finally jumped down off the horse, and it was only once he had that Janet realized the boy was withdrawn and somber for the first time since she had met him. "But there would seem to be no other way. I shall move slowly so you can keep up."

\* \* \*

Andre led them off to the east, towards another cliff face. It was a different cliff from the one that housed the entrance to the crystalline caverns, in fact it faced that cliff. It almost seemed the forest through which they rode was book ended by the two.

The boy traveled as he had before, jumping from branch to branch above them. Yet, somehow, there now seemed a grim purpose to his movements, like he was set to go where he must even if he did not want to. Janet thought back to his words about "guardians" and wondered just how difficult it would be to get around them.

That thought, naturally, had her mind drifting to Malcolm. She did not want him overusing his powers again, and not because it might lose them the extra day Andre claimed they would gain. She feared what extended bouts of using that power, and then collapsing might do to his health. She was prepared now to admit that her feelings for him ran deeper than friendship, and she might even want to see if things could go further once they returned everything to normal.

But she needed him well for that. And watching him continually risk his wellbeing on her account was not sitting well in her heart.

She could not go about stopping him the same way, not after the results of the argument earlier in the day. But there were other ways to keep him from overdoing. And if she was right about the way her powers worked, then she might have an avenue to pick up some of his burden in battle.

They could and would get through this. And once it was all done, once they broke the curse and saved her family, the two of them would talk. She swore it upon her own power.

Andre dropped from the branches several feet from the rocky face and carefully scanned the stone. "There," he said as they joined him. He nodded at what seemed a faint depression in the stone, a circle the size of a man's palm and chest-high up the cliff.

As Janet looked, her eyes made out an even fainter raised edge surrounding the circle. It arced high enough that a man could ride on another man's shoulder and fit beneath it, and wide enough that three horses might stand within.

She had come across the description of such a thing in her studies of the ancient arts. The old wizards had called them *walk windows* and *spectral portcullises*, though only in apocryphal texts. That she might one day find and travel through one had never once entered her mind. Yet, here she stood, about to do just that.

If Andre would only open it. The boy seemed quite reluctant, standing there, and staring at like it was some obstacle he dreaded trying to defeat.

Rowena slid down off Psyche and laid a hand on her cousin's shoulder. "You led us this far," she told him. "Now, you must lead us through."

"I know." But Andre's hands had balled into fists at his side, and his jaw was tight with tension. "She made me promise."

"Yes." Rowena patted his shoulder. "But I believe she would understand in this situation."

Andre nodded and stepped up to the rock. He slipped his hand into his tunic and pulled something out on a silver chain. He lifted it to his mouth and Janet glimpsed bronze and red in his palm as he murmured something. Then he shifted and laid his hand over the circle in the rock.

There was a profound click that somehow made Janet think of a lock and key long separated finally being reunited. A grinding sound followed, a torrent of rocks tumbling downhill that faded into a shimmering bell tone.

That tone filled the air as Andre stepped back and as he took his hand away the section of rock gleamed. It brightened, shade by shade, until it was a glowing white. Andre looked over his shoulder and beckoned to them before he walked into the white and vanished.

\* \* \*

They emerged from the portal into a verdant

jungle that smelled of ripe fruit and lush flowers. For one brief, terrifying moment, Janet feared they were somehow in her own dreamscape. But then she heard the birdsong, a song she had only ever heard once, when a carnival had come to the capital on her tenth birthday.

"This is Mi'Kam'Wo," she said in amazement.

"Impossible," Malcolm scoffed. "Mi'Kam'Wo is on the other side of the world."

"I am afraid Janet is correct," Rowena told him. "There are tunnels like this that lead all over the world. They are how Merlin has appeared in the various kingdoms throughout history. He can only leave his tower for a set length of time, and so requires a fast mode of travel."

Malcolm's tone was dry as he said, "And you know all this how?"

"Because she is my cousin." Andre looked about with an expression of abject misery on his face, as if just being here was physically painful. "My family is sworn to protect these passages. Besides Merlin himself, we alone know their secrets. Their risks."

It was the way he said the last part, in the solemn whisper of a funeral attendant, that reminded Janet of his conversation with Rowena before he opened the door. "Who did you promise you would never use this path?"

"His mother," Rowena said when the boy did not respond. "Lady Beatrice has forbidden him to enter the paths unless a matter of life or death."

"Death is what this place is!" Andre snapped suddenly. "We walk in the blood of my ancestors just by being here!"

"Your ancestors?" Malcolm asked calmly. "Or your father?"

Janet, too, had clued into the meaning beneath the boy's outburst. She slid down from the saddle and went to him. "I know nothing of your father," she admitted. "But if he was anything like the son he sired, then he must have had the heart of one of the lady's own agents."

Andre's lips quirked into a sad smile even as tears glittered in his eyes. "You will make Avanna a fine queen, Princess. A fine queen indeed."

Janet smiled and turned back to remount Shadow, only to see Malcolm look quickly away. She started to follow his gaze, fearing another attack, but stopped when he walked the horse up to her and stopped to wait. He had simply been watching her again.

Their talk, she decided, might need to come sooner than planned.

As they rode, she noticed how the trees they passed beneath arched above their heads. The way they met so smoothly at the top they resembled the vaulted ceiling of a castle hallway. Oddly, it reminded her of the northern hall of her own estate in Morrberry-by-the-Sea.

When she voiced this observation—minus the bit about her estate—Andre nodded, though his usual laughter was still absent from his tone. "It is an enclosed passage. There is no way to get into it from the outside. In fact, we might walk right through a building or a person, and they would never know."

"Impossible."

Janet nudged him playfully. "You grew up with me and can move faster than the eye. It amazes me that despite that, you can be so close-minded. This passage is not truly in Mi-Kam-Wo, but passes through the space it inhabits."

He turned in the saddle to study her with a raised brow. "Your studies progressed significantly while I was gone if you are so familiar with such an abstract theory."

"It is not all that abstract." It made her feel better he could jab at her that way. But she must have let too much relief—or something else—into her eyes, because the friendly light in his went out like a snuffed candle.

She cursed inwardly as he turned away and caught the sympathetic look from Rowena. The woman's eyes were sharp, Janet reminded herself. She had sniffed out some of what Janet felt for Malcolm as well, even before the princess had accepted it was there.

"What did you use to open the gateway?" she asked of a sudden, remembering the way he had done so. "It has to take more than a spell."

"It does." As he had before at the cliff face, he reached under his tunic to draw out the silver chain. This time, though, he showed them what hung on that chain.

It was roughly the size of his palm, a disk of hammered and weathered bronze. On it, the relief of a goat's head was carved, standing out sharply despite the obvious age of the piece. And the eyes gleamed a deep, bloody red within the sockets.

"That is a bloodstone," Janet said, recognizing the color of those crystal eyes. "The crystal— Is it actually set *within* the pendant?"

"Sealed inside," Andre confirmed. "Merlin did it himself, and all made since have used the same type of crystal, though none of the smiths who forged them knew that. It is the lady's own crystals, mined from the caverns of the Ariagne, from the queen's chamber with her permission. Another secret held by my family."

He toyed with the circle of bronze and crystal, his eyes still so sad. "It is the first of the bloodstones. The Criotaur Coin."

Janet was about to ask after that, for a 'Criotaur' was something of which she had never heard. But at that moment the air grew cold and a heart-stoppingly familiar fog crept in from among the trees.

# CHAPTER 13

"Rowena, protect Janet," Malcolm instructed as he hopped down off the horse. "Keep her from doing anything foolish."

"Blast you, Malcolm!" Janet snapped. "Not this again!"

"This is not the time for your ego, Janet. Stay here and find a way out of this. Andre." And with that man and boy ran towards the shadows already emerging from the trees.

Janet started to leap down from the saddle and go after him, but Rowena caught her arm. "This is not what you think," the redheaded archeress said.

"Is he telling me to stay back while he goes and fights and puts his health on the line?"

"Yes, but—"

"Then it is *exactly* what I think." Janet shook Rowena's hand off and jumped down. She got two steps before the other woman maneuvered Psyche into her path. "Blast it, Rowena, I will send you flying if you get in my way."

"No, you will not." Rowena joined her on

the ground. "Malcolm is not doing this to protect you, he is giving you time to find the solution."

"What on earth does that mean? What solution?"

"Whenever we have faced this spell, at least a few of us have gotten hurt. That is something we cannot afford at this point. And so, we must break the spell without that happening. Malcolm is trusting you to find a way."

Before Janet could say a single thing to that, Rowena yanked an arrow from the quiver, shoved her aside and took down a shadow that had been coming at her back by stabbing the projectile through its head. In a smooth move, as if it were something she did every day, Rowena pulled the arrow back, nocked it, and let it fly. It took two more through the throat, tearing them into shadow before it *thunked* into a tree.

Janet looked back up the passage to where Malcolm and Andre battled the sword-wielding shadows. Amidst the close confines of the trees Malcolm's speed was all but useless, and Andre and Rowena's acrobatic talents would fair little better. Rowena was right. It was up to her.

She considered earth magic again, but quickly rejected the notion. If she did not destroy the passage outright, she would block their path again if she dared use such spells. The air was also too cold and damp from the fog for her to draw enough heat to use fire magic.

Wind, she decided, would have to be the method. But when she tried to stir the air, it responded sluggishly. It was heavy, damp, like a sodden blanket.

Too heavy. *Too* damp. Even in a rainstorm there was wind. The air should not be so inflexible. The spell was blocking the movement of the air. But why?

She lowered her gaze to the fog lying heavy on the ground. The unmoving fog. That, she realized, was the weak point of the spell. It needed the *fog*.

But how could she move it without wind? How could she exploit the weakness of a spell when that weakness kept her from using her own magic?

*The best weapon against magic is magic.* One of her earliest lessons from the court wizard came back to her. *A wizard's greatest strength is also their weakness. But the stronger wizards already know that, and so they will guard against your magic. You must find a way through their guard if you are to succeed.*

A way through the guard. There had to be a way through the guard, a way to channel her magic to—

Channel. By the gods, that was it!

She darted for Rowena, ignored the woman's shout of, "What are you doing?" when she grabbed the quiver. She lifted it onto her shoulder, aimed the opening at a shadow and shoved her power into it.

The blast of pure magical energy that shot out obliterated the creature, shredding it into smoke that faded quickly into nothing. She turned, keeping up the assault with her power as she erased more and more of the shadows.

With the source of her arrows out of reach, Rowena dropped her bow and drew the long hook-pointed daggers as she stepped up to defend Janet's back. While the smaller woman worked to destroy the spell, Rowena kept her from being stabbed in the back.

Janet started feeling the strain as she swept the area, shredded the shadows, and shoved away the fog and the damp. Sweat beaded on her forehead, but she could not give up. She had to end it, or there would be nothing after.

Malcolm and Andre had spotted what she was doing and fell back as her spell neared where they fought. The boy jumped into a tree to get away, while the man ducked nimbly under it as it passed by.

She kept going; the sweat getting worse and stinging her eyes. Her vision was going blurry, her head lightening, but she bore down. Everything rode on her completing the job.

The air became sweet and clear, warm, and bright as the last of the fog cleared. The job done, she pulled her power away from the quiver and lowered it.

And it slipped from her suddenly

nerveless fingers to tumble to the ground. It seemed to fall forever through an endless expanse of space. The sound of it hitting the ground was a dull, echoing *thud* heard from a great distance.

And the only reason she did not join it was Malcolm's speed. He caught her the instant her knees buckled and lowered her gently. "Easy," he murmured. "Just take it easy."

"I just need to catch my breath." Her arms felt inordinately heavy when she tried to pat his arm. "I have never used so much of my power before. Gods, that took a lot of energy."

"How did you know that would work?" Rowena asked as she collected the fallen quiver.

"Implement theory." Janet's smile was as tired as the rest of her. "Your quiver generates arrows to replace the ones used. All I needed to do was change what it put out with my own magic, then direct it."

Rowena shook her head in amazement. "Will the two of you never stop impressing me?"

"Oh," Janet laughed. "Perhaps someday." She laid a hand on her stomach, which felt as empty as if she had gone two days without food. "Is there any food left over from last night?"

\* \* \*

A little food, some water, and twenty minutes of rest, and she was perfectly fine. After all, she joked, it was not as if she had suffered any physical harm.

Malcolm was clearly unhappy with that joke and walked away for a time, leaving her feeling uncomfortable. She did not like this gulf that had grown between them over the last day, but she could find no way to bridge it. Malcolm's feelings towards her were obviously conflicted, and he seemed to care for her more deeply than she wished.

She was quite afraid he could not be satisfied with a friendship anymore, not after that kiss. She mourned the loss, for it had been quite dear to her.

Once her strength had returned, they mounted up and headed on, as there were still several hours of daylight left. Janet reluctantly rode with Malcolm, even though they were both increasingly uncomfortable with the arrangement. Still, her riding with Rowena would likely cause even more problems between them, so she was stuck.

As they rode, Andre explained more about the passage and what they faced. "The guardians I spoke of do not have actual forms, nor are they truly in place to bar the way. They are tests, meant to judge the worth and ability of the groups that pass through."

"Groups?" Janet asked. "I thought that only your family could travel through here."

"Only Merlin can travel it alone. When my family uses it, we must have companions, or the portal dumps us back out again. And the passage tests each of those companions along the way before we can leave."

"So, then, we will all go through something like that?" Janet asked.

"Every one. And it will focus on more than our abilities. It will judge our hearts and courage as well." He looked off into the woods. "What we are inside."

\* \* \*

It was as they were making camp that night that something occurred to Janet. "Andre, what if Cedric slipped through the portal behind us?"

The boy, who was in the middle of building the night's fire, sat back on his heels, and considered. "The portal would consider him part of our group if he moved fast enough. Which would mean it would lump in his test with ours."

"Then the next test might not be solvable by any of us. What would happen then?"

"You have nothing to worry about," he assured her. "The test's target must be physically present when it begins, so they can solve it. For us to be caught up in Cedric's test, he would have to be on top of us."

"But present does not mean at the very center of it, does it?" she pressed. "You and Malcolm were quite a way from Rowena and I during my test."

"Janet." With a sigh, Malcolm jiggled the pot she was supposed to be filling with water magic. "We can worry about being ambushed when Cedric ambushes us. Doing so before he does is useless guesswork."

She stared at him, then shot to her feet and ran off into the dark.

"Really, Malcolm." Rowena set aside the dried foodstuffs she had bought at the tavern in case they found themselves without game to hunt. She rose and dusted off her leggings. "Sometimes, you go too far."

Malcolm watched as she walked off into the trees after Janet, his jaw working as he ground his teeth. Finally, he tossed aside the pot and got to his own feet, storming off in the opposite direction.

Andre looked around at the campsite, then raised his eyes to the sky. "Like camping with mother," he muttered and went back to stoking the fire.

\* \* \*

It took Rowena almost ten minutes to find Janet. In fact, she nearly walked by the princess in the dark. The woman had her head bowed, her dark hair falling over her face as she rocked and wept, wept and rocked.

When Rowena kneeled next to her, she saw what Janet was weeping over. The princess held the Seven Moons Amulet cupped between the fingers of both hands. Four of the six diamonds were dark.

"Only two moons left," Janet sobbed. "Once the whole amulet—all the moons and the face itself—I shall turn, and all will be lost. *I* will be lost."

"You do not know that. We do not know whether the process begins once the Dread Queen lays the curse upon you or whether you have to turn someone first. And if it is the latter—"

"It will be Malcolm first!"

Rowena closed her eyes as Janet devolved into a fresh spate of tears. She had wondered if the woman would ever say it, would ever voice the most primal fear in her heart. "Do you think he would be so weak as to allow himself to be turned? I thought you respected him more than that."

"He loves me." Janet bit off each word like it was tough meat. "I know he does. It is why he was so upset when I used mind magic to reach into his heart. He hides it because he knows I do not love him, and he does not wish to change things between us. But they have changed already."

The princess pushed up, running her fingers through her long hair as she paced back and forth, up and down. "We do not even know what act leads to the transformation. It could be something as simple as a touch, or as profound as a kiss."

"Then we will keep you from both him and Andre." Rowena stood and reached out to stop the woman's frenetic action. "You can ride with me and not go near them until we reach the Tower."

"And if you do not watch me every second? If I go for one of them? Who will stop me? Are you prepared to kill me to keep me from turning Malcolm or Andre? Because Malcolm will never do it. He will never bring himself to raise his hand to me, even if I am at his throat with a knife. He will turn, and he will die. And I will be lost. We will all be lost."

\* \* \*

Malcolm stormed about in an absolute fury. It was not entirely directed at Janet or Rowena or even Andre. Most of it was directed at himself.

He had worked so hard over the years to hide his feelings from Janet. It was wrong to let her know how he felt when there was nothing that could happen about it. He had known better than to let it show.

But he had needed to keep her from delving too deep into his mind. He could not let her know the whole of things. His past, his heritage, they had to remain hidden. Janet could never, ever know who he truly was.

Still, he had gone much too far by kissing her. So far, he could not possibly see a way back from it. He would have to leave her, would need to make his way through the world without his old friends.

This adventure would be the last time he saw her in life.

A sudden flicker of movement off to the left caught his eye. *Another shadow?* he wondered. *Or something worse?*

Cautiously, he drew his sword, the rasp of steel on leather somehow thunderous in the silence of the night. The blade seemed to whistle in the air as he spun it once, twice, three times in his hand while he searched the darkness.

The attack came from behind him, as he had expected it would. Steel rang against steel as he blocked the strike that would have split his spine lengthwise without even looking.

The figure that had attacked him was black-garbed, but it was not one of the hooded shadows he recalled. The black clothing was a loose, baggy sort of tunic and breeches. Black gloves backed by a dull metal plate covered his hands, and his black boots were fronted by overlapping layers of that same dull metal. A black cloth was wrapped around his head, leaving only hard beetle-black eyes exposed.

The weapon he used was as strange as his outfit. Though he held it in both hands, it was as slim and agile a weapon as Malcolm's own. It had a long, curved blade that slashed the air with the sound of a diving falcon as he forced Malcolm back with deadly sweeps.

It was only the amazing agility and versatility of Malcolm's own sword that enabled him to keep up with that splendid weapon. He struck it away again and again, often deflecting it at the last moment to keep it from laying him open or slicing his throat.

But as he fought this strange foe, his sharp eyes measured his opponent. He noticed the way the fighter—silent as he was—would shift before a certain cut or drop his shoulder a fraction when he was going for a wider swing. Soon, a pattern emerged, and Malcolm took advantage.

On the next swing, he caught the descending blade in the forked hilt of the Sword of Lions. Before his foe could react, Malcolm rolled the weapons over, bent the black-clad wrists backwards and slid his sword into the notch between the collarbones.

The man jerked, the shock that always came with a death blow. As his body went limp, Malcolm yanked his weapon free and let him drop.

No sooner had he done so than another attacker came from the darkness. While the silent, black-garbed swordsman had been unfamiliar to Malcolm, he could easily identify this opponent. The horse-hide vest, leather breeches and the red-died leather thong that held back his coal-black hair would have instantly identified him as a Mi'Kam'Wo warrior.

Once again, Malcolm was forced back as he dodged and deflected the two ironwood cudgels. Once more, he used the fluidity of his sword to weave a defensive network of steel as he patiently looked for an opening. But when he thought he had found one and struck, the warrior bent over backwards to avoid the blow. Malcolm had to roll away from what was obviously a prepared counterattack before the warrior could shatter his arm.

He could not use the same trick again, he realized. He would need another method. And so, as he continued to battle, he allowed his mind to focus little by little on the roar that was forever in the back of his mind. And as he did, the roar grew louder and louder inside him until at last it tore loose in a primal howl of defiance.

His magnificent weapon flashed at inhuman speeds, slicing the steel-hard wood into chips and chunks that fell like rain. As the warrior fell back, Malcolm went in for the kill. The warrior's head rolled along the ground, coming to stop in position to stare at its own fallen body.

The next attacker was a Three Seas corsair, his scimitar a bright flash of metal in the darkness. Unlike the two previous weapons, this was one Malcolm had faced before, but its wielder was far more skilled with it than the castle armsmaster. Malcolm kept having to roll away from the slicing weapon as he tried to find an opening.

Finally, he found what he was looking for. The corsair's swing required him to pivot his upper body, and that meant he had to set his feet to keep his balance. The next time he rolled,

Malcolm went under the swipe rather than away from it. When he came up, a backhanded slash hamstrung the man, sending him pitching to the ground. A slice across the throat ended the threat for good.

An *en garde* heralded the arrival of an Avannion captain, leading with his rapier. By now, Malcolm was becoming annoyed and chose not to allow the man to get far. He rolled and threw his weapon right into the man's belly. As the captain's knees buckled, Malcolm took hold of the hilt of the Sword of Lions, drew it out, and took the man's head in one fluid motion.

"Was this your plan, then?" he asked, flicking the blade about to clean it off. "To wear me down, then come at me yourself? She has robbed you of more than your good sense if you have taken such a cowardly approach."

"Needs must," Cedric said dismissively as he stepped from the shadows, his sword hanging negligently in his grip.

"Needs must," Malcolm repeated with a shake of his head. "You are truly lost."

He came in fast, trying to end things early, but Cedric was ready. A pivot, a roll of the shoulder and steel clanged on steel as blades intersected. Malcolm pivoted, sweeping out in his usual second attack, but quickly reversed the angle of his wrist to go low rather than high. Cedric was ready for that move, too, batting it up and away.

Now, the knight went on the attack, using the weight of his much heavier weapon to beat the speed of Malcolm's. Only Malcolm's well-honed instincts allowed him to dodge what would have been a beheading blow, ducking under the swipe and driving his free hand into Cedric's midsection.

He might as well have punched a stone wall for all the good it did. The hilt of Cedric's sword came down on the back of his head and rang his bell but good. Malcolm's legs went, and he dropped to his knees. Cedric kicked him full in the chest and sent him sprawling, the Sword of Lions spilling from his numb fingers.

"You say I am lost," Cedric taunted, taking one step, then another with menacing slowness. "Yet you are the one who fights for a lost cause. My mistress will have what she wants, and this kingdom will fall."

Malcolm struggled to roll, to reach out for the Sword of Lions. But Cedric put one foot on his wrist and pinned his hand as he leveled the tip of his broadsword at Malcolm's face. "But at least you will not be there to see your princess fall with it."

*That* pushed Malcolm over the edge. His other hand came up, grabbing the end of the sword and tearing it from Cedric's grasp, overbalancing the knight. Using that, Malcolm twisted, hauling with all the strength in his biceps, and shoved Cedric off, sending him spilling to the ground.

Malcolm rolled, lurched up and dove—not for his weapon, but for the man he had just downed. There was none of the artistry of a sword fight now, but the savagery of a brawl as the two of them rolled on the ground, trying like hell to beat each other's face in.

Finally, Cedric shoved Malcolm off him with a mighty heave and both men scrambled to reclaim their weapons. They snatched them up and faced each other down on their knees, blades leveled and chests heaving.

"Is this how you want it, Cedric?" Malcolm asked, getting slowly to his feet while his foe did the same. "The two of us dueling until one gets lucky and tears Rowena's heart in two? Will you abandon her this way?"

"She abandoned me by putting in her lot with you." Cedric feinted with his weapon, a quick jab Malcolm easily dodged away from. "Imagine, her throwing in with royalists rather than the man she professed to love."

"She loves you." Malcolm came in with a high, sweeping cut that was easily deflected, and quickly redirected into a second from the other side that was similarly blocked. "But she will not join herself to evil."

"Then she will die like you."

Cedric came in hard and fast now, stabbing his powerful sword at the center of Malcolm's chest. Malcolm caught the blade in the forked handguard of his own weapon, as he had with the strange black-clad attacker. Turning his wrists, he shoved it clear and drove his knee into Cedric's side. The *crunch* of a breaking rib rewarded his efforts this time, and he followed it up by ramming his elbow into Cedric's throat.

Now the knight stumbled back, gagging, and grabbing for his injured windpipe. Taking advantage of the distraction, Malcolm charged. His weapon flicked out fast as a snake. Once, twice, three and even four times as he scored each limb deep.

As the knight fell to his knees, too wounded to continue, Malcolm leaned in and laid the blade of his weapon against Cedric's throat. For a long moment, there was only the sound of their breathing, one tired from a prolonged fight and the other labored with pain.

"Finish it," Cedric urged him at last through clenched teeth. "If you do not, I will hunt you to the ends of the world."

Malcolm's fingers tightened around the hilt of the Sword of Lions. He knew Cedric was right. The Dread Queen would send him after them again and again. It would be better, smarter to end it all here.

But then he thought of Rowena, of the future she had wished for and the look upon her face when she had been separated from the man she loved. He could not do it. He could not deprive her of her chance at happiness.

"Come after us, then," he said, pulling back and sheathing the Sword of Lions. "I will beat you as often as I must in order to save the kingdom."

And with those words, Cedric and the fallen warriors all vanished as they had never been there in the first place.

# CHAPTER 14

It took Janet some time to get herself under control, and more time to clear away most of the signs of her weeping. By the time she and Rowena returned to the campsite, Malcolm was just arriving himself. To say the encounter was awkward would have been roughly the same as saying her hair was black. Fortunately, Andre had done the cooking in their absence, so at least there was food to go with the awkward silence.

Or, at least, it was silent until Malcolm spoke without warning, "At least we are halfway done now. We should be through the passage by nightfall tomorrow."

Janet's head snapped up from her bowl of stew. She recognized easily he must have had his test while she had been off panicking. She wanted to ask about it, but something inside told her not to. It was far too likely it had had something to do with her.

Rowena dipped into the pot for a second bowl. Andre had made far too much, so there would be seconds for everyone. "There is an old tale in my family," she said in a conversational tone. "It was back in the days of my ancestor, Robin of Loxley, and shortly after the death of the Lionheart while on campaign. He had no heir, and so John the Greedy became king once again. But the lords of the kingdom were not willing to give him free rein again, for they feared that might cause the citizenry to revolt. In such a case, many of them might very well end up with their heads on the block.

"John was ever the opposite of his older brother. A cowardly bureaucrat with no talent for warfare. So, when the nobility presented a united front and threatened to depose him, he had little choice. He allowed them to institute a council of lords with the authority to countermand or approve his orders. It was the foundation of what became the royal court we know today.

"Though he had spent many a year robbing them all, none had as much experience countering John as Robin. And so, they came to him at Loxley Hall and asked him to aid his country once again as First Minister. He agreed, with his new bride's permission, and assumed the job.

"At first, he found it easy to split his time, his focus between his official duties and the duties of a new husband and, after a time, a father. But bit by bit his wrangling of King John took more and more of his time and attention. Soon, he did not return to Loxley Hall for months at a time, and when he did, he would argue with Marian. And when they fought, he would react by staying away longer, for under it all he loved his wife and did not wish to fight with her.

"But fight with her he did, and the longer he stayed away, the worse the fights became. Until Marian, in desperation for her husband and her marriage, turned to an old friend."

Rowena set aside her empty bowl, shifted to sit more comfortably. The others sat silently, listening to the tale, but Janet snuck looks at Malcolm and saw the anger and defiance leeching from him little by little as the story went on.

"Little John had been named sheriff of Nottingham Forest," Rowena went on. "And when Marian asked him to intervene, he came to the capital. And there, in front of every man in the court, he challenged the Archer as he had once done when they had been younger men. He baited him, taunted him until at last Robin accepted the challenge.

"The previous challenge had ended with Little John on his back in a creek, but this time was different. For the man who was now sheriff had remained a tough woodsman, while the former leader of the Merry Men had grown soft sitting on his backside and administrating. And when Robin was down, thoroughly embarrassed by a solid clubbing, Little John spoke.

"'Is this the great Archer?' he asked. 'The

hero of the forests? Is this a man who would defend his home and family, or a man who would sit and wring his hands while raiders sacked his home and made off with his wife and children?'

"And Robin understood. He had betrayed himself, for a warrior is a warrior and a woodsman is a woodsman. And so, he left his post as First Minister and went home to teach his son the ways of the forest."

Malcolm's bowl made a sharp click against the ground as he set it down. He rose and came around the fire to kneel before Janet. "My life," he told her. "My loyalty has ever been to you, and you alone. I can be nothing else but your protector."

She raised a hand, touching her fingers gently to his cheek. "Your loyalty was something I never asked for. I waited not for a protector, but only for my best friend. It was him I wanted back."

She saw the shadow flit through his eyes, the moment of pain in those wonderful tawny orbs. "He has not come home yet," he told her, reaching up to take her hand away. "And he may never. I fear he died upon the battlefield with so many others."

She shifted to link their fingers together, a gesture more intimate than she might have been comfortable with under other circumstances. "He is not dead. I would have felt it if he had."

She leaned in and kissed his cheek lightly.

"And so, I shall wait for him to return to my side, no matter how long it takes."

* * *

Because of the intimacy and sentimentality of the exchange, Janet chose to ride with Rowena the next morning. She wanted a bit of distance from Malcolm to sort out what was going on in her head.

To save some face about it, though, she made up an excuse. "Rowena is likely to be the next one tested, I think. As the Le Fay among us, it would make sense for Andre to be the last test."

"And what does that have to do with our riding arrangement?" Malcolm asked as he set Shadow to a walk.

"The same thing it did during my test," she countered, doing her best to ignore the way he was refusing to look at her. "My magic will be more useful at the core of the test, defending and aiding her while you and Andre meet any enemy at close range."

His shoulders and back set as if her words had turned him to stone. "Very well," he bit off. "I suppose I shall just go off and guard against enemies coming at us from ahead, shall I?"

"Malcolm." But before she could give voice to her apology, he spurred his horse onward and into a gallop.

"Why are you so determined to hurt him?" Rowena asked quietly enough that only Janet and Andre—walking next to the horse—could hear her.

Janet sighed. "I do not wish to do so, but a little pain may do him some good."

"But will it do you? You love him."

Janet's back went up immediately. "I do not love him," she hissed.

"Then why do you look so hurt whenever he slaps at you?" Andre asked with a smile. A smile that fell away as she gave him her most venomous glare.

"You have known me," Janet said spitefully. "For less than a week. Do not presume to know me, my mind, or my heart. This is an absurd notion, and I shall have it stop here and now."

"Forgive—" the boy began, but she rolled right over him.

"To have my feelings guessed at by a boy barely old enough to even have an interest in girls is bad enough. To have them assumed by a woman who has been stabbed in the back by her own betrothed is far worse."

"Cedric did not—"

"Is he here with you?" Janet demanded. "Is he beside you, helping you save this kingdom? Or is he working against us? Some warrior you are, Lady Loxley. Did you even try to fight him, or did you climb onto the back of that Dread Knight and simply wait to be secured to its back?"

An angry command from Rowena stopped Psyche in her tracks. The archeress' movements were jerky with rage as she swung her leg over and dropped down to the ground. Even so, Janet was unprepared for the woman to spin around, grab two handfuls of her dress and throw her from the saddle.

When Janet started to scramble up, Rowena planted a boot in her chest, and then jabbed a finger in her face. "If you so much as try to get up before I am finished with you, it will be a solid month before you can walk on your own again."

Janet scowled, but made no further attempt to rise, and Rowena took her foot away. "I make no pretenses of being an expert in love. Throughout our relationship it has always been Cedric who needed to be patient with me because I am far too headstrong. He has never tried to change me, though, for the woman I am is the woman he fell in love with. But there is one misstep I have never made, and that is to take his love for me for granted."

She pointed her finger up the trail to where Malcolm could barely be seen in the distance. "You have a man much like mine, who loves you and accepts everything about you. He would die for you."

"I do not want him to die for me!" Janet all but shouted. "I have never asked that of him!"

"Oh, I know. I know because that is something I would never ask Cedric. But I have done what you are too afraid to do. I have asked him to do something much harder than dying. I asked him for an even bigger sacrifice."

Rowena kneeled, bringing the two of them to an even level as she looked the princess in the eye. "Do not ask him to die for you, and do not ask him to give up on you. He will never do the latter and is all too eager to do the former. The true test of a man's devotion and loyalty is to ask him to live. Ask him that, Princess, for I guarantee that is what you want from him."

Of a sudden, both women blinked as if coming out of a trance. "What on earth just happened?" Rowena asked.

"You passed your test." With another wide grin, Andre crouched beside them both. "And with quite the flourish, I might add."

"My test? Andre, all I did was yell at Janet."

"Oh, you did more than that, cousin." He shifted to look at Janet. "Her words reached you, I presume?"

"I—" Janet had to swallow. "Yes. Yes, they did."

With a satisfied nod, he turned back to his cousin. "The tests are about more than our abilities. They are about discovering who we are inside. Janet's test was a unique problem requiring a unique solution because, as a ruler and wizard, she will face many such situations. Yours was about proving yourself a true heir to the Archer."

"But I did not shoot anything."

"Robin of Loxley was more than a marksman," he pointed out. "He was a leader, one who could change hearts and minds and could see through to the core of a problem. Last night, you proved the first part by persuading Malcolm and Janet to reconcile. Just now, you proved the other by recognizing what Janet wants from Malcolm, for him to stay."

Both women stared at him, then at each other. "I said it before," Janet said finally. "And I will say it again. He has the makings of a hero."

"That he does. That he does." Rowena held out a hand, and when Janet took it, pulled her to her feet. "Come, we should catch up to Malcolm."

\* \* \*

Malcolm, in truth, was not as far away as he seemed. He had made sure not to get so far ahead he could not hear if they needed help. He could never seem to get far from her. Even when he had been in the army, she had always felt so close by.

Blast it all! Was this then to be the price paid for the sins of his blood and hers? Was all the chaos of their lines meant to reduce them to misery for their entire lives?

She was so near. Gods, she was *right there*. Everything he wanted. All he had ever wanted. He loved her. He had always loved her. And he could never have her. They were doomed, both of them, to being half of a whole.

They were done back there. Whatever argument Rowena and Janet had had was clearly passed. Odd he had not heard the whys of it, given how he had kept his ears peeled for their conversation. Perhaps it was some trick of the passage.

He recalled what Andre had said about tests being centered to the person they were for. Had Rowena had hers, then? Was that what had gone on back there? If so, that would leave just Andre's to pass.

Perhaps once he had gotten Janet to the Forest Tower, he would be able to find some way to free himself of her at last. A way, he hoped, that did not include falling on his sword.

With a sigh, he turned his horse and began riding once again. They would doubtlessly catch up.

\* \* \*

Janet sighed as she got back on Psyche. "He is already moving off. He truly does not want to be around me."

"Can you blame him?" Rowena asked, setting the horse to walking.

"No," Janet admitted. "He is angry with me. And, I think, with himself. Why does he not simply come and be done with it?"

"Because you have so far given him no reason to think you would be receptive."

That, Janet thought, was the most penetrating sentence she had heard thus far from Rowena, and it was a high bar to clear. She had been very firm about not loving him, and

Malcolm was unlikely to feel free to try to change her mind. Gods, she was still not ready to change it herself, though she was ready to admit what she had seen in her dreamscape was the truth. She was falling for him again.

"He always kept himself to himself," she blurted, memories from childhood flashing in her head. "Growing up, he would listen to me, would play with my sisters. But he rarely talked about what was happening on his end of things, and most of that had to do with Martin."

"He was the same in the army," Rowena concurred. "I was not even aware he had grown up in the capital until Cedric was being discharged and Malcolm recommended some places in the city to visit. He said nothing about his family or friends, and certainly nothing about you. I thought that letter was from some sweet-faced little shopgirl or chambermaid, not the crown princess."

"The letter." Janet almost laughed. "I wrote only the one, you know. It was just before I came of age. We share a birthday, and I wanted him to come home for the celebration. He never did."

"I do not think he came off the line all five years he was in the service." Rowena shook her head. "How he did not go mad, or die is beyond me. It was like he was possessed. He had to fight, had to be the best there was."

"Father had already invested him as a Purple Rose before he went off to the wars,"

Janet explained. "He was always going to replace Cedric as my bodyguard."

"And so, trained for that," Rowena finished. "Well, that makes sense. You are the core of his world. He wanted to defend you, no matter what."

The woman truly had found her ancestor's power, Janet realized. Her words hit the target relentlessly.

And yet, something did not fit quite right. She had given no sign as children she did not love him. Rather the opposite. So why had he fled her back then if he had loved her all along?

There was a piece yet she did not have. One last question she knew when answered would solve the entire mystery that was her oldest friend.

"Do you suppose he knows more about his origins than he has said?" Andre asked as if he had been privy to her thoughts. "If he holds back as you both have said, what if he has done so because he has known all along who he is? Maybe an enemy to your family, Janet, or even to the kingdom."

It was an interesting notion, she thought, and might well be that missing piece. Still... "He has known me and my family all his life. He knows we do not hold the father's sins against the son. Why would he think that would ruin things between us?"

They all were silent for a bit, thinking it

over. Then Rowena muttered, "The Lion. The Golden Lion."

"What?" Janet asked, but Rowena never got a chance to answer. For at that very moment a hideous scream ripped through the air.

* * *

"Ride!" Janet all but shouted in Rowena's ear, terror spiking her voice. "By the gods, ride!"

Rowena spurred Psyche on with a barked command and the mare shot into a gallop. "How did a Dread Knight get into the passage?"

"It did not." Janet's fingers tightened on Rowena's waist and her eyes were wild and scared. "It is the last test. *Andre's* test."

"A Dread Knight? How is that a test for him?"

"A hero's heart." *Faster*, Janet urged silently. *Oh, gods, please go faster*. "The tests force us to prove what we are inside. Who we will become. Andre is still a boy."

"And thus has the greatest potential," Rowena finished. "So, his test will be the greatest of the four."

Janet nodded, but she said nothing more as she strained to hear the sounds of battle up ahead. Malcolm would surely confront the creature, and it would be the one and only time the powers of his weapon would be useless.

"But would not the test have centered on Andre?"

"A hero is not just one who slays evil. He

saves the innocent. Malcolm is alone!"

And just like that, the man she spoke of flew over their heads. High over, much too high.

Janet screamed. His name, a protest against fate, a spell, she could never be sure. But she cast that spell all the same, using wind to cushion his fall.

Without waiting for Rowena to stop or even slow the horse, Janet threw herself from the saddle and took off in a loping run. She had to get to him. She had to make sure he was alright in order to breathe again.

She never got there. At the edge of her awareness, she heard Rowena shout her name, but it was far too late. She gave a surprised yelp as the Dread Knight's hand closed around her and plucked her off the ground.

"Janet!" Rowena unslung her bow, drew an arrow, and let fly in a blink. It shattered against the monster's forearm just above the wrist without doing the slightest bit of damage.

And then, Andre came flying out of the trees to land atop the hand which held the princess. His blades cut so fast they were only flashes of light scything through the air.

The creature screamed as its fingers fell away and Janet went into free fall. Summoning her focus and will she cast another wind spell to cushion her fall. It went wrong, of course, but at least all she did was send herself tumbling a short distance into a landing that jarred but broke nothing.

Andre spun, hurling both swords into the opening in the monster's face plate. It screamed again, jerking and twisting like a man being assaulted by flies. The boy backflipped off the hand rather than be flung off in some unknown direction.

As he tumbled down toward the ground, Janet saw him dip one hand into his tunic and draw out the Criotaur Coin. He held it to his forehead, closed his eyes, and chanted. He was nearly to the ground when he suddenly shoved the coin out before him and shouted something Janet could not hear.

The second he hit the ground, the coin flared into brilliant light, and the boy vanished in a cloud of dust. The cloud grew, spun, and whirled, climbing up and up and up until it was as high as the Dread Knight itself.

There was a howl unlike any she had ever heard. It sounded, oddly, like a wolf crossed with a goat and funneled through a ram's horn trumpet the size of her tower back home.

The dust spun faster and faster, coalescing inward as it went. And then, with a second cry, it flew apart once more, evaporating into nothing.

What stood in its place was a man tall as a giant, its heavily muscled chest gleaming and bare. Its legs were clad all in black, and whatever covered them was too tight to be any form of cloth. The feet were cloven hooves, and the head was that of a shaggy bearded goat with burning red eyes.

It was, Janet realized, the very essence of the bloodstone of the Le Fay family. This was the Criotaur, the goat-man.

It threw back its great shaggy head, and that howl issued from its lips in an undeniable challenge. The Dread Knight faced it screamed, the cry ringing defiance. And they fell upon each other.

This was no battle, no meeting of warriors and arms. This was, to put it quite plainly, two beings trying to kill each other by hand in whatever manner was possible.

They punched. They kicked. They threw elbows and knees and gouged at joints and skin with their fingers. The Criotaur bit the Dread Knight's shoulder, and the Dread Knight responded by bashing its skull into the Criotaur's nose.

It was as if two young children the size of the royal castle were brawling in a courtyard, only with the goal being bloody death. And the death, when it came, was bloody indeed.

The Criotaur drove a vicious blow into the Dread Knight's chest, which caved inward with a sound of tearing metal. The goat-man's hand sank through into the cavity beneath, and the Dread Knight's scream was one of mortal agony.

And when the hand which had invaded the body was pulled free once more, it held a dripping, beating heart. Deliberately, maliciously, the Criotaur held up the organ and slowly squeezed it into pulp while foul-smelling blood oozed down its arm.

And then both combatants shrank and withered, the monstrous forms fading away into what they had been before. Andre was left standing over the fallen body of a courtier, swaying like a man who had spent all night in a taproom getting drunk.

And all around them the passage faded into a more familiar pine forest. For with the last test passed, they were now back in Avanna, and only hours from their goal.

# CHAPTER 15

They had gained that extra day after all, and as the entire party was in a rather sorry state, they all agreed to make camp and rest.

Malcolm, naturally, was the worst off the lot. Though Janet's spell had saved his life, he had nevertheless landed badly. He had racked one knee, and his back ached. He was in for an awfully long night, even with the healing abilities of his sword.

And Janet was only making it worse. Her ministrations were not particularly painful, but it was annoying the way she clucked over him. And that damned brew she gave him tasted awful.

"All of it," she snapped when he set aside the earthenware cup. "It works better when you drink the entire thing."

"I do not need it to work better," he shot back. "This is hardly the first time I have been injured, Janet. I will be fine by mor—"

She had snatched up the cup while he spoke, and now she took a fistful of his hair and yanked. When his mouth fell open in a reflexive grunt of pain, she poured the rest of the drink down his throat.

"There," she said as he sputtered and coughed. "Now, you will be fine *before* morning. This would hardly be the first night to be interrupted on this journey."

"Worry about yourself then," he snarled. "Or better yet, worry about Andre."

Janet looked over at where the boy was napping. "The only thing wrong with him is the use of that coin exhausted him."

"Fine. Then just see to dinner and leave me be."

She turned back to him, and her expression was dangerous. "*That* will not happen any time in the next several years, Malcolm. We have quite a few things to work out between us."

Dammit. He had been afraid she might have this reaction to what he had done. "It was a way to derail the argument, Janet. It meant nothing."

"Oh, do not even *attempt* to try that! You have lied to me enough!"

"What on earth have I lied about?"

She stared at him. "Your father! Your heritage! Your feelings! Your plans to leave the capital! Your plans to be my bodyguard! You told me *none* of it!"

"There is a difference between telling a lie and not saying anything!" But he came up short as he realized what she had said. *Your father. Your heritage.* "Dammit, I told you to stay out of my head!"

"When you refuse to tell me the truth, you give me no other choice! Dammit, Malcolm, did you think I would be upset? Did you think I would look at you differently? Nothing could ever change how I feel about you!"

"I am your enemy!"

"No!" Her shout was so loud it woke Andre and the boy jerked up, blinking in astonishment at the furious fight he had emerged into. "By the gods, Malcolm, you had nothing to do with your father's treachery!"

"I am his son! His heir!"

"And I am heir to John the Greedy! Does that instantly make me a weak, money-obsessed failure? You are far more Martin's son than Geoffrey's!"

And there it was. His greatest secret out in the open at long last. Uttered by the one woman he had never wanted to know.

In the echoing silence he drew himself up, getting slowly to his feet. "Just because I have never used the name," he said coldly, "does not mean I am not Malcolm de Bergiouac. That name and the legacy of it are curses far worse than what you bear, and no wizard can remove them."

The sound of clapping, edged with a faint note of metal and leather slapping against each other, came from the trees behind him. Cedric, his armor shimmering red in the firelight, emerged from the shadows. "Well, well, well," he said with a mocking smile as he continued to clap. "So, that is what you have hidden all this time. How brave of you, Malcolm, to deny yourself what you desire most because of your father's sins."

The smile fell away into a dark look that promised nothing but pain. "And how useless. The line of the Lionheart ends here."

* * *

Malcolm never hesitated. His hand blurred to the handle of the Sword of Lions, and he shot across the distance to Cedric. Steel rang against steel as Cedric blocked his first strike with his gauntlet rather than his weapon.

Still moving too fast for the normal eye to see, Malcolm reversed his grip, spun back the other way, and attempted to stab low. This time, the breadth of Cedric's sword blocked the attack, drawn halfway from its scabbard to block the attack with the flat of the blade.

Malcolm pulled back again, but rather than go into another spin, he once more switched his grip and came back in on the same side. He stabbed out rather than slashed, jabbing and jabbing like the sword was a rapier. Cedric, who had not had time to get his weapon clear of the scabbard, had to dodge back and away.

But Malcolm's speed was increasing, the blood-red stone in the handle of his sword starting to glow. The familiar lion's roar was echoing in the air. And Cedric's defenses could not keep up with the power of the Sword of Lions.

Malcolm's jabbing strikes battered the knight's armor whenever Cedric failed to dodge in time. He was going to get through. It was only a matter of—

Cedric's fist plowed into his gut, ending his assault by taking away his wind. He had no time to recover before two lightning-quick steel-clad punches rocked his jaw, knocking him to the ground. The sound of Cedric's sword leaving its scabbard at last was the evil hiss of a snake.

But he did not slay Malcolm, for Andre struck from behind with a flying double-booted kick to the back. It knocked the man off balance, sending him stumbling away from the fallen swordsman.

Now the boy picked up where Malcolm had been stopped. His blades flashed in his hands, slicing and stabbing as he backed Cedric towards the trees.

But no matter how fast he cut or how sinuously he snaked out his arms, Cedric was always just a bit too quick. Every slice and jab either missed by a few inches or was batted aside with a gauntleted fist or the edge of a sword blade.

Unlike the more experienced Malcolm, missing so routinely frustrated young Andre.

The boy threw more and more into the attacks until he was overextending enough to unbalance himself if he put so much as a toe wrong.

And then Cedric's back hit the trunk of a tree and Andre's eyes lit with triumph. He went in, putting everything he had behind a last cut.

Halfway in, the blade flew from his hand as Cedric slammed a vicious blow into the boy's chest, putting a violent halt to his momentum. The knight's other hand grabbed the back of Andre's head and threw him face-first into the tree.

Improbably, the massive pine shattered under the impact, and Andre went flying through the shards. But as the boy fell, a gust of wind picked up the falling fragments of wood and sent them spinning around Cedric.

It was Janet, her face set with rage as she used her power to batter her former bodyguard over and over again. She twisted the wind about him, faster and faster. She tightened the whirlwind until the man within could not be made out through the spinning, tumbling wood.

Then there came a sound that seemed a cross between a ringing bell and a plucked harp. It echoed louder and louder, overpowering the sound of the wind and the wood. And as it reached a crescendo, another sound joined it: the whistling slice of a massive blade being swung impossibly fast.

The whirlwind flew apart, the tumbling

shards of wood shredding into nothingness. And Cedric stood unmarked with his sword held high. Runes shone along the length of the blade, glittering with energy that hummed in the air.

He had lifted his face to those runes, staring up at them in rapture. And there seemed about him the air of a man profoundly changed. He appeared possessed by the energy of those runes.

Janet, fearing what might come from that power when it was unleashed, gathered in her own. Before she could make use of it, Cedric brought that sword down, and a lance of pure force caught her full in the chest. The blast tore her off her feet and sent her flying.

Malcolm caught her before she could hit anything. He set her down gently, but the look on his face was murderous. "There is no saving him," he said, his fingers tightening around the hilt of his sword. "He dies. Here and now."

"Malcolm—" she began, but he had already rushed off, the lion's roar thundering in the air.

The Sword of Lions struck against Cedric's enchanted weapon with a brilliant flash of light, knocking it up and away. The swordsman's fist flashed up, catching the blond knight hard on the chin. But he might as well have punched a stone wall, for Cedric's head did not move so much as an inch.

The answering blow from Cedric had a much different effect. Malcolm flew like a child's ball hurled with a man's full strength. He crashed into Janet, and both fell to the ground in a tangle of limbs and bodies.

A pair of arrows struck the breastplate of Cedric's armor, and he staggered back as if struck a heavy blow. A small crack opened in the metal, and he stared down at it in amazement. Three more thudded into the crack, and it spiderwebbed across the entirety of the metal.

Then, with a great creaking sound, the breastplate shattered like a window with a rock thrown through it. And in the wake of that, another trio of arrows slammed into Cedric's chest. A second later, one last shattered his wrist and the enchanted sword clattered to the ground.

His knees buckled and his undamaged hand came up to his chest, his heart bracketed by the arrows. "Well," he said. "So, finally, you betray me completely."

"Please, Cedric," Rowena said, her voice thick with tears. "This must stop. Let us help you."

"Help?" His head snapped up, his blue eyes burning with hatred. "You betray me, side against the kingdom's salvation, and you wish to *help*?"

"Do not do this," she begged him. "Please, Cedric. Do not make me kill you. Come with us. Come to the Forest Tower and Merlin can make it all right again."

But he had begun to laugh, a rich, rollicking laugh. The kind a man would make if he had heard a spectacular joke. "Kill me?" he said, throwing back his head as the laughing got louder and deeper. "You ignorant fool! I am my lady's champion! I am immortal! All powerful!"

His laughing grew deeper, turning hideous and evil. And he doubled over.

And grew. He grew and grew, his body contorting and changing. His breastplate regrew and all his armor warped and turned an ugly metallic red. His blue eyes blackened like a bug's, and his mouth and nose vanished beneath a fold of metal. Horns erupted from his temples and his fingers curled into claws.

From the ground, Janet stared up in horror as her former bodyguard and friend became a Dread Knight. His words, his power, all of it now made a very terrible sense. Cedric Ivanhoe was the ultimate champion of the Dread Queen.

"The transition was his own," Malcolm said, and she turned her head to stare at him.

"Malcolm, you cannot kill him. You cannot mean to do that to Rowena."

He shook his head. "No, I mean just the opposite. If the transition is his, then he can turn back. We can still save him."

He looked over at Rowena, who stared up at what had become of the man she loved. "They will not end up like us so long as I draw breath."

\* \* \*

Malcolm leaped as high as he could, aided by the power of his sword. There was no leaving something for later in this situation, even if they did not plan to kill him. Holding back was a sure path to death.

His first strike showed the proof of that philosophy, for the magnificent blade of his weapon simply bounced off Cedric's hide. And before he could recover or set himself, Cedric swatted him aside as if he were only a fly.

Still, at least Janet had taken precautions. The princess had encased the entire area in a bubble of wind, and it carried him to the ground without harm. She was proving to have gained considerable insight into her abilities over the last few days.

Rowena loosed another trio of arrows, but whatever power they had had to harm Cedric was gone now. They shattered against his armor like sticks hurled at a wall. She had to dodge a second later as he swiped at her and nearly hit.

That, Malcolm thought grimly, was not good. The Dread Knights they had battled up to that point had been fast, but Cedric was much faster. *Not good.*

Andre, who had seemed to have been taken out of the fight, hurled his swords higher than Malcolm had jumped. He summoned himself to them, flipped over and threw them down into Cedric's back.

The move had proven successful before,

but now it did no more harm than Malcolm's sword or Rowena's bow. The blades bounced off the armor at the very moment the boy summoned himself to them. He went tumbling down and only saved himself from hitting at terminal velocity by using the technique once more to reach the ground safely.

Cedric laughed, in a voice so hideously twisted it was no longer recognizable. "Is this all you can do?" he asked, spreading his mangled and warped arms to indicate the battle and the bubble. "Is this the best defense offered by a dead and dying regime? Worthless."

He staggered under an invisible blow, then was rocked by another.

"Worthless?" Janet spat, stepping forward. Another blow, a gust of wind propelled by her magic, cracked into his gut as her eyes flared with rage. "Dead and dying? Do not measure my family by the witch who has warped your mind, Cedric."

More blows rained down, driving him back even as she advanced. "This is how much life flows in *my* blood," she hissed, raising clawed hands to the sky. "Witness it for yourself! *Dakla!*"

The storm swirled into being above their heads, roiling black clouds that pelted the giant figure with hailstones and stinging rain. Rain and ice, which froze in thin layers on his gruesome armor. Cedric strained against the restricting frost, taking one halting step, then another as he reached out for Janet. His clawed hand stopped only a foot from her as he froze solid.

Janet's angry defiance faded away over the next several seconds into smug satisfaction. And in that, in her letting go of the temper which had fueled her magic, she lost the reins of the spell.

Lightning flicked out of the clouds, forked tongues of destruction that fell indiscriminately. One struck the tip of Malcolm's sword, and he jittered and jerked. Seeing that, she screamed his name and ran for him, though what she might have done to aid him she would never know in her life. By the time she reached him, he had stopped the awful dance and lay smoking on the ground.

"Malcolm!" She dropped to her knees and reached for him, then paused, too afraid for a moment to touch him.

Then he moved, groaned, and her heart started up again as he pushed up. His eyes when his head came up were a bit foggy, but they cleared as they focused on her. "Of all the times for you to lose control," he grumbled.

"My apologies," she said, though she could not hold back the smile.

Not until she heard ice cracking.

She spun around and her eyes went wide. Another bolt had struck Cedric, perhaps several, and they played along his gigantic frame. Cracks were forming in the ice, and they were spreading. Beneath the rime, muscles bunched, strained against the restriction.

*No*, she thought. *Oh, gods, no.* Her spell had been the only strike that had had even the slightest effect on this new form of his, and it had taken far too much of her energy. She did not have the strength for more. There would be no defeating him.

They had failed. They had come so far, gotten so close to the goal, and it was all over. She turned to Malcolm, prepared to apologize for the futile efforts and for dooming him and to say the one thing she needed to tell him before they all died.

But he grabbed her before she could open her mouth, and he pulled her in close. She brought her arms up to hold him, but the roar of his sword's power sounded in her ears, and she pulled back. He had hauled her away from the danger area, gotten her clear.

"Rowena and Andre," she said, pushing away from him. "You must go get them too. Malcolm, please."

"Not necessary," Rowena said, appearing from out of nowhere as silently as the night.

"Is Andre right behind you?" Janet asked.

"No."

"Then it is necessary!" She rounded on Malcolm again. "Go get him."

He simply smiled. "Did you forget what the boy has? He was more than a match for that test."

The test. Janet looked in the direction of where they had been. Cedric's horns could just be seen above the tree line. And as she watched, the horns of the Criotaur joined them.

\* \* \*

They ran as if the entire host of the seven hells were on their heels, but their flight was not completely heedless. They did have a goal after all, and off in the distance they could just see the top of the wooden tower jutting above the trees.

They were so close. They were nearly there. They were nearly safe.

The sounds of the battle behind them were enormous. Cedric was roaring. The Criotaur was howling. Trees were felled, of rocks the size of handcarts smashing against the ground. The two were likely hitting each other with whatever came to hand like a pair of tavern brawlers.

"The transformation has a curious flaw," Rowena said between quick breaths. "He cannot use his swords. Fortunately, it seems Cedric has no access to his own sword either, so they may be evenly matched."

It was at that exact moment the noise of the fight cut off as if by a knife. The trio of them all but skidded to a halt. Rowena nocked an arrow and Malcolm laid his hand on the hilt of his sword as they listened for any sound of movement.

Slowly, the sound of footsteps came to their ears, and they all turned. The treads were heavy, but not the thunderous ones of a Dread Knight.

Janet narrowed her eyes, trying to peer through the gloom and dark. The sun was starting to rise but was not yet high enough to provide any real light. So, when she caught the glint amidst the trees, her heart sank.

Cedric stepped into view, Andre's beaten and battered body slung over his shoulder. With a contemptuous shrug he tossed the boy down onto the ground, and the Criotaur Coin fell from his limp fingers. It rolled across the ground, coming to rest at Janet's feet. She stared down at it, at the blood staining the bronze metal, then slowly raised her eyes to the former knight.

He flashed a sinister smile. "Next?"

Malcolm shoved her at Rowena. "Go!" he snapped, drawing the Sword of Lions as he charged at Cedric.

"No!" Janet tried to shake off Rowena's hand when the woman took her arm. Rowena simply slung an arm around the princess' waist and threw her over her own shoulder. Even as Janet struggled, the woman bent her knees and leaped into the trees.

"Damn you, Rowena!" Janet cursed, thumping her fists uselessly against the redhead's back as the woman jumped from branch to branch. "Go back! He cannot hope to hold Cedric!"

"Do not discount his strength," Rowena

told her. "There is no man in the kingdom who can outfight Malcolm in fair combat. Even Cedric."

But it was not fair combat that concerned Janet. Cedric's strength was clearly far beyond that of any normal man now. Malcolm would not be strong enough to use the powers of the Sword of Lions for long, and Cedric would overpower him.

As Rowena leaped from yet another branch, Janet slammed her elbow into the back of the woman's head. It stunned the archeress just enough for her to miss the landing. Rowena's boots slipped on the branch, and they both tumbled down, down, down to the forest floor.

They hit together but Janet, prepared for the impact, quickly rolled away from Rowena. Gaining her feet, she took off back the way they had come. Her hip ached, her shoulder twinged from the fall, but she ran all the same. Fear for Malcolm, for the safety of the only man who mattered to her, fueled her steps.

Had she not been in such fear, she might have considered the fact that now, with the prospect of losing him lying in her path, she had given up all pretense. She loved him. She needed him. There could be no one else. And so, he had to survive.

She tripped, heard the tearing of cloth as she fell. She could not even begin to care. Pushing up, she took off running again and promptly stumbled into a tree. She bounced off it and hit the ground once more. Pain sang up her right arm, yet she pushed up once more.

She got another few steps before she turned her ankle and went down a third time. Twigs scratched at her face. Her left leg screamed bloody murder and would not support her weight when she tried to get up again.

She might have laid there, simply laid there and wept, but the cry ripped the air and her heart. It was a shout of such agony it spurred her to motion again. Tears flowed freely from her eyes as she clawed at the ground, desperation forcing her to crawl. She had to reach him. She just had to. She could not let him die alone.

And then her hand touched a foot. A man's foot, clad in an armored boot. She stared at it, pain and fear clouding her mind so it took her some time to recognize what she was looking at. Slowly, slowly she sat back and looked up the long, muscular frame to the blue eyes and blond hair.

Blood smeared the tunic Cedric wore, and his gauntlets. One shoulder hung looser than it should, the pauldron deeply scored. His cheek bore a fresh cut that ran from jaw to ear and oozed yet more blood.

But it was his sword, his enchanted, evil sword, that bore mute testimony to her greatest fear. For it fairly dripped blood she knew could belong to only one man. She was too late.

Malcolm, the man she loved, had been slain.

Cedric's gauntleted fist coming down to knock her unconscious was a mercy against the agony of her shattered heart.

# CHAPTER 16

When Janet first roused, she thought it might all have been a dream. A horrible, terrible dream. Malcolm could not really have died, or Andre. They were perfectly fine and waited for her to get up and have breakfast. Then they could go on to the Forest Tower and...

Someone was carrying her. She was slung over someone's shoulder. Someone wearing armor that glittered in the morning sun. Oh, gods, it was *Cedric.* It was real. It was all real.

Fear shot through her, and she struggled. Cedric held her fast, but she fought as hard as she could.

"Enough." He stopped walking and tossed her negligently to the ground. She rolled and came up ready to fight.

And saw once again the blood splattered on the front of his armor. Her throat slammed shut, her heart stopped beating. It was real. That was Malcolm's blood.

"Tell me," She managed through gritted teeth. "Please, tell me you did not kill him. Please, tell me you have not sunk to that, Cedric."

He sighed. "This all could have been avoided, Janet. All you would have had to do was stay in the castle and accept your fate. Malcolm would have never known, and Andre would have never even seen it all. It is your fault. All this is *your* fault."

Her fault. Yes, oh, gods, *yes*, it was her fault. She had doomed them all. Her head bowed, and she shook as tears streamed down her face.

Then she shot to her feet and shoved at him. It did no good, but she nevertheless pushed again. "Damn you!" she spat between tears. "Damn you to the seven hells, Cedric! You betrayed us all! Malcolm was your friend! Your captain!"

"He betrayed me!" Cedric thundered back, fetching her a backhanded blow that knocked her to the ground once more. "He and Rowena both! What love has she for the royal family? What did you do to her, you evil *bitch*?"

He kicked her, anger and frustration pouring from him as her grief flooded from her. And she snapped. She grabbed his arm and let loose with all her power. Lightning shot up his leg, shoving him back. With the beginnings of distance between them, she switched to wind. Blows battered him, shoving him back further.

Then, with enough distance between them, she slapped her hand against the ground, curled her fingers into the dirt and yanked up a column of earth. And as it came, he sank, sank up to his neck.

"I am no traitor!" she snarled at him, gaining her feet again, her hands clawed at her sides. "And I am not evil. You are the one who sided with the darkness!"

"You cannot kill me," he scoffed. "You cannot even hold me here."

To demonstrate, his shoulders heaved. The ground restraining him cracked, shuddered, and burst. To her horror, he climbed out of the hole she had buried him in.

She shot another blast of lightning, but he swatted it away with one hand. She switched to wind, but it did nothing.

"Do you not see?" he mocked as he pulled his legs free. "Do you not see how utterly weak you are? You are nothing compared to my lady. To *my* queen."

And then she understood. The Dread Queen herself had laid this power upon him. And she smiled. Magic, she reminded herself, was the best way to defeat magic.

She reached for her bracelet, yanking it off her arm. "You think I am so weak, Cedric? Then take this!"

She flung the enchanted piece of jewelry at him. It was only a short distance to throw it, but he still snatched it out of the air. "Was that supposed to do—"

The bracelet flared with a brilliant light, and he cried out in pain. His fingers convulsed around it. The dweomers worked into the metal and stones had him bucking and jittering like a puppet on a string.

Janet never hesitated, and she took no time to attack him again. There was something much more important she needed to do.

She ran. Cedric, she reminded herself, could not be counted on to tell the truth. His goal was to bring her back to the Dread Queen so the ancient evil could finish laying the curse on her. It would be to his advantage for her to feel hopeless, for her to think Malcolm was already dead. If she had no reason to stall him in hopes of a rescue, his task would be much easier.

The blood smeared on Cedric's armor could have easily come from his own wounds. The blood on the sword had to be Malcolm's, but its presence did not mean he had been dealt a mortal blow. He had been debilitated, undoubtedly, or else he would have come after them. But he could easily still be alive.

She charged in a straight line back the way they had come. Cedric, she knew, would have been best served heading straight from the spot where he had captured her. Which meant all she had to do was get back there and head towards where she and Rowena had left Malcolm. He would be there, with Rowena and Andre. She would find him, help him to the Forest Tower, and it would all be alright.

It took her perhaps ten minutes to reach a

familiar section of forest, and she immediately turned and ran towards where Malcolm would have fought Cedric. And it was not long before the coppery smell of blood reached her nose. Rather than cause her steps to falter, the scent spurred her on. She was close. She would find him soon.

And then she ran into a newly cleared section full of fallen wood and splattered with blood. Too much blood.

Her knees went out from under her. There was too much blood. Too much for someone to survive it. Too much, even with what Cedric must have bled.

By the time the knight caught up with her, she was in no mood to put up any further resistance. Her spirit was broken.

* * *

She did not fight Cedric again. She did not have the willpower to do more than put one foot in front of the other.

Malcolm was gone. Malcolm was *gone*. She would never see him again, never have the chance to tell him what was in her heart. There would be no talk, no chance at a future for them. He was dead, and she would become a monster.

At least once that happened, she would no longer remember him. She hoped. Gods, please, let her have that small mercy. Let her not suffer through eternity knowing what had happened to the man she loved. Knowing his death was on her head.

Cedric bound her to a tree when they made camp, though, again, there was little need for him to do so. She would not run. There was nothing to run to, or for.

Still, even in her grief, she had enough presence to ask him a single question when he brought her food. "Why? Why did you have to do this? Why did you have to betray us all? Me? Malcolm? Rowena? Gods, did your love mean so little in the end?"

"That is a good question, Princess." Silent as a panther, Rowena had stepped from the trees and approached Cedric and now she held a nocked arrow right behind his left ear. "What could have possessed you to do this, Cedric? How could the man I love become this filthy, evil creature?"

"Me?" Cedric chuckled. "Am I the one betraying what I believe in, or is it you? The end of the royals, Rowena. Your greatest desire. We could have it."

He turned his head slowly to look at her. "Join me. Join my lady's efforts and avenge all the wrongs done to your family. Generations of harm and slights. Get your revenge."

"You know," Rowena told him. "That might have worked. You might truly have convinced me at one point. But I have seen what your lady has done to innocents, and I have seen what you are willing to do to gain an upper hand on Malcolm. You are no longer the man I knew. Goodbye, Cedric."

But she had hesitated for just a second too long. His hand came up, bumping the bow aside so the loosed arrow zipped harmlessly past his head. He jammed an open palm into her stomach, doubling her over, then followed it up with a hard punch to the face. She fell back, tumbled to the ground, and he rose, drawing his sword.

Andre's booted feet hit him in the back of the head, the boy's full weight and the drop from the tree behind the attack. Both man and boy went spilling to the ground and the younger of the two rolled through and came up to kick the older full in the face. But Cedric's enhanced abilities came into play once again, and he caught the kick, twisting Andre's leg and forcing the boy to spin with it to keep his leg from being broken.

Cedric scooped up his sword and went for Andre as the boy summoned his own blades to defend himself. Andre spun and whirled his blades, backing up and away from Cedric's swings and stabs.

With her former fiancé occupied, Rowena all but fell upon Janet's bindings. Frantically, she hacked at the ropes with her daggers, finally cutting the princess free. "Go," she told Janet. "Run for the Forest Tower! Hurry! There is still time!"

Janet stared blankly up at her. Time? There was no more time. There was no further need to fight. Why would this woman keep trying when it was all lost?

Andre was in no good shape to fight, and his battle with Cedric was nothing but a diversion. Within seconds, the knight had fetched him a hard blow to the temple with one gauntleted fist, turning the boy's legs into loose yarn as he collapsed. Rowena shoved Janet towards the trees with a last, "Go!" before turning to face Cedric with her daggers in her hands.

Janet watched the battle dispassionately. She had not seen Rowena do much fighting with those daggers, but she appeared to be every bit as agile and competent as she was when she used her bow. She easily avoided Cedric's longer, heavier sword and dug furrows into his armor with her knives.

Her feet and knees and elbows came into play as well as she knocked aside his arm and tried to debilitate him. But that proved her undoing, that reluctance to try for a fatal blow even after having given up on him. She caught the hilt of his sword in the stomach, his elbow to the shoulder, and one dagger fell from nerveless fingers.

In desperation she grabbed at his sword arm and pulled him to the ground where they rolled, locked together in an ugly parody of passion. She was beneath him when they stopped, his sword at her throat and the hand that held her remaining dagger pinned to the ground. For a long moment, she looked up at him, her breathing heavy and labored.

"Do it," she hissed at him. "If you are truly lost to me, then this world holds nothing for me. Kill me and complete your descent into darkness. Destroy yourself."

He stayed like that for a time, his shoulders straining as if he were battling some internal compulsion. Finally, he eased back a bit, taking the blade from her throat.

Rowena blinked, started to reach up for him. Then she went limp when he struck her in the side of the head with the hilt of his weapon.

He continued to kneel, his breath heaving as he looked down at her. Then his eyes changed, as if another person took over him. He got to his feet and sheathed his weapon, then walked over to scoop Janet up.

She did not even look back to the fallen cousins as Cedric carried her away into the night.

\* \* \*

He walked through the night, still carrying her, and never stopped to rest. She said nothing, too mired in her own grief and shock. Part of her wished Rowena had shown her mercy during the fight. A slip of one of those daggers between her ribs, a slash across the throat, and it all would have been over.

The amulet bumped against her chest, and she glanced down at it with little interest. Odd, how a square piece of etched silver could so change someone's life.

Something stirred in her mind. Something to do with that amulet. Was the shape wrong? The material? Why? It was the same one she had worn all along, was it not?

And what did it matter? Everything was lost. She was too far from the Forest Tower now to reach it even if she had the strength of will to try. Even if her world was not crushed beyond all repair.

Something flitted amidst the trees, drawing her attention from the amulet. It was a dark shape, and it was not Andre or Rowena. For the briefest of seconds, hope rekindled in her breast at the thought it might be Malcolm. After all, Andre had recovered and come after her. Maybe he was alive after all.

But another glimpse of the figure brought that hope crashing back down. It was much too broad, much too muscular. The arms were too long, the legs bowed. It was not him. Whatever that might be was nothing and no one she knew.

She slumped once again, losing interest as she had with the amulet. Nothing mattered.

"Why do it?"

She blinked, looked up at Cedric. There was a confused expression on his face, his eyes flicking back and forth as if he was studying something only he could see. "Why do it?" he said again. "It would have been so easy."

He stopped, seemed to shake himself like a dog coming out of the water. His eyes changed, focused, and he continued walking for a few feet before stopping once again. This time he looked around carefully, searching the surrounding trees. He muttered something she could not quite hear and started off again.

The attack came at midday. Andre leaped from the trees once more. Rather than kick Cedric or slice at him as he had done before, the boy instead caught him in a lunging dive, wrapping his arms around the knight's neck. The weight of the boy leaping so far so fast took Cedric off his feet and flipped him head over heels.

Janet bounced free of Cedric's arms as he hit and went tumbling away. Andre ignored her and went for Cedric with a pair of flying knees to the face as the knight rolled and tried to get up.

Had Janet not been so lost in the world of her own emotions, she might have appreciated that Andre fought with everything he had. No more were the quick cuts and fancy tactics the boy had displayed all that week. He was out to get Cedric's blood on his bare hands.

He struck hard, and he struck often. Fists. Elbows. Knees. Feet. His forehead. He used all of it until his own skin was cracked and bloody from the assault.

And none of it had more than the most minor of effects. Cedric withstood the entire assault and waited until Andre had exhausted himself before counterattacking. A fast, hard uppercut and the boy was down.

A pair of arrows slammed into his shoulder pauldron, shattering it. Cedric rolled and sliced another trio from the air with his sword. "Do you not know when to lay down and stay dead?" he snapped at Rowena.

"If you wish me to stay dead," she shot back, drawing, and loosing another arrow in a smooth motion, "you will have to kill me."

He deflected the arrow with the flat of his blade. "Fine, then."

His burst of speed shot him across the distance before Rowena could draw another projectile or even take a step to the side. His weapon sliced out, and she fell back with a cry, holding her hand over the deep cut in her biceps.

Deliberately, Cedric brought his foot down on the shattered remains of her bow and ground it into the dirt. "You throw away your life needlessly, Rowena. It is not too late."

"It is for you." She spat, the glob landing on his cheek. "You are dead to me."

His face went dangerous, his eyes flat and hard. "Then die."

The figure that burst from the trees should have never moved that fast. It was too ungainly, too misshapen to move like that. But it did, and one gnarled, warped hand grabbed Cedric by the front of his tunic. The thing hauled him up and slammed him back down with such speed and force that his sword flew from his fingers to land on the ground at Janet's feet.

She looked down at it as if it were no more than a clod of dirt. Nothing mattered to her anymore.

Until the misshapen creature crossed to her and took a diamond-shaped piece of bronze from within its tunic. It laid the shard of metal on her forehead and spoke a single word in a voice deep and rich. The chain of the silver amulet broke, and it fell away to the ground. Janet blinked, looked down at the amulet and the skull etched into the silver.

Everything roared back in her mind. Her grief, her anger. Cedric had killed Malcolm. Cedric. Had killed. Malcolm.

She started forward, gathering her power to avenge the man she loved, but the wretch laid a hand on her shoulder. "No," he said, in a voice as articulate and refined as he was ugly. "You will regret that later on."

"I could regret nothing," she spat. "He killed Malcolm!"

"No." Rowena stepped around the fallen form of Cedric, keeping her eyes on Janet's. "Malcolm lives. That is what I have tried to tell you all this time. He *lives*, Janet."

\* \* \*

The misshapen being opened a magical path to the Forest Tower, and Janet all but ran through it. When she emerged, it was within a large, circular room with walls that shone like the brightest silver. Light glowed at the tops and bottoms, and there were odd panels of onyx set with glittering gemstones in strange patterns here and there.

But she scarcely noticed, for her eyes were all for the table set in the center of the room. And the man who sat at it, his chest and right arm wrapped in bandages.

It was quite the most curious of sensations. Her heart felt as if it had resumed beating after an extraordinarily long pause. Yet, she could not seem to breathe.

She took one hesitant step, then another, and he shifted to look at her.

At the sight of those tawny eyes, she was across the room in a flash. So relieved was she that she tossed aside all pretense of proper behavior, grabbed his face, and kissed him with everything she had. "I love you," she told him, throwing her arms around his neck, and holding him tight. "I love you," she said again. "I love you, I love you, I love you. Please, never allow me to forget to say it again."

"Janet." To her surprise, he did not embrace her, but gently took hold of her waist and pushed her away. "This cannot happen."

She gaped as he rose and crossed the room

to a strange contraption that sat against one wall. "What do you mean, this cannot happen?"

He turned a knob on the contraption, and water flowed from it into a basin. He filled his cupped hands with the water and splashed it on his face twice before shutting off the flow. "I mean, you and I are not the right match. I am not the one."

"Malcolm."

At that precise moment, a section of the right-hand wall slid aside, and a gray-bearded man bustled in. "Ah, good," he said, noting that not only was Janet in the room but the others had come through the portal as well. "You are all here. And just in time for tea."

He stopped and noticed the way Malcolm had Janet had yet to look away from each other. "Hmm," he said to himself. "Some things truly do never change."

"Merlin."

"Yes, yes." The gray-bearded man waved off the admonition of the misshapen creature with a weary sigh. "I know. Everything in its time, and every time in its place."

"Yes." The warped wretch lumbered across to another contraption with a strange door on it. With a surprising deftness, he opened the door and withdrew a tray laden with earthenware cups and a steaming pot. "And I daresay, they have all had a rather trying time, so if you would mind getting on with it?"

The gray-bearded man raised his eyes to the ceiling with another windy sigh. "You have been quite petulant of late, Quasimodo."

The wretch placed the tray on the table and began pouring out tea into the cups. "Yes, well, I have been watching the situation more often than you, now, haven't I? It is rather depressing all in all."

"True enough." The gray-bearded man walked to the table, and the other handed him the first cup. "Thank you, love," he said, and lifted the cup to his lips, only to pause when he saw Janet, Andre, and Rowena stared at him in utter astonishment. "What now?"

"Merlin?" Janet asked. "*You* are Merlin?"

"Well, who did you think I was, Saint George the Dragonslayer?" With a chuckle, Merlin sipped at his tea before giving his companion a wry look. "Honestly, you would think a future queen would have a faster mind."

"Well, you don't exactly look the part, now, do you?"

The warped man set the rest of the cups out for the younger people to drink and returned the pot to the cradle on the tray.

"Still?" Merlin asked in amazement. "Good gods, what has it been, better than threescore and ten centuries since those bloody woodcuts?"

"About that." The man lifted the tray and walked it back to the contraption. "But then, it has been roughly five for me, and they still portray me as an idiot."

"And look how far you have come in that time. Oh, very well," Merlin said when his companion sent him a baleful glance over his shoulder. "It is neither here nor there, I suppose. Sit, sit," he bade the still shell-shocked trio. "Tea is much better hot. And we do have quite a bit to talk about."

They all continued to stare, though, except for Malcolm, who had filled a cup of his own with water and had sat down as far from Janet as he could. "Merlin?" Janet asked again.

"Yes, yes. Really, child, there are more pressing matters just now than whether I have that blasted chest-long beard or those silly robes."

"Sorry," she said, rubbing at her temples. "I just— Quasimodo?" She turned and looked at the big man as he lumbered back their way. "The Bellringer of Avannion Chapel?"

"Once upon a time," he admitted, sitting down with a cup that smelled faintly of strawberries. "I always find it interesting how far from Le'Mane that story can go."

"I believe it reached the Isle of Broken Skulls in the Five Seas not twenty years ago." Merlin pulled a pipe from gods only knew where and lit it with a flick of his finger. "Though it appears to have changed somewhat. They now have Phoebus and Esmerelda dying on the gallows and you throwing the judge from the belltower."

"He slipped," Quasimodo said heatedly, and Merlin reached out to pat his deformed hand.

"I know, I know. There is not a more peaceful soul in this world than you, dear heart. And we both know that Phoebus and Esmerelda lived quite happily in the aftermath, and their descendants still farm the lowlands of Avannion. You must permit them their embellishments, as there is little we can do from here. Though not," he said, turning back to Janet, "in your case. Do drink that tea, dearie. There are going to be some things that will come as quite the shock later, and the tea will help quite a bit."

Andre and Rowena finally sat, but Janet continued to stand and stare. Something had clearly shaken her world to the core. "Forgive me," she said, seeming to form each word before speaking it. "But— How are you alive? You obviously are not a wizard."

"He hardly needs to be one," Merlin said with a shrug. "Most wizards have a normal lifespan."

"But you have not lived one," she countered.

"Well, no," he agreed. "But I am of quite a different stock than most. And I have this place," he added, looking around at the room. "It does tend to help defer the time."

"Defer?"

"Well, yes, dearie." Merlin nodded at Malcolm. "Your young friend's sword is quite the marvel, if I do say so myself, but it hardly has the power to take someone from the brink of death to nearly healed in a matter of hours. He has been in here for days."

Her eyes about started from her head and, had he been on the other side of the room, she would likely have snapped her neck spinning around. "Malcolm?"

He waved dismissively but continued to avoid looking at her. "It was not quite as bad as all that."

"Not as bad as all that?" Merlin cocked a brow. "My dear boy, I may be the greatest wizard of all time, but it was still a near thing to get your insides back inside before you bled to death."

"*Bled to death?*"

"I am fine, Janet." Malcolm knocked back the rest of his water and rose to get more. "Merlin, would you just get on with it already? We have wasted enough time." He glanced over his shoulder at Janet, his expression deliberately cold. "Unless you have given up on saving the kingdom and your sisters."

She opened her mouth to make a smart remark, then wisely chose to let it drop. "Very well," she said, and took the tea Quasimodo held out to her with stiff grace.

# CHAPTER 17

The tea was an appealing, tangy blend that tasted of fruits Janet could not name. It was refreshing and went well with the unusual food Quasimodo took from the same contraption he had gotten his drink from.

Thin slices of meat and cheese folded between triangles of bread. Oddly shaped biscuits full of jam. Small green fruits that were salty rather than sweet. She, Rowena, and Andre had not eaten in nearly a full day, and they downed all of it gratefully.

Merlin had left the room briefly while they ate and returned with a special guest in tow. While Janet and Malcolm watched him in apprehension, he crossed to Rowena, dropped to his knees, and whispered something to her. Rowena's eyes filled with tears. "I missed you."

"Several times."

She gave him a playful shove, but she was smiling in a way she had not in days. Cedric, it appeared, was back to normal.

Malcolm rose from where he sat and joined the pair. "I knew you were still in there," he told the knight. "You are too good a warrior not to finish the job."

Malcolm's words suddenly reminded Janet of how Cedric had twice refused to deliver a death blow to Rowena. This, she realized, was at the core of his actions. Even under the Dread Queen's control, he had kept enough of his faculties to keep from slaying his comrades. It gave her hope.

But then his gaze moved to her, and she watched pain and regret come into his eyes. He rose, leaving the side of his fiancé and comrade to come around the table to her. "Can you ever forgive me?" he asked. "Do I even deserve it? I have betrayed you and your sisters, my oath, in the most egregious manner imaginable."

Janet shook her head. "There is no need to ask, Cedric. I know the kind of man you are. You would never have done what you did without the Dread Queen's influence. Even then, I have little doubt you never stopped screaming inside. You have suffered enough."

She shifted her gaze to Rowena. "And you, Lady Loxley, have earned far more than we bargained for. The land, I think, will not be a sufficient payment for what you have done for the kingdom."

"It is more than enough already," Rowena protested, but Janet cut her off.

"It is far from enough. You have redeemed the honor of your family beyond even the actions of your renowned ancestors. I only wish I were able to return your ancestral homeland along with your fortunes. I know not what my father might agree to, but if he does not declare you and Cedric heads of a house than I swear on my life to do it once I become queen."

"I fear the people of the kingdom may protest against my receiving a reward of any kind," Cedric said soberly. "The Purple Rose have become something quite different."

"It has only been a week."

"The capital became a prison within hours of your fleeing," he explained. "Once the king disappeared—"

"Disappeared? *Father*?"

He looked at Merlin, who nodded. "Come with me," the gray-bearded wizard said and walked to the far wall. Mounted upon it was a long onyx panel stretching from the floor to just above his own height.

Unlike the other panels on the walls, it bore only a single gemstone, a square-cut diamond two-thirds of the way up the right-hand side. When Merlin reached out to touch it the onyx panel turned a brilliant, glowing white before shimmering into an image of the capital's walls seen from half a mile away.

"A magic mirror." Though she was deeply troubled by the potential of what Merlin planned to show them, Janet rose and crossed to study the rare object with the fascination of a scholar presented with a unique relic. "I have only read of these. One has not existed within the kingdom since the days of lore."

"My sister had a habit of using them to control others," Merlin said quietly. "We were forced to round them up and destroy them."

"We?"

"The Agents of Fate," Quasimodo said. He stood at the back of the room in a semblance of parade rest, a strangely formal stance for one like him. "There were considerably more of us back then, and it took us quite some time."

"Five years," Merlin agreed. "And we lost several to Morgana's slaves before the deed was done. Here now."

He had moved the diamond up and down the panel as if he tried to calibrate a direction on a siege engine, and now it showed the city within the walls. The sight was quite the shock to Janet. The buildings were in shambles, walls broken, and roofs torn up.

The once-proud residents who had gone about their day with a kind of honorable pride only found in those with the satisfaction of an honest day's work now seemed as broken as their homes. Their clothes were near to rags, and every face was dirty, with expressions of abject misery.

She reached out one hand and tentatively touched the panel, finding it smooth as glass and slightly warm. "What has happened?" she asked.

"How could this have happened in only a week?"

"It is easy to break spirits if you use the right pressure," Cedric said mournfully. He had seated himself at the table with his back to the panel, clearly unwilling to look. "And a private army of well-trained knights can apply a great amount of pressure."

"Janet."

At the look on Malcolm's face, she turned back to the panel. A trio of Purple Rose knights dragged a man from his home. He kicked, struggled, and screamed, the action somehow darkly comical without sound to convey the terror. One of the knights fetched him a heavy blow with a gauntleted fist, and he went limp.

"No one is doing anything," Andre said. "Why is no one doing anything?"

"Those who have," Cedric told him. "Have been lucky if they were only slain in the streets like dogs."

"And the unlucky?" Rowena asked.

He buried his face in his hands. "Watch."

They did watch. They watched as the now-unconscious man was borne through the streets of the city with all the care one might show a bag of dirt. He was brought to the castle, brought inside and to the throne room. Inside, he was brought to the throne, upon which sat a familiar man.

"Uncle Regis?" she asked in confusion. "Why would he sit the throne?"

"Because there is no one else to do so," Cedric replied, still not turning around. "And because she wills it."

He did not need to say who *she* was, for at that very moment a woman descended the steps of the platform with the grace of centuries. Lady Maria looked down at the man, her expression one of utter disdain. With cold indifference, she gestured to the alcove, wherein were chained six hideous creatures. Creatures with unnaturally long arms that ended in claw-tipped hands and backs even more hunched and warped than Quasimodo's.

The unfortunate man was dragged to the alcove and tossed unceremoniously within. One of the creatures lumbered over, parting its curtain of limp, colorless hair to reveal the most monstrous face Janet had ever witnessed. It fell upon the doomed man, seeming to feast upon his face as his legs kicked and drummed on the floor like a child having a tantrum. Slowly, his thrashing eased until he lay still, and the monster pulled back to howl to the heavens.

"Behold," Merlin said, his solemn attitude in sharp contrast to how jovial he had been before. "The Dread Mothers, tools and slaves of my sister, Morgana Le Fay."

\* \* \*

Janet lay awake in the chamber Merlin had given her to use. Only the magical luminescence seemed to denote whether it was night or day within the tower, and she was far from used to it. But that was not what kept her from sleep, for she had had such a trying day she could have easily slept through the brightest morning in the history of the world.

So much had happened in only the handful of hours they had been within the Forest Tower. The woman who had descended the platform had been none other than Lady Maria, meaning their elusive enemy had worn the face of a friend after all. A woman who had systematically and cruelly turned Janet's sisters into monsters with the sole goal of setting her consort upon the throne, that she might control the kingdom from the shadows through fear and intimidation.

And even if Janet could get beyond what the Dread Queen had done, what she had turned her sisters into, there was yet more. For Merlin could not free her from the curse she bore. The Seven Moons amulet, the very thing which had kept that curse at bay, prevented him from undoing it. Only dislodging the Dread Queen would serve to release the seven princesses now.

But while Merlin could open them a path directly into the throne room to battle Morgana Le Fay, they were in no shape just now to do so. The entirety of their group was injured or ill-equipped. They would need rest and training to succeed.

She sat up and slung her legs over the side of the odd bed upon which she lay. Climbing down, she walked over to one of the strange devices Merlin called *sinks* to get a drink of water. At the very least, her curse would progress no further. Merlin had managed to pause its progress, which meant she no longer lived under the weight of the hourglass.

But then, another weight had replaced that one. Malcolm would not even look at her anymore, and that hurt more than any wound. She did not know how to bridge the impasse, having never been in this situation before. But there surely had to be a way. She knew he loved her, but something still held him back.

Deciding that wondering would solve nothing, she chose instead to seek him out. If they could just talk, like they had in the old days, then surely there would be some way forward.

Malcolm's chamber was in the next hallway over, but she could not recall which of the five doors it was. They all looked the same, recessed in the walls with a small panel on the right jamb. She had seen Merlin use the one on her door, but it took her some experimenting with the gemstones before she figured out how to use it herself.

From there, it took a frustrating ten minutes to figure out how to see whether the room within was occupied. It took her another ten to find which chamber was his and gain access.

The door slid aside with that strange little

airy hiss, and she hesitated. The room within was as dark as hers had been, and there was no sign of movement. Blast it, she had not expected him to be asleep. Waking him up to talk about an obviously sore subject was only going to annoy him.

But then his voice filtered out of the darkness, clear and alert. "Janet, either come in or go away. Do not stand in the door."

"Sorry." Quickly she stepped through, and the door slid closed at her back. "I thought you might be asleep."

"That's a pretty strange reason to come and find me." He sat up in the bed, and his eyes studied her in the dim light. "I guess you couldn't sleep either."

"Not really, no." She rubbed at her neck, which was a bit stiff after lying on that strange bed. "I, um, thought we could talk a little. About what happened earlier."

He said nothing for a while. "I get the feeling you don't mean what Merlin showed us, or your curse."

"No."

He sighed and pulled at his nose. "I didn't think you'd just let it go."

"Do you— Is it the crown you object to? Is that it? Because there are ways for us to be together without you becoming king."

"It is not the crown. Or not just the crown."

"Then it's me." She waited for him to

respond, and when he did not, she nodded. "It is me. Well, I feel a complete fool."

"Janet—"

"No, no. Go back to bed. I will leave you be."

He caught up with her halfway to the door, and she spun back, ready to fight again. She should have expected the kiss, that bone-melting kiss that had her mind going numb and her body pressed against his. But she had not expected it, and she was so wrapped up in it that when he pulled back, she nearly toppled over.

"Why?" was all she could manage.

He looked so sad, so tortured as he smoothed his thumb over her cheek. "Good night, Janet."

Deliberately, he turned his back on her and walked back to the bed, leaving her more confused than ever.

\* \* \*

In the morning, Merlin began Janet's training. Or tried to. She had thought her powers were getting stronger, but for whatever reason she was suddenly worse than she had ever been.

She could not manage even the simplest of spells without them collapsing. Attempting to light candles ended up in a bonfire. Trying to create a small breeze sent her flying across the room to slam into the wall hard enough to bruise.

Merlin, thankfully, had the patience of a saint. No matter how badly he failed, he never seemed disappointed or talked rudely about her lack of talent. He simply watched, quiet and sympathetic.

When an attempt to create an ice spear ended in her hands and feet covered in ice, he stepped in and defrosted her with a simple gesture and a quiet word. "Let's take a break, shall we?"

"I just don't understand," she groaned, dropping limply to the floor. "I haven't been this bad at magic since I was ten."

"An unsettled mind can cause considerable trouble." Merlin brought her a cup of water from a sink at the far end of the room.

"My mind has been unsettled this entire time," she countered. "I haven't had that much trouble so far."

Merlin sat on the floor facing her and took a pipe from up his sleeve. "Quasimodo hates when I use this," he explained as he lit it with a touch of his finger. "I always have to hide it from him."

He puffed for a while, his blue eyes measuring her. "You know, I had a student once with a similar problem. He had considerable potential, just as you do. He had a great ability to control his energies, just as you do, most of the time. And just as you do, he could never settle his mind enough to gain full control."

Janet sipped at her water and settled herself more comfortably on the floor. She loved stories and knew that when a storyteller paused like that, he waited for a question. "What was bothering him?"

"Well, he had quite the conflict in his soul. He had sworn to slay a certain dragon with his powers, and the dragon knew it. The creature had taken a sinister step. He had abducted the girl my student loved and bound her soul to his, so that to slay him was to slay her as well."

Janet shifted again, though it was now out of nervousness. She had a feeling she knew where Merlin was going with this. "What did he do?"

"Failed. Again and again. Each time he went to slay the dragon to try to save his beloved, he found his powers failed him and had to flee for his life. It was not long before the villagers lost faith in him and as he continued to try, they mocked him, which only made things worse.

"He came to me for help but could not control his power any more than you are just now. I told him what I have told you. Only a clear mind can control magic."

Janet was now quite certain she knew where this was going. After all, only one thing had truly changed since they had reached the tower. "How did he get past his problem?"

Merlin puffed on his pipe and studied her. "There was one other thing he shared with you, an affinity for mental magic."

As she shifted again, he smiled. "It is a

rather subtle school, and not one most dabble in. Connecting soul to soul is a very profound act. It was so for him, but it was his salvation.

"He meditated for three days, and at the end of the last his mind reached that of his beloved. United, they planned, and they plotted, and they strategized. And when they were ready, he went to battle the beast.

"The villagers mocked him as they had become prone to do. But he ignored them and strode to the very center of the village. And there, he summoned his energies and challenged his foe.

"The dragon emerged from his lair, certain that with all the people watching he would at last be able to destroy his enemy. But when the dragon arrived, the young wizard easily destroyed him. For the dragon had been unaware of one thing: through the link of the mental magic, the young wizard had freed his beloved from the dragon's soul, removing the doubt of slaying the beast."

\* \* \*

As it was nearly suppertime and with no further progress in the offing, Merlin sent Janet off, though that was scant comfort. The others were also training to master their abilities or simply restore their bodies to peak. And so, she took to wandering the halls alone. And thinking.

She knew what Merlin's story had been getting at. The young wizard, the infamous

George the Dragonslayer, had been afraid to use his powers for fear of harming the one he loved. That fear had caused his powers to fail again and again until he had connected to his beloved and their hearts and minds had worked as one to save her.

Her problem was a bit different. Using her abilities would not harm Malcolm. But Malcolm was still the basis of her issue. She was far too confused where he was concerned, and it split her mind to such a degree she could not hope to center herself. If they could just get past whatever held him back, she was sure she would be able to use her powers again.

The sound of a lion's roar drew her from her reflections. It was Malcolm, training to use the powers of the Sword of Lions. She hesitated for a moment, deciding whether it would do it any good to go and watch him train. Seeing her would distract him, likely cause more trouble. Was it worth it?

When the roar cut off suddenly and was followed up by the sound of a body hitting a wall, she made her mind up. She sought him out.

It took quite a bit of time, as the halls not only looked the same, but they appeared to create a confusing echo of any sound. She went down several halls, trying to track the roars and slams before she finally found the room where he was training. She walked through the open door just in time to see him go flying once more, flung by one of Quasimodo's powerful arms.

She watched Malcolm hit, roll, and come back up for another charge. He drew the sword across his chest, the stone in the crosspiece glowed brilliantly, and he vanished. Janet watched as Quasimodo turned slowly, his eyes tracking this way and that, obviously searching for Malcolm's attack.

The misshapen man suddenly lurched, ducked, and swung around. One elbow shot out and Malcolm reappeared with a grunt as that elbow buried itself in his gut. This time, he lost his weapon when he landed, and lay there breathing heavily.

"You're concentrating too much on your speed," Quasimodo told him.

"So, you've mentioned a half-dozen times." Malcolm rolled and started to push up, then spotted her standing in the doorway. His eyes went through several emotions in the spate of a few seconds before settling on resignation.

Quasimodo, who had noticed Janet as well, walked across to the sink. "As good a time as any to take a break, I think. I do need to get supper on." He got himself some water, then lumbered towards another door at the far end where he paused and looked back. "Perhaps a walk before dinner?" he suggested. "A rather good way to clear the mind."

Janet said nothing until the hunchback had left. Malcolm looked defeated, though also rather delicious. He had dispensed with his tunic and the ripple of muscle sheened with sweat was a very appealing sight. Though she was not entirely sure how she felt about the scars on his chest and arms. Particularly the one that trailed down his abdomen and under his leggings.

Because of how he looked, she nearly made a salacious remark when he asked, "What do you want, Janet?" As it was, she stood there and watched him walk to the sink before she responded.

"I, um, thought we might talk a bit."

The moment the words were past her lips, all other words abruptly fled her mind. She was too busy looking at him. There were more scars on his back, proof of a life led on the battlefield. He had left a boy, she realized, and come home a man. A warrior.

Rowena's words from her trial came to mind now. *Do not ask him to die for you. Ask him to live.* Janet had puzzled over how to do that for several days. But now, she suddenly saw a way through.

"You pledged your life to my service," she began.

"To your protection," he countered, keeping his back turned. "And neither of those requires me to give into emotion, so don't use them as an argument."

"You came home a coward, then."

That got him to turn around. "After

everything we have gone through this last week, you would call me a coward to try and get your way?"

"Oh, not to get my way. It is the truth." She took a step forward. "Dying for someone is easy, Malcolm. All it takes is stepping in the path of a sword or an arrow. Then it is all over."

Another step, and she watched his struggle to remain where he was. "Once you are through the gate of the death god, you cannot go back. The world you left behind fades."

A third step, and now his nostrils flared like a beast, readying itself to strike or flee, for she was near enough for him to touch. "It is harder, much harder, to live for someone. To go through each day with them, beside them."

With one last step, she was scant inches from him and looking directly into his eyes. "Can you make such a pledge, Malcolm of Bonaparte? Can you pledge to me that you will not again turn my life upside down and inside out by leaving me behind?"

She reached out, laying her palm over his heart. "I have already seen what lies in here. You have no secrets from me, and I know you to be a fine warrior. Perhaps, for once in your life, rather than be modest and self-effacing, you should take what is freely offered."

He did. And, oh, was it everything of which she had ever dreamed.

His hands came around her, pulled her in.

His mouth feasted on hers. Her hands slid up that splendid chest and broad shoulders until she fisted them in his hair, pulled him deeper.

His hands roamed, skimming down her sides, up her back. She shivered from his touch, arched into him, wanting to be closer even though she was already right up against him.

He bit her lip, and she reveled in the pain. He nipped at her jaw, then her throat as he cruised down, eliciting gasps. His hands were on the ties of her riding dress, pulling the garment apart to expose swaths of flesh. And when his mouth roamed even lower, the first moan slipped from her lips.

By the gods, how did he know to do that? How did he know it would make her respond this way?

She heard her dress tear and did not care one bit. The need was an ache, a burning that had to be sated if she was going to survive. It had to be now.

She pulled back from him, kept her eyes on his as she freed herself from the garment. She saw the hunger in his eyes and felt it answer in her belly as he freed himself from his own clothing. There he stood now, right in front of her eyes. A most perfect specimen that any woman would desire.

Their mouths met again, and she reveled in the contact of skin to skin. She tumbled with him to the floor, rolled with him so that he was above.

He broke the kiss to look down at her, eyes full of naked hunger and a question. Was she sure of this?

She did not have to hesitate. She had made her choice, and she was not a woman to go back on what she deemed important. So, it was her hand that fit him against her most private place, her look of acceptance and trust and love that said she was ready.

And her cry that filled the room when he took her.

# CHAPTER 18

That night, Janet lay awake in her chamber as she had the night before. But now, it was not only worry in her head.

Making love with Malcolm had been the most incredible experience of her life. It was amazing and had been well worth having to return to her chambers to change out of the damaged dress before going to supper. She had thought it had been the same for him, given the stunned look on his face when they'd finished. But he had not looked at her throughout the meal, had barely looked up from his plate come to that.

Was he ashamed? He had made the first move, had been so eager to be with her. He had wanted her. She knew that. So why?

She sighed. Wondering about it was not going to help her. She needed to center herself or she would be useless the next morning.

Pushing up, she folded her legs under her and closed her eyes. The dreamscape spell was easier than ever, so easy she was in the garden within the beat of a heart.

It was still lush, but no longer as wild. The flowers and trees were in full bloom and the air smelled sweet and clean. It was soothing, life-affirming to walk through the space and just take in all the color, scent, and sound.

But as she walked around a fruit tree, she found Malcolm. He stood, looking around in utter confusion.

"What in the five hells?" he said, and when he did, she realized it was not a mental representation of him. She had somehow pulled him into the dreamscape with her.

She took a single step, and he whirled around on her. "Janet?"

"Hi." She gnawed on her lip. "I, um, was trying to calm myself down."

"Uh-huh." He looked around again. "And you did that by...?

"It is called a dreamscape. A kind of representation of the inside of my mind."

"I see. And...I am here because?"

"Not really sure." She rocked back and forth on her heels. "I guess it's because you're why I needed to calm down."

"I see," he said again. "And I am going to guess you're not going to just send me back until we've talked."

She started to bristle at the temper in his voice, started to send him off so she could do what she came to do. But she realized suddenly he was deliberately trying to goad her into doing just that. She also realized the two of them talking now was the best way to end this dilemma. In here, soul to soul, they could not lie to each other.

"Are you upset with me?" she asked. "Are you sorry we did what we did?"

"No." He blinked at the reply. "No, I am not upset with you."

"And what we did?" she pressed. "Malcolm, we cannot lie to each other in here. This is not us talking out there in the world, where we can indulge in pretense and hide things. These are our souls. I love you, and I do not regret anything more than waiting all this time to tell you."

He sighed. "There are times I wish I had said yes to your father's offer. You are all I've ever wanted."

"And what you won't let yourself have," she finished. "Why? Why is it so necessary for you to deny what we both want?"

"Do you know what would have happened if my father won at the Idenian Plains? His goal was never to take the crown for himself. He wanted to make me king. *Me*, Janet. And if he had gotten what he wanted, you would never have been born."

It stunned her. This was what he had carried around all their lives, the weight around his neck ever since they had been children. It was so damned *stupid*.

"And you think that just because your

father lost means you're not supposed to be happy?" she demanded.

"The Lady doesn't make mistakes."

"No. No, she does not. But we cannot know what her real plan is until it happens. That is the truth of existence. There is plenty of other ways this could have been meant to turn out. She had Merlin rescue you, bring you to Martin, to the capital. Martin's position as the blacksmith for the Purple Rose came from the creation of the Sword of Lions, which led to you being around my sisters and I. We grew up the way we did because of that. And none of it happens without the battle of the Idenian Plains."

"What in the blazes does that have to—"

"The lines of John and Richard have been divergent for centuries. They have come down through all the years to us. What if this is her plan? What if it has all been to reunite the lines? What if she saved you so that all these years later, I'd have you beside me? To save me, to bring me to the Tower so we could stop the Dread Queen's plotting?"

She stepped in closer, reached up to lay a hand on his cheek. "This is meant, Malcolm. I feel that. You are the only one I've ever wanted. You are the only one I can ever want. Please, do not turn away from me anymore."

\* \* \*

She did not feel any better the next morning. Oh, she felt rested - she and Malcolm had spent the entire night walking through her dreamscape, talking of days gone past. But they had shied away from continuing the conversation about what the lady's plan might have been. It hurt, she realized, far more than him leaving had hurt. He was nearby, and yet so very far away.

With no appetite, she skipped breakfast and instead went straight to the chamber where she had been training with Merlin. And there, she discovered something incredible. Her magic *worked*.

In fact, it worked flawlessly for the first time in her entire life. She produced spell after spell, summoning fire cages and cyclone-like gusts of wind and torrents of water and not even one got out of her control. In fact, her magic was easier than it had ever been. Just like casting the dreamscape spell.

When Merlin arrived, he needed only one look at her face to say he had nothing more to teach her. She was now a full-fledged wizard.

Excitedly, she ran out, wanting to tell the others the news. And remembered they would all be at their own training. She would have to wait.

The rumbling of her stomach signaled to her that she was hungry after all. Thinking there had to be some food left over from breakfast, she headed for the main chamber.

And nearly turned right back around and left when she found Malcolm sitting at the table with his sword laid out in front of him. But before she could, he turned. Still riding on her elation, she crossed to him, took his face in her hands, and kissed him soundly. "I love you," she told him, not caring at that moment whether he returned it.

He did not. Instead, he took her hands and said, "We need to talk."

"I am not going to stop saying it."

He smiled. "Just sit, would you? Please?"

She sat but kept hold of one of his hands, determined not to let him forget she was there. "Malcolm—"

"Did you ever wonder where Martin got the materials for this?" he asked, laying his free hand on the sword.

Resigning herself to the fact he still did not want to talk about it, she shifted to study the magnificent weapon. "I always assumed he had them lying about."

She cocked her head as a thought occurred to her. "But that is wrong. The handle is gold, *solid* gold. But not soft, like normal gold. It is hard as steel, so it's a special kind."

"There is a sword they use in Qin Han. It has similar properties to long-sabers, designed to slice rather than stab or hack. Fast and agile and strong as diamonds. They make the blade by folding heated steel dozens of times with carbon in between the folds."

She lifted her gaze back to him. "Carbon gold?"

"And carbon steel." He lifted the weapon, let the unnatural light of the tower play off the blade. "Legend has it, there was another sword with those properties. A sword that is shattered remains supposedly lie within these very walls."

She stared at him, slack jawed, for ten full seconds. "Excalibur." The name of the legendary sword of King Arthur came from her lips in a reverent whisper. "Your sword is Excalibur reforged."

"So, it would appear. The sword that waits for the hand meant to wield it."

"The hand of a king," she finished, remembering the last part of the legend. "Arthur reborn. *You*."

He placed the sword back down on the table and turned to take her other hand so he held them both again. "You were right," he said. "I am meant to sit the throne and meant to sit it beside you. But" he added as she opened her mouth to celebrate, "I want you to promise me that you won't push. I want us to take our time."

She hesitated. It was not an unreasonable request, given how long he'd blamed his own heritage and refused to be with her. But there was something in the back of her mind, a niggling possibility she had not wanted to voice. "Malcolm, my father is missing. He might be dead. If he is, I am going to have to take the throne. The kingdom will be more at ease if it is at least announced that I am betrothed."

Now, it was his turn to hesitate, to struggle. Finally, he nodded. "Alright. But if the king still lives, then we wait. Agreed?"

"Agreed." She leaned in and kissed him. "But no more running away from me. And no more shouldering blame for what your father did. In fact, he is not your father. Malcolm de Bergiouac does not exist. Agreed?"

He nodded. "Agreed."

"Good. Now, is there any breakfast left over? I am starving."

\* \* \*

Merlin and Quasimodo had been busy. Or, more accurately, Quasimodo had. It turned out the legendary wizard was useless when it came to crafting magical objects. It did explain why he had sought out a smith to forge the Sword of Lions, though.

In any case, Rowena's bow and Cedric's armor had been completely remade, with new enchantments laid into them as well. Cedric's sword had needed to have its new powers stripped from the metal as they were in fact how the Dread Queen had kept her hold on him. To make up for the loss of strength, Quasimodo had laid new enchantments upon the blade and handle.

The result of all of this was they had to learn to use the new weapons. Without accidentally annihilating themselves or each other in the process.

Rowena was finding the wind rune the hardest to master. Quasimodo had laid in three, enabling her bow to imbue the arrows with fire or ice or wind depending on her own choice. Focusing her mind to make that choice was difficult enough but controlling them was so much worse. She had, in the three hours since receiving the newly empowered weapon, gained a new respect for Janet's difficulties in mastering her magic.

But the wind rune was becoming an absolute pain in her backside. Literally. The backfire kept knocking her off her feet and onto her bottom when she tried to use it.

"Blast it all," she snapped, tossing the bow aside and rubbing at her face.

"I think you just did."

She shot Andre a vicious look. "Maybe I am just not aiming at the right target."

He ducked behind Cedric. "Save me!"

With a long-suffering sigh, Cedric reached back and hauled the grinning boy back out into the open. "Quasimodo," he said conversationally. "Could you do something with this? It is getting annoying to have underfoot."

The hunchback smiled, an expression that was somehow sweet and endearing in that hideously ugly face. "I did forget about you, lad, now, didn't I? Cannot send the others in with new powers and weapons and not you."

"I've got plenty to use," Andre boasted.

"Morgana helped forge the Criotaur Coin."

The boy's face fell like a stone dropped from a parapet. "S-she did?"

"Mm-hmm." Quasimodo took a sip of the strawberry-scented drink he seemed to favor, then set the cup aside and rose from the bench he sat upon. "And she knows every single weakness that form possesses. You will not be able to use it in this battle."

"Then I'll use my swords." Andre's eyes went stony. "Blast it, I am not about to start learning a new weapon. I am not a knight."

Rowena and Cedric traded amused glances. Andre did not mind a fight, but at the core, he was still a thief. His style was to get in, strike, and get out fast. There were few weapons that afforded him that freedom, and even fewer he could master in the length of time they had to work with.

"Those swords have quite a bit more to them than you've been using."

The defiance and anger faded into suspicion. "And you know this—?" Quasimodo's response was to glance at Rowena's bow, and it had the boy's jaw dropping to the floor. "*You* crafted them?"

"One of my finer pieces," the hunchback said with pride. "Arsene was a most unique young man, and he needed a unique weapon."

He pushed up to his feet and lumbered across the room to the boy. "Hold out your arms."

When Andre did, Quasimodo took his right wrist in one clawed hand. He turned it just so, and something on the skin of the wrist gleamed in the light of the tower. "Wolf's head," he murmured. "Interesting. I would have expected the raccoon, like your mother. You are quite the interesting specimen, lad."

Now, Andre struggled, clearly wanting to ask a half-dozen questions all at the same time. "What other powers do they have?" was the one he settled on.

"That," the hunchback said with a secret smile. "Is the magic of them. They do not respond the same to each owner. Nor do they appear the same in the hands of each owner. For Arsene they were stilettos. For his son, a hooked kind of blade called a *kukri*. When your mother bore them, they showed up as long climbing claws. Now, with you, they are butterfly swords."

Quasimodo let go of his wrists and stepped back. "Attack me with them," he directed, then added, "You will not hurt me." when the boy hesitated.

With a reluctant sigh, Andre summoned his blades and charged at the hunchback. Before he could manage to swing, he took a hard, ham-fisted blow to his chest that sent him flying across the room.

"Again," Quasimodo instructed, and Andre dutifully picked himself up and tried again. This time, just before Quasimodo would have punched out, the boy ducked, rolled, and tried an upward sweep from the side. Quasimodo fetched him a blow to the back of the head which sent him sprawling, the sword he had tried the cut with falling from his grip.

Quasimodo stepped away and turned around. "Again."

Now the boy was starting to become annoyed. He scooped up the sword and hurled it. Quasimodo dodged the throw, then spun around just in time to strike Andre as the boy summoned himself to the weapon. Andre hit the ground, tumbling along it, then came up with a snarl of anger to rush at his deformed opponent.

Now, he went in with his swords twirling and spinning over each other. He dodged Quasimodo's blows, and Quasimodo dodged his slices. They circled each other, striking, and dodging as each sought an opening. Rowena watched in fascination. She had never seen her cousin so determined to do harm.

But he was more than determined. He was frustrated. He had never spent so long fighting without landing a blow. And that frustration, rather than making him sloppy, urged him to focus his energies.

The swords glowed in his hands, shimmering with a bell-like tone that filled the air. His movements took on a more circular quality, his arms arcing and weaving as he cut. And then, improbably, the swords grew, turning into longer, more traditional-length weapons that featured an arcing edge.

Amazed, he stopped, holding them up to study them. And they faded back into the familiar butterfly blades.

"A very interesting specimen," Quasimodo said again. He relaxed his posture and shambled back across the room to pick up his drink. "It seems you are not entirely ready to use your full power yet. And so, it has locked itself away, allowing you only the most basic level. Curious that this would reappear so soon."

"So soon?"

But Quasimodo did not answer Andre's question. Instead, he walked from the room like he was in a dream, saying over and over to himself, "Curious. Quite curious indeed."

* * *

"It was amazing," Andre gushed at supper. "I am swinging my blades, trying like bloody hell to hit him, and...I guess I just started wishing for a longer reach or something. And they start growing."

"Andre," Rowena admonished. "Slow down and chew before you choke to death."

Cedric laughed and nudged Malcolm. "Some things never change, eh?"

"Oh, I do not know," Malcolm replied. "Her concern with you was more that she *wanted* you to choke. Especially when you criticized her cooking."

"She over-seasoned a lot," the knight said in his defense, then had to duck as Rowena threw a piece of bread at him.

"You under-season," she accused. "At least I shall not have to spend overmuch on salt for the table as you all but refuse to use it."

"You shall have the money if that changes," Janet reminded her. And the entire table went dead silent as Rowena and Cedric traded a look. "What?"

"We have come to a decision regarding your offer," Cedric began.

"It isn't right for me to do that," Rowena cut in. "That land is yours and will belong to your children after. It is not right for me to take away from you and Malcolm like that."

"Rowena- No!" she said when Malcolm laid his hand over hers. "By the gods, their families have suffered long enough!"

"What are you going to do?" he asked calmly. "Force her to take the land?"

She opened her mouth twice to argue but could find no voice to do it. "Very well," she sighed at last. "But this is far from fair."

"We still have Raven's Rock," Rowena reminded her. "Cedric and I will not be left destitute." She reached out to take her betrothed's hand. "And it is a step up in his family's lifestyle, anyway."

Janet had forgotten that. Ivanhoe, Cedric's great-grandfather, had become disinherited because of his father, who gambled away name and deed and title without thought. "At the very least, you should have a title better than lord and lady," she pressed. "Saviors of the kingdom should receive *some* honor."

"How about we save the kingdom before you start planning honors?" Malcolm suggested.

As if on cue, Merlin entered the room with Quasimodo. The hunchback led Shadow and Psyche, crooning softly to the two horses.

At the sight of her faithful steed, Rowena jumped to her feet and ran over, and both horse and rider had a happy reunion. Shadow's reuniting with his own master was more sedate, but then the horse always had been unflappable.

"We have been caring for them in another chamber," Merlin explained. "It didn't seem prudent to leave them out in the world while a year passed."

"A *year*?" Janet gasped. "We have been here a full *year*?"

"I did tell you time passed differently in my tower, child," Merlin admonished.

"Yes, but...an entire *year*. I know, I know," she added when Malcolm sent her a pitying look. "Not really the point just now. Carry on."

Merlin gestured to Quasimodo, who produced five mud-brown hooded cloaks he handed out. "I do not believe my sister will be able to detect you when you emerge, but these should at least serve to disguise you somewhat."

"I suppose we shall have to do the entire ride in reverse," Cedric mused. "Minus me trying to kill everyone, of course."

Merlin shook his head. "She is sure to be watching, and the entire way would be one long running battle to reach the city. There is a much easier way."

So saying, he lifted his hand and waved it in a small circle. A shimmering portal wavered into being. "This can deposit you within the city walls. I cannot risk sending you into the castle itself. Morgana has probably warded it against such an intrusion, and the outcome could be... unpleasant for you all."

"Maybe I should go through before the rest of you," Andre suggested as the others mounted up. "Do a bit of reconnaissance."

Malcolm, Rowena, and Cedric traded looks. "Too risky," Cedric decided. "The longer you are over there, the long the portal would have to stay open. And if, gods forbid, they happen to catch you—"

"Bite your tongue!" the boy said, mortally offended.

"If they do," Cedric repeated, rolling over Andre's outrage. "The portal may stay open that much longer."

"And if that happens," Rowena added before Andre could give voice to another outburst. "The Dread Queen's forces could gain access to the Forest Tower. Which would mean the Dread Queen *herself* would gain access."

The boy winced. "Eesh, fair point. Alright then, no reconnaissance. But I do not think the horses are going to be a good idea."

Malcolm raised a brow. "Explain your logic."

Andre shifted nervously. "Well…the point of the cloaks is to disguise ourselves, right? So we will not be spotted so quickly? Well…a pair of Shadda-Dar are not exactly incognito. We will get spotted way too quickly if we're mounted."

"Hmm." Malcolm glanced over at Rowena, nodded. "He is pretty well-educated. Nice work."

The redhead shrugged. "His mother did most of the training. Arsene Lupin did match wits with Holmes and Dupin, after all."

"True." Malcolm hopped down from the saddle and reached up to help Janet dismount. "You are right, Andre. The horses would be far too noticeable."

Janet pulled down her pack and slung it over her shoulder. "Will you watch them for us?" she asked Merlin and Quasimodo. "It should not take us long by your reckoning."

"Hardly more than a few seconds," Merlin agreed, laying a hand on Shadow's flank. The look of longing on the old man's face had Malcolm stepping around to look his steed in the eyes.

"*Matakana toh*," he said, giving Shadow a stroke on the nose. "*Kotemi kata zo, paka*?"

"Do you think that's wise?" Rowena asked. "You're twisting the demon's ears."

"Just a precaution."

"And an honor," Merlin added. "*Kota toke zento,* Master de Bergiouac."

# CHAPTER 19

What they emerged into was not the city Janet remembered. She recalled buildings with a definite shape and clean streets. This was filth and tumbledown and ruin. What had they done to her city?

"The ghetto." Her teeth nearly cracked as she ground them together. "This is the Dread Queen's ghetto. He put us down right in the middle of the suffering."

"This kind of suffering will spread if we don't stop her."

"Then why did you put us in so much danger by tweaking the Joker's ear?" Rowena demanded, rounding on Malcolm in a fit of temper. "Giving Shadow that command was the height of arrogance!"

He shrugged. "It was practicality."

"What did you do?" Janet demanded of him.

"That command is acknowledgement of a hopeless fight!" Rowena snarled, her voice rising with her mounting rage. "No rider has ever given it and come back alive!"

"That's because riders generally give it when they're already half-dead."

"Stop," Janet hissed. "We are supposed to be hiding. If you keep yelling, they are going to spot us."

She swore as an alarm bell set to pealing. "Well, so much for *that*."

"Split up," Malcolm ordered. "We'll find each other later."

They all abandoned her before she could say another word, vanishing like smoke into the night. It was those warrior instincts, she knew, those skills they all had learned she had not.

But she was not without her own talents. A subtle push with her powers, a quick rush of wind, and she had a nice minor dust storm that covered her own flight into the dark.

She did not know where she was going, though. Could scarcely see, as she had whipped the dust storm a bit too hard in her haste, and it was blocking out what little light there was. She tripped over something, went spilling to the ground and heard something—cloth, flesh, she was not sure—tear.

"Here," a voice hissed out of the dark, layering over the increasing sound of running feet. "This way! Quickly! Before they find you!"

She pushed up, and from the pain in her leg she had a feeling it had been flesh that tore after all. But she ran, desperately chasing the voice that continued to beckon her to what she prayed was safety.

She caught a movement, a burst of light from one hut, and rushed for it. She nearly bowled over the woman who had held open the cloth covering for her as she charged inside. Her legs, recognizing she was safe even before her mind, gave out, and she dropped to her knees, chest heaving for air.

"It's alright, child." The woman moved briskly to grab a pail of water and a ladle. "Your first raid, I assume?"

She kneeled beside Janet, dipped up a scoop of water. And promptly dropped it. "You!"

She scrambled back, knocking over the water bucket, her eyes wide with fear. As the woman trembled, Janet realized she knew her. It was the wife of Towrick, the silversmith who had forged her coronet. "Mrs. Towrick—"

"Stay away from me!" The silversmith's wife held the ladle up to ward her off. "Stay away! You will not get me!"

"Calm down. I am not going to harm you." Janet started to reach for the woman, then pulled back as she flinched. "Mrs. Towrick, you know me."

"Where's my James?"

The demand had Janet blinking in surprise. And then she understood. "You think I am like my sisters."

"Aren't you?"

"No." Slowly, Janet reached into her dress

—she had torn the bodice some, it seemed—and extracted the Seven Moons Amulet. "You know this, don't you?"

"My husband's grandfather made it."

"Then you know what it does."

"It holds off a curse so long as not all the moons are black." Mrs. Towrick, smirked. "And all of them *are*."

"No." Janet turned the amulet so the light, which came from a small cooking fire in the center of the hut, played off the surface. "The six diamonds are black, but the seventh moon is the amulet itself, and that is still white. I have not fallen yet."

Mrs. Towrick studied her for a long moment, and Janet watched the calculation, the assessment play in her eyes. And she saw the moment the woman believed her. "We've been gone all this time, and we've come back to set things right."

"We?"

Janet smiled. "Malcolm. Did you really think he would just vanish and leave me?"

"Malcolm." Mrs. Towrick sighed and put down the ladle. "Oh, gods, child. I am so, so sorry."

Now, the hair on the back of Janet's neck prickled. "Why?"

"His father was the first to be arrested."

The guilt was a hard blow. She had never given a moment's thought to the smith in all their travels. Yet, she should have known that, for helping them escape, he would have become a target for the Dread Queen. And if he had been the first arrested, then he had most likely been turned into a Dread Knight long ago.

Gods. How would Malcolm handle that? Martin was his father, no matter what he said about his true heritage. To find out he was dead—

No. Merlin had already said that they could turn her sisters back to normal if they defeated the Dread Queen. That had to mean the surviving Dread Knights would also turn back. There was still time.

"We can undo what's been done," she said. "Malcolm and I are not alone. We have allies with us, and we are going to take down the Dread Queen and free everyone."

The woman sagged. "Child, they eat the prisoners. There is no one left to save."

"That is where you're wrong. They did not eat anyone. My sisters have become the Dread Mothers, and they are turning those brought to them into Dread Knights. They are very hard to kill, which means most of the affected are probably still alive."

"Then— My James." Hope, long since extinguished, rekindled in the old woman's eyes. Hope and gratitude. "Thank you, Princess. Thank you."

\* \* \*

Heading on towards morning, Janet sat with her

back against the tumbledown wall by the sheet-covered door. She had managed to coax Mrs. Towrick into getting sleep, but it was not coming to her.

Things had gone wrong too quickly. There had been no time to plan or outline a place to meet back up before they had been forced to scatter. And now there was no way to reach the others.

No. *No*, that was not true. She had accidentally pulled Malcolm into her dreamscape before. If she could figure out how she had done it, she might be able to pull them *all* in.

The garden felt cold now, even though the sun was bright, and the birds sang their sweet songs. The nip in the air was her own fears, she knew, her sympathetic pains for what Malcolm had likely lost. No matter what she had told Mrs. Towrick, Janet knew Martin might very well be gone.

But there was not time to indulge in those fears. She could not help Martin, but she could help those who hadn't been gone as long. She needed to reach the others.

She focused on her impressions and memories of each of them. Andre's irrepressible humor, brave heart, and quick hands. Rowena's strange mix of cold defiance and fierce passion. The kindness and sense of loyalty and duty that had kept Cedric from slaying them all.

And Malcolm, both the boy she had known

so well and the man he had become. The man she loved. The man who would willingly sacrifice everything to save her.

She built the images of them, crafting them as statues in her garden with all their aspects and facets. And then she reached out for the people, the souls that went with those statues. They shimmered, flickered. And turned into those she sought.

Cedric, Rowena, and Andre all looked around, amazed. Malcolm, however, just looked annoyed. "I thought you were going to stop doing this."

"I had to reach you all somehow."

"Where are we?" Rowena asked.

"This is my dreamscape spell," Janet explained.

"Okay. And that is?"

"Mmm, we're basically inside my mind."

"Your mind." Rowena took another glance around. "Oddly, this doesn't shock me in the slightest."

"You're going to get us caught," Malcolm snapped.

"I only brought a portion of your awareness in," Janet told him. "I am not peeking into anyone's mind, and you're perfectly aware back in the real world. There is no danger."

She reached out and took his hand in hers. "I keep my promises, Malcolm. You know that."

He sighed. "Are you alright?"

She smiled. "I found Mrs. Towrick, the silversmith's wife. She is doing okay, but her husband's been taken to the castle."

She nearly told him about his father, but the words stuck in her throat. She could not do it, couldn't do that to him just now. He had enough on his mind.

"I am at the west end of the ghetto," Cedric said. "There's a refuse pile."

"Oh, lovely." Rowena rolled her eyes skyward. "You're taking a bath before we share a bed again."

"They brought out dogs," he protested.

"You're still taking a bath if you want to get within five feet of me."

"I am at the other end from you," Malcolm cut in, though there was a small smile on his lips. "They never filled in the livestock trough when they built this place. The scent's enough to fool the dogs."

"You got the smart one, I see," Rowena said to Janet. "I am off to the south, near the city gates. I got out of the ghetto without being spotted. I am currently following a pair of guards on patrol to see if I can find some way into the castle."

"If you can't," Andre said. "I might be able to. There is a tower in the center with a view of the whole place. I got in through an upper window."

His cousin rolled her eyes. "And I suppose

you've already stolen a few items."

"Well, yes. What, I was supposed to pass up the easy pickings? Guards never expect to have their purses lifted."

Janet just had to laugh and, in doing so, she felt the garden warm. When the others gave her a questioning look, she just shrugged. It was not important.

"We might not need to trail the guards," Malcolm said. "They might not know about the tunnel."

Janet had a sudden flash of the ceiling of her chambers dropping down into a staircase with Sonya tumbling after it. "My tower is quite a distance from the court. If we are found out, we could wind up fighting every inch of the way."

"I am sorry," Rowena interrupted. "But what in the blazes are you talking about?"

"One of my sisters enjoys finding back passages in the castle," Janet explained. "Such as the old escape tunnel that leads from my chambers to the outside."

"It leads to more places than just your chambers."

She gave Malcolm a wry look. "I believe we are going to need to talk about how often you were in that passage."

He grinned. "That passage actually doesn't lead to the outside at all. It leads to the dungeons, where another passage leads out."

"So, you want us to fight our way up from

the dungeons rather than down from Janet's tower?" Cedric asked. "That's hardly a choice, old friend."

"We'd have to go through the dungeon anyway," Malcolm pointed out. "It's a shorter route."

"And a narrower one," Cedric argued back. "The dungeon is several levels, connected by winding staircases. The amount of potential choke points is absolutely staggering."

"As opposed to coming down from the tower where we could end up facing an army all at once."

As they argued, Rowena had moved around to stand between them. Now, she raised both hands and smacked the two men smartly on the back of the head. "Fighting about this can wait until we get inside. We must enter the dungeon anyway, so once we're there we can figure out the next step for ourselves."

* * *

As dawn was breaking, Janet slipped from the hut and made her way in the early morning light to the wall surrounding the ghetto. The palisade wall was high, but not stout enough to have guards patrolling the top. That did not mean there weren't guards on the outside keeping watch, but they wouldn't be looking for someone doing what Janet planned.

She had oriented her position by using the rising sun and knew exactly where the nearest building would have to be. All she had to do was reach the roof, and she would be off and running. She gathered in her power, set herself, and cast.

The wind spell sent her sailing neatly over the wall and arcing out across the road that had once surrounded the market. She had judged her target perfectly but- as seemed to forever be her fate- she overshot the mark. She had to scramble, fighting to turn so she could use another blast of wind to make sure she did not miss the roof entirely and hit the alley behind it. She made it, but it shook her enough she had to stop and wait for her breathing to slow down.

"Are you alright?"

She jumped, cursed. "Gods, Malcolm, *please*, announce yourself? I nearly fell off the roof."

"I would have caught you. Maybe."

She sighed as she stood and dusted herself off. "Alright. I am sorry about the spell. I had to find a way to reach you all."

"I thought we had a promise."

"I connected our minds. I did not intrude into your thoughts."

"That's not what I am talking about, Janet." He reached out and lifted her chin so she looked at him. "Where's Martin?"

"I assume he's safe."

"Janet." He did not raise his voice or chastise or even look angry. All he said was "Janet."

"Alright," she snapped. "He was the first one arrested! I am sorry! I am sorry for not wanting you to hear it because I didn't want to hurt you! I love—"

She did not get to finish, because his mouth had closed over hers in a kiss that was heartbreakingly tender. A kiss that brought tears to her eyes. "I am sorry," she said again, but the heat of temper she had used as a defense was gone.

"I'd already prepared myself for that possibility," he told her. "It did not seem likely he'd gotten away or been left alone after he helped us defy her. And I am glad you thought enough to protect me, but I am alright. If he is alive, we'll save him. If he is not, well avenge him."

"How?" she whispered. "How are you that strong? The thought my father might be dead has me terrified."

He just smiled. "Look in a mirror."

She understood instantly. He held off the fear because of her. It was his need to protect her that staved it off.

"I need you," she said. "I don't think I can live without you anymore."

"Then we will get through this together. And if your father's dead, we will do what needs to be done."

"Alright." She slid her hand into his and felt steadier with the contact. "Let's go."

\* \* \*

"This escape tunnel is pretty well-made," Andre observed as they walked along it. "And it looks pretty secure."

"Sonya has a gift for finding hidden routes." Janet touched a wall, then immediately pulled her hand back as it felt quite slimy. "The dirtier the better."

"Dirty just means it isn't well-used." Andre grinned back over his shoulder at her. "She and I could cause a lot of trouble together."

"You know, working with her older sister won't really save you from Alexis' wrath."

His grin just got sharper. "Can't wait."

"Let it go," Rowena told Janet. "You're only egging him on at this point."

Janet sighed. A feeling of trepidation and dread had been growing more and more as they had gone along. They were so close to the end of the journey, and she was afraid of what they were going to find when they got there.

Was her father still alive somehow? Was Malcolm's father? Was it possible to save her uncle? Was it even possible to kill the Dread Queen? Those questions cycled through her head again and again, and they were driving her mad. It was getting harder and harder to put one foot in front of another.

And then, up ahead, Malcolm stopped and looked back. Those tawny eyes gleamed in the gloom of the tunnel like golden gems and made her stomach jump all the more. "We're here."

Janet held her breath as he eased open the hidden door, then jolted when he gave a shout and rushed in. There was the sound of a short, vicious fight that involved a lot of clanging steel and slams and grunts. By the time the rest of them had come through the door after him, four Purple Rose knights were groaning on the ground, and he had a fifth by the throat.

"I've got questions," he hissed in the man's ear while the knight fought for air. "And you are going to answer them. If you do not, if you try to run or call out for help, I will split open your belly and shove you face down in your own entrails to die like a dog."

As she was quite afraid the man would do it anyway and get himself killed, Janet stepped forward and laid a hand on the side of his head. A quick murmur of a spell, and she was in his mind. The information they wanted was right there in front of her, and it took her breath away.

"He is here. *They* are here."

Malcolm gave her a shocked look. "*Both?*"

When she only nodded, too overcome with relief and emotion to speak, he let the man go. His hand flashed to the hilt of his sword, and the knight flinched, readying himself for the deathblow.

But, instead, Malcolm vanished with the roar of a lion filling the air. Cedric prudently stepped up and drove a gauntleted fist into the man's face, dropping him to the floor.

"Where did he just go?" Rowena asked.

"To save—" Janet had to swallow against the lump in her throat. "To save our fathers."

\* \* \*

It did not take an expert tracker to follow Malcolm's path. Janet was not entirely sure it even took eyes. He had obviously learned a considerable amount of control over his sword's powers because he appeared to be using them without hesitation or cease.

There were the fallen knights he had beaten to a pulp and strewn across the floor like broken toys. He had ripped cell doors off their hinges as if they were straw. And the occupants of those cells stood in the hallways, looking as confused and stunned as survivors of a natural disaster.

At the sight of the first group, Cedric slowed to a stop. "Move them on," he told Janet. "They won't be comfortable with me."

She did not need him to tell her that. The freed prisoners were already inching back, eyes wary. She made a deliberate choice by stepping away from him, placing herself between them and Cedric. "You're safe now," she told them, making certain to keep her voice light and soothing. "You're free."

"Princess Janet?" one man said and, to her surprised pleasure, it was Mr. Towrick. "Y-you're back to normal?"

"I was never cursed, Mr. Towrick. And I have come back to save my sisters and this kingdom, to undo what's been done."

His gaze flicked to Cedric, and Rowena stepped up behind Janet. "Sir, Cedric is as much a victim as you. He was under mental domination."

"Oh, is that what you call it?"

"Yes." Janet stepped forward again, drawing Mr. Towrick's attention back to her. "That was Malcolm who saved you, Mr. Towrick. We have just spent the last year in the Forest Tower getting stronger, so we can throw the Dread Queen out of this castle and out of this kingdom. If you do not want to trust Cedric, I can understand that. Your impression of the Purple Rose probably is none too good after the last year. So run."

She jabbed a finger the way they had come. "There is a hidden door two levels down that leads to an escape tunnel. It is in the third cell on the right from the stairs. Take it."

Still, the silversmith hesitated, looking nervously at Cedric. So, she took another step closer and said, "Your wife is waiting for you outside, Mr. Towrick. Do not make her wait anymore."

She looked around at the dirty, ragged prisoners staring at her with mixtures of fear and hope on their worn faces. "This is not a place for any of you to be right now. Please, leave here while you can."

That finally got them moving, and it was not long before the four were alone in the corridor. It was only then she turned to Cedric. "You were under someone else's control," she reminded him. "And you are about to make up for what's happened by helping to save this kingdom. You are a hero, Cedric, never forget that."

"Well spoken."

Her heart skipped a beat. There he was, more unkempt and leaner than she was used to seeing him. But the man standing there beside Malcolm and Martin was undoubtedly her father.

Her feet moved on their own, taking her to him. She threw her arms around his neck, and he gathered her in to a warm embrace. "I feared for your safety," he whispered to her. "You had me so worried."

"Malcolm would never allow me to come to harm."

"No." The old king smiled. "He most certainly would not."

After a quick conference, they decided that sending Ardent off with the other prisoners was not only insulting of his honor, but needlessly indulgent. And so, Martin, Malcolm, and Cedric quickly stripped a downed guard of his arms and armor and outfitted the king.

To Janet, it felt strange to see him clad in such ordinary and unornamented attire, but he rather enjoyed it. And as he gave the simple broadsword a few testing swings, she was reminded Ardent of the Red Dagger's talents in combat were a large part of his legend.

Her gaze drifted from him to Malcolm, and she thought it fitting she should fall in love with a man so like her father. Recalling that, she moved over to the young swordsman and spoke in a low tone to him, "My father has not been on a battlefield in twenty years. I am counting on you to keep him alive."

"I will." But he reached out and took her hand for a moment. "No unnecessary risks."

"Speak for yourself." But she stood back and let him lead the way up the stairs, leaving her with her father and his.

"He has become a fine man and a fine warrior," Ardent said. "Finer, I believe, than any of us ever anticipated. You have done an incredible job with him, Martin."

"The job was only partly mine, I think," Martin replied with a small smile. "A man can only become a true hero when he has something to fight for. Wouldn't you agree, Princess?"

She smiled. "Quite."

"He is the spitting image of his ancestor," her father said as she started towards the stairs, and she whirled around to stare at him.

"Y-you knew?"

"That he is Malcolm de Bergiouac, you mean?" Ardent smiled. "I faced Geoffrey myself, and the son has his father's eyes. Fear not, my daughter. I would not have offered him your hand if I did not think him worthy of you and the throne."

So, he had known *that*, too, she realized. She might have guessed. "We have…" She cleared her throat. "Promised not to announce it right away. We want to take some time."

"Then it shall be so."

# CHAPTER 20

The stairs to the dungeon exited out into a back section of the castle and should have been easy to get through. Apparently, though, the Dread Queen had anticipated their point of entry, as what seemed to be every Purple Rose in the kingdom waited.

Malcolm struck first, the roar of his weapon's magic filling the air as he flew across the intervening distance in the blink of an eye. His blade flashed this way and that, batting aside swords and slicing through the straps of armor. Metal and bodies thudded to the floor in a cacophonous symphony.

Close behind his assault was Cedric, whose newly forged sword now proved its own mettle and power. Each swing carried a force that extended far beyond the blade's own path, felling men like ninepins before a well-rolled ball. His armor also showed off its new powers, allowing him to match Malcolm's unearthly pace without effort and easily protecting him when the odd sword strike got through his defenses.

Rowena's arrows fell less like rain and

more like a meteor storm. Ice and wind and flame erupted in staccato bursts across the length and breadth of the space. Every strike, every blast of magical power, sent a handful of men flying into the air.

Each one who flew up, Janet sent slamming back down onto the stone with her own wind magic. Their arms and armor shattered on impact like glass hurled to the ground.

The ones who still moved after that caught Andre's feet in flying stomp-kicks and sweeping strikes. The boy's acrobatic talents were on full and prominent display as he leaped and lunged and tumbled about the area with the speed of a rabbit.

Martin and King Ardent simply stood back and watched. It was an absolute scene, more of a pageant than a vicious battle.

"They have grown up quite a bit, haven't they?" Martin asked idly.

"Oh, undoubtedly," was the king's reply. "Malcolm's swordsmanship is impressive enough, but I never really imagined what my Janet could do once she finally got her magic under control."

"I had reconciled myself to that never even happening," Martin admitted, adding an appreciative whistle for Cedric and Andre coordinating in a particularly inventive takedown of a trio of knights. "My, they're all rather good."

Ardent chuckled. "To think what I could have done with them at the Idenian Plains. I could have saved many lives with powers like theirs. That was always my greatest regret in that conflict. The waste of it all."

Rowena's arrows blew a pair of the knights clear of the fracas, and they landed near to the two men. Ardent quickly and prudently clobbered them before they could rise. "Hmm." He rolled the shoulder of his sword arm.

"Problem?" Martin asked.

"Have not really swung a sword since Alexis was born. I am not used to the strain of it anymore."

"It might not be the worst idea to start working with the weaponsmaster once this is done with."

"Agreed." But Ardent looked sadly at the fallen men who littered the floor. "It appears I will not be the only one who needs it."

With the fight over, Malcolm, who had fought his way across the length of the corridor several times, strode back to them from the far edge of the carnage. "We got lucky."

Ardent cocked his head. "That's an interesting level of faith in your own abilities, son."

"He's right," Cedric called out. He had crouched down and was inspecting the armor of one of the downed knights. "They are outfitted the same way I was. This battle should have taken ten times as long and left us in terrible shape. We did not even go for deathblows on the whole."

Rowena stepped to him and laid a hand on his shoulder, looking around at the fallen men. "They were fighting the Dread Queen's control, just like you."

He reached up and linked fingers with her, though continued to look at the man at his feet. "They were either fighting it harder than I was, or her control is weakening. They let us win."

"No," Janet said quietly, turning to look at Ardent. "They were doing what they are trained to do. They were protecting the royal family to the best of their ability."

Ardent took another look at the men strewn across the floor, and once again felt the waste of it. His fingers tightened on the handle of the sword in his grip and his teeth gritted. "No more," he said. "No. More. I swear upon all I have ever done in my life, this ends today."

He strode through the bodies and, with each step, his anger melted away the years. By the time he reached the doors to the throne room, Ardent of the Red Dagger had returned from the mists of time.

Andre had beaten them all there and ran his hands over the surface of the doors, knocking on them with his ear pressed close. "Not locked," the boy confirmed, "but I can't open them."

"Barred." Ardent turned to his eldest daughter as she arrived, flanked by the rest. "Can you break it down?"

She stepped around, motioned Andre away, and extended one hand towards the doors. "Hmm. No wards that I can feel. Odd that she has gone to all this trouble to slow us down but doesn't ward the last barrier. Well, well, she *wants* this."

She took a half step back and raised both hands so they were nearly against her shoulders. She gathered her power, collected the energy into a focused ball of solid air. And *hurled*.

The explosion hurled them all to the ground, blown over like trees before a vicious storm. Even as the doors crashed to the floor in the opposite direction, Malcolm sat up and grumbled, "You know, it comes to me that your training in counter-magic was practically nonexistent."

"So it was." She shook her head, lightly rubbed her temple with the heel of her hand. "And she seems to be exceptionally good with wards. Not too much emphasis on redirecting the force, which saves considerable energy."

"If the two of you are quite done," Rowena growled. "I'd really like to give this harpy a good stomping for what she did to us all."

\* \* \*

The throne room was in even worse shape than it had been in Merlin's magic mirror. Gods, Janet thought, how many months had passed since that scene had played out? How long had her people suffered after she had finally learned of their horror?

The rich tapestries, centuries upon centuries of the banners belonging to Avanna's rulers, were torn and filthy. The elegant rug that lined the passage from the main doors to the throne dais lay shredded and tattered, ruined by the feet of all the men dragged across it to their doom.

One of the Dread Mothers, still chained in an alcove, raised its head, nose sniffing. As it did, Janet saw it had no eyes whatsoever. "Janet?" it asked in what was clearly *Rebecca's* voice. "Sister? Is that you? And—" More sniffing. "And *Malcolm*? By the gods, you did it! Please! Please, help us!"

Around the room, the other monsters raised their own heads, and the voices of her other sisters came from their deformed mouths, begging her to save them. She started forward, though what she would have done she could not have said. But Malcolm grabbed her arm to stop her. "No," he said. "It's not safe."

"They're still in there!" she protested.

"You do not know that. Cedric was able to speak and move about on his own, but he was not free, and he wasn't himself."

It was true, and she knew it. It did not make ignoring their cries for help any easier on her conscience. And so, she threw her efforts in another direction—*anger*. She shook his hand off and stepped forward. "Maria!" she shouted out. "Or should I say Morgana! Let us end this!"

"Look out!" Malcolm called, just as a shadow loomed over her.

In another second she was at the far end of the court by the main doors, cradled protectively in Malcolm's arms. The sound of something huge smashing into the ground told her he had saved her once again.

It was a Dread Knight, one last defender. This one was smaller than the others they had faced, its head topped by a crown of arcing black horns. A grimy black cape streamed down from wide shoulders and hideously clawed fingers curled around the handle of a long black sword.

Janet had little doubt who this was. "Uncle Regis," she sighed. "I'd hoped we could save him, too."

Malcolm ran a hand over her hair, soothing, comforting. "There's never a way to save everyone."

"Do you like it?" Maria—Morgana—walked into view from out of nowhere. Her beautiful amethyst eyes glowed with energy, delight, and cruelty as she all but glided to her hideous creation. "My finest work."

She grinned at all assembled. "My finest work for my greatest performance. The snake in the midst of Eden coming into her own at long last!"

"You haven't won yet," Janet spat at her. "And you are not going to because you can't secure your position until you get me. Until I am the same as my sisters. And I will die before I let that happen."

Morgana laughed, a silverly, bell-like tone edged with madness. "Oh, my dear little stripling. Didn't my brother tell you anything at all? Turning you is not necessary. It does not matter how you're removed from the line of succession, only that you are."

She caressed the arm of the beast beside her. "Regis has taken care of that."

The last piece fell into place, the final stitch that completed the tapestry. "So," Janet said, "that is it. That is why you waited until now to spring your surprise. You have been here in the capital for seven years. If my sisters and I were your goal, you could have struck at any point. But you waited until now because you did not have the key you needed."

She looked around at the chained, hideously warped forms of her sisters. At her father. And last of all, at Malcolm. "Seizing the throne means nothing without a way to secure your legacy. You need to ensure that your rule extends beyond yourself."

She watched the recognition come into his eyes, watched the pain and sorrow of what she meant hit home and forced herself to turn back to her enemy. "An heir," she continued. "With my mother dead, my sisters transformed and the true king missing, I would ascend the throne. But if I am gone, too, then there's only one person left with royal blood. Only one person capable of producing a new heir to the throne. The bastard brother of the late queen."

"Every queen needs a king." Morgana stroked a possessive hand down the arm of the beast beside her. "At least, that has been the case since Arthur. Before him, when the great queens ruled the world, a king was not necessary."

She sighed. "My sister queens never could see the benefit of them. It was why I helped Arthur oust them in the end."

"No," Janet agreed, her belly going hot and her heart cold. "No, of course not. They could not see, could they? They did not know what the ultimate step was, did they? How long does your kind remain pregnant, Morgana?"

"Oh, three years." The ancient beauty's eyes shifted from Janet to Malcolm. "At least, that's how long it took with you."

Janet half-turned to Malcolm but got no further before the familiar roar of the Sword of Lions filled the air. He shot forward, the magnificent blade of his weapon scything through the air.

The creature that had been Lord Regis—what they could term the Dread King—blocked the strike with his own sword as Morgana laughed. "Temper, temper, Malcolm. Oh, you are so much like your father."

A blast of wind struck the woman across the face like a hard punch. "You don't get to speak to him that way," Janet seethed. "You may have been his mother, but you know *nothing* about who he is."

Morgana shrugged. "It hardly matters. You are a failed experiment, one that has continued far beyond your usefulness. Time to end it."

\* \* \*

The battle was titanic. The most explosive and bitter of the entire journey. It had to be. There likely had not been so much magical power unleashed in a single conflict since the fall of Camelot.

Morgana had unbelievable power. Thousands of years of practice and experience gave her an array of spells the likes of which Janet had never seen. Using fire, wind, and lightning, she crafted spectral versions of ancient creatures. She forced Janet and Rowena and Andre to keep one step ahead of a burning dragon, an airy basilisk and a screeching thunderbird that flew about on six electric wings.

Malcolm and Cedric and the king fought against an unceasing army of hooded shadows that rose like smoke from the very stones of the floor. They had to keep watch for the Dread King as well, for he charged in and out of the melee, a rampaging bull that targeted friend and foe alike.

Even Martin was forced into the battle, bashing the shadows that came towards him with a fragment of the destroyed door. And all the while they fought, the Dread Mothers screamed and howled and rattled the chains holding them in their alcoves.

It was too much, Janet thought as she dodged a swipe from the thunderbird's talon. Even with all their own power and skill and the magic in their weapons and equipment, it was still too much.

They were being worn down. It had to end, had to end before they were too far gone to keep fighting. It was time to use what she had learned.

She planted her feet, used the slightest bit of earth magic to ground herself as the six-winged bird came back for another go. She reached out, extended her will and hands out to the construct. It struck her, vanishing with one last defiant screech.

The power she had absorbed was enormous. She could feel it coursing through her body, standing every single hair on end. Her heart and lungs strained with the stress of holding it back. But she did not intend to hold it for long.

She pointed at the dragon and basilisk and spat out a single command. The blasts of lightning she loosed obliterated them in an instant.

And there was still more power locked inside her, power she had saved for an even more specific purpose. She directed it downward, sending it skipping out along the stone of the floor. It obliterated all the shadows at once and surged up the legs of the Dread King, causing him to jerk uncontrollably.

Malcolm and Cedric acted immediately, as if they had waited for her to do that. The two young warriors struck hard and fast, carving deep gouges in the monster's back and arms, and the creature howled in response. King Ardent followed their assault, coming in from the front while the Dread King was distracted. His unornamented, unenchanted blade pierced the creature's belly, drawing another pained cry from it.

A blast of force sent him flying back to land at the foot of the Golden Eagle Throne. Two more blasts sent Malcolm and Cedric tumbling along the floor to join him. Morgana spun to Janet, batting two of Rowena's arrows from the air with a negligent flick of her hand.

"Worthless," she hissed, using another blast to send Andre crashing into his cousin. "Pitiful. You. Are. *Nothing!*"

Janet answered with a gout of flame mixed with wind, which she wove into a burning maelstrom around the ancient sorceress. She poured more power into it, weaving it tighter and tighter, faster and faster. Her intent was incineration, obliteration.

She heard the rumble of the Dread King rushing at her and rolled away before he could bowl her over. Her concentration broken, the firestorm broke apart, freeing the Dread Queen. Morgana erupted from within the dissipating flames, lightning crackling between her clawed fingers as she lunged for Janet.

Malcolm intercepted her. The lightning played along the blade of his sword, streamed down to the handle. The blood-red stone in the crosspiece glowed like a burning flame. And the lion's roar was an explosion in the charged air.

"Morgana," he growled in a voice Janet had never heard before, as if someone else came from his throat.

"Arthur." The woman smiled, her eyes bright, and sharp, and wicked as a thornbush. "Again and again, you stand before me."

"Again and again, you ply your little games, your grand schemes. How many times do you intend to have me come back from the abyss to stop you?"

"'Tis your own choice to return."

"Hardly." He turned his head to study the seething form of the Dread King. "So, this is where your magic has progressed."

He flickered, vanishing for a brief second before he returned. The Dread King dropped to its knees, its head hitting the floor a mere moment before its body. "You still need work."

"Hmph. So showy." With a contemptuous flick of her hand, she set the fallen corpse alight. "Really, Arthur, why make these displays when you know you cannot harm me yourself? The magic I used all those millennia ago to empower you to depose my sister queens binds you to me. You cannot touch me."

He smirked. "That was always your flaw, Morgana. You never saw the value of cooperation."

She jolted as Rowena's arrows caught her in the back, then ignited. Andre and Cedric came in next, taking her arms off at the elbows as neatly as chopped wood. Ardent struck next, driving his sword into her gut from behind, burying it deep.

Even as she screamed, Janet used her magic to turn the burning arrows into another fiery maelstrom. Her screams turned louder and louder, got higher in pitch until they were not the screams of a woman burning alive but, oddly, a bird.

Without warning, the flames turned black —not oily, but black like midnight. And from them emerged the very bird that had been crying out. It was a phoenix, with feathers black as the flames and eyes like burning coals. It hovered above their heads, wings flapping, flapping. It threw back its spectacular head and cried one last time.

And vanished like smoke.

\* \* \*

While the defeat of the Dread Queen restored the other princesses to normal immediately, the rest of the capital took a while longer. There was the ghetto to disassemble, buildings to repair across the city. Lives had been uprooted, commerce all but ground to a halt. The scars of what had happened would last for years.

Fortunately, the loss of life had been minimal. Except for the ones who had vanished during the early days of the crisis, Morgana had fed only those with experience in war to the Dread Mothers. The rest of the arrests had either agitated against conditions or been arrested solely to keep people frightened. As a result, only the Dread Knights sent after their little group had died, and the survivors made their way back to their families without incident.

Because of all this, it was nearly a month before King Ardent honored those who had saved the kingdom. They held it in the marketplace, so everyone in the city could attend, which was part of the point. Rowena's family had a bad reputation in the kingdom, and Cedric was not well-liked because of what the Purple Rose had done. Honoring them in public would tell everyone the full story of what had happened.

He provided a full honor guard. Not Purple Rose, but officers of the king's army. That too was meant to comfort. The army had not been part of the Dread Queen's coup, and it reminded those present Malcolm, Rowena, and Cedric weren't only heroes but veterans of the monster wars. As a further honor, he greeted them on level ground and hung the medals around their necks himself.

Then he turned to those assembled and spoke. His words were both soothing and inspiring. He reminded them all there was always a way to stand against evil, that courage was a blessing, and one that lived in the hearts of all. He praised those who had stood up to the machinations of the Dread Queen, all who had endured the challenging times of that horrid year.

Then he shifted to a different topic, one that surprised everyone. "Over the past years," he said, "two mysteries have plagued this kingdom. One has been around for a quarter of a century, the identity of the hand destined to wield a most magnificent blade, the Sword of Lions. The other is not nearly as old but is more central to the future of the kingdom. All have wondered whom my eldest daughter, Crown Princess Janet, would finally choose as her husband."

Janet flicked her gaze to Malcolm, saw he had also guessed where this was headed. Happily, he did not seem upset by it.

"Many have guessed at the answer to one or the other," King Ardent continued. "But none have ever realized the answers were one and the same."

He turned, gestured towards Malcolm. "I

give you now that answer. Ladies and gentlemen, I present to you the bearer of the Sword of Lions, the choice of my daughter. Malcolm de Bergiouac!"

A buzz went through the crowd, and not a happy one. Janet's heart sank. It was the one thing she had feared about revealing their relationship, that Malcolm would be right about the reaction to his identity.

"And now we see nothing ever changes." It was Rowena, stepping forward with her eyes hot and hard. "Avanna, the kingdom of heroes, casting aside someone because of what their family did. As you did to my family, to Cedric's family, all because of the actions of one man in a line that stretched back centuries. You make me sick."

Before anyone could speak, before Malcolm or Cedric could step forward to stop her, her bow was in her hand, and she was launching an arrow into the sky to explode in a burst of flame. As people cried out and ducked, she nocked another and aimed it at the crowd. "On. Your. Knees."

Malcolm was there in a flash, his hand closing over the bridge of the bow to keep the arrow from firing. "Have you lost your damn mind?" he snapped, wrenching the bow from her grip.

Her response was to hit him, full in the face. As his head snapped back, she snatched up one of her daggers and lunged.

He blocked her first strike, but she cut his sword belt with the second. Then Cedric grabbed and hauled her back, pinning her arms to her sides. "This isn't going to help," he told her as she struggled to free herself. "Dammit, Rowena—"

"Pick it up!" she shouted out. "Pick it up and show them! Let them see!"

A new buzz went through the crowd now, and she stopped struggling. "There, Avanna, there's your proof!"

Just as Rowena had directed, as the woman had clearly planned all along, Janet held the sword aloft for all to see. Cedric released Rowena, and he and Malcolm both stared in amazement.

"There is your proof, Avanna!" Rowena shouted again. "None but a de Bergiouac may wield the Sword of Lions! Lady Fate herself ordains this union! Who among you will deny the will of the gods?"

The buzz grew louder and was no longer so angry. Taking it as a sign, Janet walked to Malcolm and held out the sword.

Rather than take it, he leaned down and kissed her. "Let me do this properly," he murmured.

And before all assembled, he lowered himself to one knee and proposed.

# EPILOGUE

*Two weeks later...*

"They look so happy, don't you think?" Janet asked Malcolm as they watched Rowena and Cedric, sitting off in a corner and completely lost in each other.

"Very happy," he agreed. "That was quite an honor you gave them, asking your father to marry them while he married us."

"They would not let me give them land. I had to do something."

He chuckled, lifting her hand to his lips to kiss the knuckles. "Your father took care of that, too."

He had indeed. King Ardent, who had known Cedric's father, Hugo, as a boy, had followed up the dual wedding ceremony by proclaiming that "We must rectify the injustices of the past". He had then named Cedric and Rowena as the new baron and baroness of Weldentore, the lands previously held by Lord Regis. The pair had been so flummoxed it had taken them a full minute to find their voices so they could accept.

She reached out and toyed with the pendant she had had made for him as a wedding present. On it, wrought in gold over silver, was a prowling lion beneath a waning moon. The coat of arms of their new union. "Do you know what I want, Malcolm?"

"What?"

"I want us to have all the years my parents did, and more besides. I want us to live, happy and well, and watch our children grow and our kingdom flourish. And to never again wonder if the other will disappear."

His eyes, those wonderful tawny eyes that saw everything in her, went soft. "That sounds absolutely perfect."

He was leaning in to kiss her when from behind them there came the sound of Alexis cursing. Before they could turn around, Andre vaulted both them and the table and beat a hasty retreat from the hall, hooting with laughter all the way. Alexis, bereft of sword thanks to the king's direct orders, charged after him, shouting for all the castle to hear that when she caught him, she was going to play knucklebones with his teeth.

"Well," Janet huffed, "so much for the moment."

"There will be others." He turned to Rebecca, who had just walked up with a goblet of wine and a big grin. "What did he do this time?"

Rebecca's grin grew wider as she sat down. "Our young thief stole himself a kiss."

"And I thought I enjoyed danger," Sonya put in as she, Jasmine, and Monica also sat down.

"They are so entertaining to watch." Jasmine winced as something large in the outer hall crashed to the floor. "Most of the time."

Abruptly, her twin made a strangled noise and took her wine goblet, draining it in one go. As Monica was not one for spirits of any kind, Jasmine gave her a worried look. "Are you alright?"

"Fine," Monica said, though she looked like she had just swallowed a toad.

"Did you see something?" Janet asked.

"I—" Monica swallowed. "I was just looking off at the wall, and I could suddenly see through it, and through the next, into one of the spare chambers."

"Farsight." Janet nodded. "I thought as much."

"Farsight?" Alarmed, Rebecca looked between them both rapidly. "Janet, what is going on?"

"It's nothing to worry about," Janet assured her. "The court wizard told me that he was fed to Monica while you were...during the crisis. Magic can sometimes react with magic to produce side effects. Monica, it appears, can now see well beyond normal vision."

Sonya, however, had been studying

Monica most acutely, and spotted that her sister was turning a deep shade of pink. "What was going on in the chamber?" she asked.

"I, um..." Monica fidgeted. "Lord Montague was in there."

"Really?" Sonya's lips spread in an eager grin at the thought of her sister spying on the exceptionally handsome Avannion politician who had come to the wedding as a representative of the national government. "Was anyone with him?"

"I, um... Lady Brentworth." Monica turned a deeper shade. "And Duchess Morrwick's niece, Alanna."

Jasmine immediately laughed. "Alanna the Stoneheart. So, the rumors of his charms are true after all."

"Or her reputation has been nothing but a sham," Sonya put in, laughing just as hard.

"Sonya!" Rebecca slapped her sister's hand, but she, too, was chuckling.

Janet was about to join in the merriment, when she noticed Malcolm still stared at the doorway through which Alexis had chased Andre. He did not even seem to notice what was going on, and that worried her.

"Malcolm?" She waited a beat for him to respond, but when he did not, she squeezed his hand and said again. "Malcolm, what's wrong?"

"By the gods," he breathed, then shook his head, seeming to come back from somewhere very far off. "Rowena told me in confidence she had no intention of letting us know she was there when we entered the tavern the day after we fled the capital. Andre alerted us to their presence all on their own."

"So?"

"He tried to steal the Sword of Lions. He tried to steal the one thing most likely to get him noticed. What use would he possibly have for it?"

Janet shrugged. "He is a habitual thief."

"Yes," Malcolm agreed, "to the point of doing it without thinking. As if something is *making* him do it."

Now Janet glanced towards the door. "You think something controls him occasionally?"

"What happens if he does not attempt to steal it?" Malcolm pressed. "We would have left the inn without knowing he or Rowena were there."

"And without him," Janet added, catching on to what he was saying, "we would never have used the passageway."

"And we would have failed. The Dread Queen would have won."

"An Agent of Fate." Janet whispered. "Well, well. By the gods, indeed."

As one, the group turned to look at the doorway once more. And wondered on the workings of the lady.

TZ KRASNER

**THE END**

Made in the USA
Columbia, SC
28 October 2022